THE BEGINNING OF
THE END

UNIVERSE IN FLAMES BOOK 4

CHRISTIAN KALLIAS

ALSO BY CHRISTIAN KALLIAS

The Universe in Flames Series

- Book 1: Earth - Last Sanctuary (*also available as an Audiobook*)
- Book 1.5: Ryonna's Wrath (Novella)
- Book 2: Fury to the Stars
- Book 3: Destination Oblivion
- Book 4: The Beginning of the End
- Book 5: Rise of the Ultra Fury
- Book 6: Shadows of Olympus
- Book 7: Armageddon Unleashed
- Book 8: Twilight of the Gods
- Book 9: Into the Fire I: Requiem of Souls
- Book 10: Into the Fire II: To End all Wars

- The **First** Universe in Flames **Trilogy Box Set** (Books 1-3)
- The **Second** Universe in Flames **Trilogy Box Set** (Books 4-6)

Rewind Series

- Book 1: Rewind 717

Anthologies

- Collateral Damage (Out Now)
- The Expanding Universe 3 (December 15, 2017)
- Beyond the Black Volume 1 (mid-December 2017)

Dedicated to Daniel, Cedric and Walter without whom I'm not sure I would have had the courage to go forward with writing professionally. Thank you for all your help, unwavering support, encouragement as well as for believing in me.

I'd also like to thank my Family and Friends.

Special mention to Paula L., Alain H., Florent Z., Val K., Russ B., Houman H., Jean-Marc D, Jean-Marc B., Sandro C., Marc M., Marc S., Jay V. E., Noel, Arthur S. & Mary H.

ACKNOWLEDGMENTS

Cover artwork by Christian Kallias

- christian@kallias.com
- www.christiankallias.com
- www.facebook.com/ChristianKallias
- www.twitter.com/kalliasx

Production Editor & Alpha/ARC Team Lead

- Paula Lavattiata Lopez

Editors

- Philip Newey
- Paula Lavattiata Lopez

Proofreaders

- Philip Newey
- Paula Lavattiata Lopez
- Miliana Chipaila (Thank you so much Millie!)

COPYRIGHT

Thank you for buying my book, here is an **exclusive freebie** for you. Get the **DAMOCLES FALL** book here:

www.christiankallias.com

DRAMATIS PERSONÆ

Earth Alliance

- **Lieutenant Commander Chase Athanatos** – Earth Alliance Fury hybrid (formerly Star Alliance Lieutenant Commander)
- **Commander Sarah Kepler** – Earth Human (formerly US Navy Commander)
- **Commander Daniel Tharraleos** – Earth Alliance Human (formerly Star Alliance)
- **Commodore Adonis Saroudis** – Earth Alliance Human (formerly Star Alliance Captain)
- **Chief Engineer Yanis Tixichos** – Earth Alliance Human (formerly Star Alliance)
- **Ryonna Isch'ys** – Droxian Warrior (a fugitive Droxian smuggler)
- **Tar'Lock** – Gorgar (Insectoid & formerly a Hellstar prisoner)
- **Admiral Ally Thassos** – Earth Allliance Human (formerly Star Alliance Admiral)

- **Commander Fillio Steriopoulou** – Earth Alliance Human (formerly Star Alliance)
- **R&D Engineer Spiros Malayianis** – Earth Alliance Human (formerly Star Alliance)

Olympians

- **Aphroditis** – known to humans as the goddess of love
- **Ares** – know to humans as the god of war (deceased, living as pure energy form)
- **Athena** – known to humans as the goddess of wisdom, craft, and war

Furies

- **Argos Thanatos** – Fury and Chase's twin brother (head of the Zarlacks)
- **Arakan** – Supreme Commander of the Furies
- **Miseo** – Arakan's son and right arm
- **Arkoolis** – top Fury General

Other Characters

- **Cedric** – Earth Human Scientist
- **Keera Hawking** – Humanoid Bounty Hunter
- **Gaia** – Artificial Intelligence created on Earth, speaks for the planet
- **Ronan Isch'ys** – son of Ryonna

- **Jonas** – Ryonna's brother-in-law
- **Sendra** – Commodore Saroudis' daughter
- **Alexandra** – Commodore Saroudis' wife

THE STORY SO FAR

Warning: If you haven't read all the previous books in the series, you're exposing yourself to **SERIOUS spoilers** by reading this part.

This section was created for readers of this series to refresh their memories (should they need to) before reading this new book. It can, of course, be used by new readers but I'd recommend you start reading the series at Book 1: **Earth – Last Sanctuary** (it's free).

Volume I: Earth - Last Sanctuary

Following a devastating attack by the Obsidian Empire, helped by the mighty Zarlacks, a band of survivors led by Chase Athanatos from the Star Alliance blind jump away from their home world (Alpha Prime) and end up in an uncharted part of space, near a planet called Earth. Guided by the Olympian goddess of love Aphroditis, Chase and his friends rescue planet Earth from an alien attack and form a new alliance (Earth Alliance). But soon the Obsidian

Empire tracks them down and decides to launch a full-scale attack on the blue planet. In the midst of the epic battle that ensues, the leader of the enemy forces captures Chase's new love interest, Commander Sarah Kepler. He reveals to Sarah that he is Chase's brother.

Volume II: Fury to the Stars

Chase learns of his Fury heritage and starts developing powers while he tries to rescue Sarah from the hands of his evil twin, Argos, currently torturing her for information. Another Olympian, Ares, trains Chase and helps him harness his emerging powers. Meanwhile, Earth is suffering random terrorist attacks that put the new Alliance's frail status in jeopardy. After going to Hellstar Prison to get Ryonna out, Chase fights Argos and is finally reunited with Sarah, but something is off. A long-range distress call from a former Star Alliance scientist (Spiros Malayianis) brings Chase and Argos on yet another collision course. Chase is put into the impossible position of choosing between preventing sensitive weapon schematics from falling into Argos' hands or saving Sarah's (and his unborn son's) life. She has been brainwashed to do Argos' bidding and is also responsible for the wave of terrorism back on Earth. Chase reluctantly destroys Sarah's ship.

Volume III: Destination Oblivion

Having had to kill the woman he loves as well as their unborn child plunges Chase into a spiral of hatred and self-destruction as he leaves the Earth Alliance. After meeting a bounty hunter (Keera), Chase joins forces with her in order to track the one man he hates more than anything in this world: his twin brother Argos whom he holds responsible for Sarah's death. Argos resurfaces on their radar after killing Ares in cold blood. When their paths cross, Chase nearly kills Argos after an epic fight in Tokyo, but only spares his twin brother's life when he reveals that Sarah is alive and the person that Chase killed was a clone. Meanwhile, a dangerous Artificial Intelligence (Gaia) is born on Earth and threatens humanity as a whole, but in the end Spiros Malayianis convinces her that she has nothing to fear from humans. In order to rescue Sarah, Chase has to reluctantly team up with Argos in order to defeat a Titan that holds a piece of tech Argos needs for his nefarious plan. When recovered, Argos requests Aphroditis to enter the piece of tech that will free his brethren, once thought to be extinct, from their dimensional prison. Aphroditis enters the machine willingly in exchange for a promise from Chase to rid the world of Argos and the threat he poses. The Fury home world (Erevos) is brought back into their reality as a result. The enemy of old (Furies) is back in play.

And now the continuation ...

C hase's eyes widened and he stopped dead in his tracks.

"What do you mean our home world?"

Argos grinned.

"You see, Olympians think of themselves as too *evolved* to exterminate an entire civilization. So thousands of years ago, at the height of the first Fury War, they devised a plan to remove us from the equation by trapping Erevos in another dimension outside of space and time itself, instead of destroying us all. That mistake will be their undoing, and today you've helped me correct this. Now that my fellow Furies are back, we'll conquer this universe that was always meant to be ours."

The weight behind Argos' words and the realization of what had just happened hit Chase's psyche with the force of ten thousand quadrinium bombs. What had he done? A million questions, images and fears rushed through his mind, overwhelming all his senses and paralyzing him to the core.

"What?" was all he could muster.

"You have a choice to make, Laiyos. You're either with us, your own people, or against us. I'm willing to put aside our differences if you're willing to rejoin your brethren. You belong with us. Deep within your heart you must know this. This is a one-time offer, though. If you leave here now, you'll forever be our enemy. So choose wisely, brother."

Darkness enveloped Chase. The shroud of pain and revenge that had cloaked him was obliterated, almost instantly, by a weight simply too heavy to bear. It had been incredibly difficult just to battle Argos, a single Fury. And only his rage and thirst for revenge had given him the abilities required to defeat him. How was he supposed to take on an entire planet of Furies? What if there were even stronger Furies than his brother? How would he defeat them?

What have I done?

Then everything turned black and Chase stood in cold darkness. Ares appeared in front of him in his old corporeal form.

"You must have known that Argos had something like this planned."

"I . . . I knew he had to be working on something big, but . . . I . . . never . . ."

"You never thought you'd help him unleash the worst scourge this universe has ever known?"

"I . . . What? This cannot be," muttered Chase.

"Get a grip, Chase! You need to shake the fear you're feeling now before it eats you alive. Even if it was never your intention, your actions make you responsible for all of this. So now you need to fix it, one way or another, and no matter the cost."

Chase's face turned livid.

"Fix it? How can I defeat a planet of Furies on my own?"

"You can't. But who said you were alone?"

"I don't follow."

"Have you forgotten your friends, your allies, those you know about as well as those you may find along the way?"

"What can they do against this new threat? I have doomed the universe in my quest to save Sarah."

"No! Only if you believe that will it become true. And don't you dare forget the promise you just made to my sister Aphroditis before letting your monster of a brother trap her in that life-sucking contraption. She and the rest of us are counting on you."

"I— I don't know that I have it in me."

"Unacceptable, Chase. And let's look at the alternative for a second. Do you want to join your brother and follow in his footsteps? Is that what you're telling me?"

Chase looked down.

"Look at me when I'm talking to you!" shouted Ares with all his might.

But right now Chase simply couldn't face his mentor and friend.

"Sarah . . ." was the only word that escaped his mouth.

"It's bigger than her. It always has been, Chase. You must have known it. At least on some level."

Tears formed at the corners of Chase's eyes as he finally mustered enough courage to glance at Ares' ice-cold eyes.

"I never imagined it could be something so dark."

"Forget about how dark or insurmountable it may seem to you at the moment. For the time being you must only answer one question."

"Which is?"

"Will you keep your promises and fight with all your might to make sure this universe isn't destroyed by Argos and the Furies? Or will you let your fears consume you? And doom us all . . ."

Chase reflected upon Ares' words. He was way beyond fear at this point. Terror engulfed him from within, paralyzing and freezing him. He felt helpless, terrified and lost all at once. What was he to do?

That was when he heard her voice echo in his mind.

I believe in you, Chase. It was Aphroditis' voice, the last glimmer of light within his quickly blackening soul.

Ares took a step forward. "Listen to her. You can do it, Chase. I know you can!"

Chase's heart pounded so fiercely that he feared it would escape from his chest.

Ares put his hand on Chase's shoulder.

"I'll always be here for you. We'll keep training, and you have all your wonderful friends too. They've just proved to you that they'll go to the end of the world to help you in your quest. And now you also have Sarah and your unborn child by your side. You must make sure you build the world you want them to live in. A world where your child can grow up in peace."

That sent a cascade of electrifying shivers throughout Chase's body, each stronger than the next. Ares was right. No matter how grim the situation felt right this moment, cowering in fear and letting darkness get the better of him was not the answer.

A glimpse of strength and determination re-infused in Chase's eyes.

Ares smiled. "You can do it. She believes in you, and so do I."

"I sure hope you're right."

"It's no longer a question of being wrong or right, Chase."

"What do you mean?"

"Follow your heart. Do what you know you must, deep

inside your soul, with every fiber of your being. Fight this new threat, and remember— you are not alone. You never were. You must release that burden from your soul now and unleash your full power."

"Easier said than done."

"And yet I feel it happening within you, building up already. You know what you need to do, deep down, past fears and the terror that's trying to get the best of you by trying to bring darkness to the core of your soul. I see that brightening light shining through the dark shroud of doubt."

"I barely feel it, and it's so small."

"Make it bigger."

"What?"

"Just like you did with your energy pool. Focus and make it bigger. Let that light shine upon you. Let it make you stronger than ever before."

"I don't know that I can."

"Chase! Close your eyes and make it bigger, *now*!"

Chase didn't really know what to do, but he had grown accustomed to trusting Ares, so he obeyed. He closed his eyes and reached deep down, within the very core of his soul where the light still shined.

"Now, make it bigger."

The mental image he was facing was terrifying. Dark, red clouds in motion around a small glimmer of light, shining through the darkness, with bright-red lightning striking at the light, trying to shut it out of existence. He pushed with all his might but the darkness was growing and the light dimming.

"Chase, if you fail now, this is the end. For us all."

"I'm not strong enough!"

"Yes, you are. Your fears are yours alone. You must defeat the darkness within yourself. Only you can do that, Chase."

"I don't know how."

"Yes, you do! Do you remember the vision-dream you had when you took the Kyrian snake venom?"

"It was just a dream. This is real."

"You make it real! We all make the world we live in real. It's your thoughts, intentions and actions that shape the universe. So ask yourself what you want? Now open your eyes, Chase."

When Chase opened his eyes he was standing on Earth. It had been destroyed. Cities had been leveled. Fires were burning everywhere in the landscape. That was when he saw them, far away, running toward him. Sarah and a young Chris, running away from the dark shadows chasing after them.

"What is this?"

"This is what will happen if you let the darkness within you win this fight. Forget the Furies; forget Argos. Right in this moment you're fighting your worst enemy, Chase: yourself."

Sarah grabbed Chris into her arms and ran toward Chase. She looked terrified. The indistinct shadows pursuing them took human form. There were no less than five Furies pursuing them.

His heart pounded even stronger in his torso, each beat like an earthquake as time seemed to slow down.

"What do I do?"

"You save her. You save Chris. In doing so you'll save everyone else."

Chase made fists and closed his eyes. He wanted to run toward them but it felt as if a dark fog kept him locked in place.

"Chase, remember . . . this battle is inside of you."

"This is just a vision. I'm gonna wake up."

"Despite that, the state in which you wake up from this vision will determine what's coming next."

A shriek resonated in the air and compelled Chase to open his eyes.

Sarah was hit by a dark-red fireball that threw her and Chris down. She had lost consciousness and all that Chase could hear was his young son cry as the Furies approached them both. Chris tried to shake his mother back into consciousness as tears flowed like rivers from his eyes.

"Dad! Help us!"

A thunderbolt hit Chase to the core and rage boiled within his very soul. In just a few seconds, the Furies would kill Sarah and Chris before his eyes. He had to act now!

Chase closed his eyes and unleashed an unearthly, animalistic roar that shook the entire planet and shattered the ground all around. When he opened his eyes again he saw that he had given the Furies pause. They now looked at him.

"Who are you?" asked one of them.

"Your doom. Step away from them and fight someone your own size, you pathetic cowards."

More energy flowed through Chase's body than ever before. Even more than when he had faced Argos. The purple aura emanating from him grew stronger, and soon his purple light was being cast all around them. Bright-white lightning bolts danced around Chase's body as his aura kept growing beyond reason.

The five furies took a fighting stance and grew fireballs in their hands. Their eyes glowed bright red.

Chase took one step from his position and teleported almost in front of them. They reacted instantly, repositioning themselves around him. They lost no time attacking him from every direction. Five fireballs came at him simultaneously.

"No," said Chase with renewed confidence.

The Furies' attacks stopped mere inches from his body before collapsing on themselves.

A bright, white aura shot from the ground and engulfed Chase. Five lightning bolts fired from his body, each striking a Fury and sending it flying backward in the air.

The column of white light rose higher in the sky and soon hit the thick, dark layer of ominous clouds above. It punched through them to let the warm light of the sun shine throughout the valley. Fires around them extinguished and buildings started rebuilding, as if time was playing in reverse.

Chase sprang into action.

Everything seemed to happen in slow motion. Chase launched himself at his first opponent and struck him so hard with his knee that he heard every bone in his torso crack. Dark, red blood shot from his mouth and death was instantaneous. While still in midair Chase performed a spinning kick that decapitated a second Fury, sending his head flying at tremendous speed toward the heavens.

The third Fury, horrified by what he had just witnessed, tried to hit Chase with a powerful blow to the head. Chase dodged his attack in midair and grabbed his arm. In a swift motion he snatched the limb from its socket as more Fury blood flew in the air. The Fury shrieked in agony and dropped to the ground, holding his limbless shoulder in a futile attempt to slow down the spraying of his blood. Chase landed in front of him and threw his opponent's detached arm away with an uncharacteristic smirk.

He lost no time sending the wounded Fury flying with a

powerful uppercut. The impact with the Fury's jaw unleashed a powerful shockwave that sent the remaining two Furies skidding backward for yards. The third Fury flew so high in the sky that he disappeared into the growing sunlight, which shined brighter and brighter upon Chase.

Chase felt an energy like no other fill his entire body. His muscles doubled in size under the pressure of the overwhelming energy building within him. His upper, black body armor ripped to reveal inhuman musculature, big, throbbing veins, pumping not only blood but Chase's life force throughout his body.

He then turned his attention to the remaining two Furies. In a fluid motion Chase thrust both his hands toward them and unleashed two white columns of energy. They hit their targets at the same time and impaled them both, punching through their ribcages.

When their bodies hit the now fully sunlit and warm ground, their lives had already been claimed.

Chase had dispatched five Furies in the blink of an eye. Sarah and Chris were nowhere to be seen, and his eyes now showed him a very different landscape. An unscathed image of planet Earth, with the sun shining bright and high in the now cloudless sky.

Ares appeared out of thin air.

"What happened? What does this vision mean?"

"It was brought on by your inner fears. I don't really know why it happened. Perhaps your proximity to Aphroditis triggered it. Nonetheless, it was important."

"Why?"

"Your fears were about to eat you alive. By fighting and defeating your enemies in this vision, you have lifted a large part of the weight that was crushing your soul."

"I do indeed feel less scared at the moment . . . Confident, even, that we will find a way to fight them."

"I also feel this when I look at you now. But this was just a flash reaction from your own psyche. You haven't defeated every one of your inner demons just yet, but you clearly bought yourself some time to work on it."

Chase reflected on his mentor's words.

"I've never felt so powerful, though."

"Good. Let's hope that means you haven't yet unlocked your full potential."

Chase nodded as Ares' corporeal image disappeared from his sight.

"I'm still waiting for an answer, Laiyos!"

That was Argos, his voice resonating within the vision's landscape.

Chase's view morphed back into the interior of his twin brother's ship and soon he was back in reality.

Chase looked at Argos and smiled.

"Why are you grinning like an idiot? What's your answer?"

"Do you really have to ask, Argos? I will never join the Furies."

"Then you have signed your own death warrant."

"I wouldn't be so sure."

Chase looked at Sarah, who was clearly still in shock at what had unfolded here in the last few minutes. She looked confused and probably wondered if any of this was real.

Chase also felt as though everything that had happened lately was somewhat surreal. But, for the first time in months, he was now painfully aware of where he stood. The full depth of the consequences of his actions were now crystal clear in his mind. He had let anger, hate and revenge cloud his judgment. But if he had to do it all over again, he would. Sarah simply meant too much to him. He didn't see the point of living without her by his side.

He would have to find a way to make things right with Aphroditis and with his friends, and deal with Argos and the Furies once and for all. Part of him felt that what had just transpired was unavoidable anyway.

Perhaps this was part of my destiny all along.

Chase took Sarah's hand and she looked at him with mixed emotions. She might never look upon him the same as she once did.

"Let's go home."

She nodded as tears slid down her cheeks.

"You're a fool, Laiyos! You will regret this decision," spat Argos as he looked with disdain at his departing brother.

Chase turned to look into his twin brother's eyes.

"My name is Chase. You're the fool and, mark my words, you'll regret ever putting me in this position. I don't think you fully realize what you've just done. I have a feeling you will though, and soon."

The fire in Argos' eyes burned as a vein throbbed in his temple.

"The next time we meet . . ." began Argos, but he let the words hang in the air.

Chase remembered what Ares had told him before, that he had felt a great deal of fear within Argos, buried deep down. At this moment, and for the first time outside of combat, Chase also felt that fear in him.

"You'd better pray our paths never cross again. We have unresolved business to deal with. I no longer care if this happens tomorrow or later in the future. But one way or the other, we have a score to settle, you and I. So long, Argos."

Argos didn't answer, but Chase could still smell fear in the air as he left the Zarlack ship with Sarah by his side.

2

O n board the *Iron Fire*, Chase and Sarah walked from the cargo bay to the lift, on their way toward the bridge.

"Are you alright?" asked Chase tentatively.

"I don't know. This all seems surreal, like a dream. Or a nightmare, more like it."

Chase softly exhaled. "I'm sorry for what you had to go through. It's over now."

Her eyes widened.

Chase felt uneasy and understood that she looked at him differently now.

"You do realize what you've done, don't you?"

"Yes, I have put everything and everyone in the universe in jeopardy to get you back."

"How could you?"

"I couldn't lose you a second time. I . . . It would have killed me."

"I would never have agreed that you sacrifice Aphroditis for me. Did you ask yourself how I would feel about it before agreeing to do that?"

"I must admit I didn't. Aphroditis went into the machine willingly."

"Only because you asked for her help in the first place. And now the Furies will destroy everything."

"Not if I have anything to say about it."

"You're just one Fury, Chase. They're an entire race. You may have doomed us all."

The words felt like a blade slicing through his heart. She was right, of course, but his intentions had been good, driven by his love for her and the baby. Which made hearing her say them all the more painful.

"I will not let this happen. If you believe anything, please believe that."

"I don't know what to believe anymore, Chase. How could you risk everything for me?"

Chase's face grew darker. "Isn't it obvious?"

"And I love you too, but how can I be responsible for the fall of the universe?"

He had put her in a tough spot and he knew it. "It hasn't fallen yet. I won't let it."

"I . . . I don't see what we can do to prevent it now."

"We fight. We give it all we've got and trust that we will prevail."

"That's not the Chase I remember."

"I don't know how or why, but I feel different also. For the first time I feel like there's nothing that cannot be accomplished."

"Look, Chase, I'm really glad you feel more confident now. God knows we will need that. But . . . the Furies, Chase, *the Furies* are back, all of them. The first time around they nearly wiped everyone out of existence. Most of the ancient races didn't just disappear naturally, they were exterminated by these . . . creatures."

They entered the lift. When the doors closed Chase put his hand on her shoulder.

"And this time we'll stop them for good, together."

She brushed his hand away as nicely as she could.

"I . . . I don't know if I can do this, Chase."

"Give it time. This has been a very trying period for both of us."

"I don't think you're hearing me. I don't know if there can be an *us* anymore."

Chase felt a growing pit in his stomach. "Surely you don't feel this way?"

"The truth is, I don't know what I feel anymore. I'm sorry, Chase. Don't misunderstand me. You've risked your life and I can only imagine what you've just been through to get me back."

"To get both of you back."

"Right . . . we . . ."

"We'll soon be parents."

"This is so much to process right now. I . . . I'm really lost."

"I know. I'm sorry for what Argos did to you. When I fired— When I destroyed the ship, when I thought you were flying it— You need to understand. The choice you're wishing I had made now is the one I did back then. When I thought I killed both you and the baby, I died inside. I loathed myself for a long time."

"What changed?"

"I'm not sure anything changed. I tracked down Argos and wanted to kill him. Revenge was the only thing that mattered to me back then. I didn't care to live anymore. In fact, I thought killing Argos would be the last thing I ever did. But then, when I was about to deliver the final blow, he told me you were still alive."

She looked at Chase and tears filled her eyes.

"It must have been really difficult for you to take that shot."

"It was the most difficult thing I have ever had to do, and I regretted it the moment I squeezed the trigger. Even though everyone around me told me to do it, to choose the universe instead of you and Chris, well ..."

"Why did you shoot, then? How did you find the strength?"

"You told me ... Well, your clone asked me to. With a really convincing tone and choice of words."

"It was Argos talking through my clone. But you should really take some comfort in the fact that, under the circumstances, I would have told you to fire upon me as well. It's so strange to have memories of both my time in that tank and of my clone. I don't know what's real and what's not."

"I know that now. But please try to understand how hard that was to do once. Doing it twice was just out of the question."

"I guess that's true. Still, try to understand how I feel."

"I understand, trust me."

Chase took a step toward her, to take her into his arms, but she took a step back.

"I'm sorry, Chase, please just give me some time here. In the last twenty minutes I feel like my entire existence has been turned upside down. I don't know what to think anymore."

Chase swallowed hard and looked at the ground. He felt sad about how Sarah was reacting but it was understandable. This was not something that would resolve easily. Sarah would need time to process it all.

"I should probably give you some space right now. So take all the time you need."

She brushed her hand on his arm and attempted to smile.

"Thank you for understanding, Chase. I'm sorry if I seem distant at the moment. I still can't believe any of this is real. I know this must be difficult for you, especially after all you've been through."

Chase nodded as the lift's door opened to reveal the bridge and their friends waiting for them.

Argos looked at the *Iron Fire* from the bridge of his capital ship. Moments later about ten hyperspace windows opened and the rest of his fleet in the area entered Erevos' orbit. His gaze was locked onto the *Iron Fire* as Laiyos' shuttle entered one of its cargo bays.

He could end his brother and his friends' lives right here and now. All he needed to do was to give the order and they would be gone, just like that. But something at the back of his mind was telling him not to. What the hell was that? Why did he feel this way?

What Laiyos had told him earlier hit him more than it should have. Was he afraid of his twin brother? Or was it something else that made him feel this way? Then again, he had given his word. His mission was accomplished, and there would be other occasions to end Laiyos. He had no doubts about that.

His train of thought was interrupted when one of his officers addressed him. "Master, there's an incoming holographic transmission from the surface."

"I'll take it in my ready room."

"Very well, Master."

Argos entered his ready room and kneeled in front of his

holographic projection area. A tall, red man stood with his arms crossed against his chest.

"Well done, Argos."

"Thank you, Supreme Commander Arakan."

"Why is there an Alliance ship in orbit of Erevos?"

"It's my brother's ship. He will be leaving shortly."

"Is he with us?"

"I've asked him to join us but he declined."

"Then why aren't you firing at his ship?"

"I gave my word that if he helped me acquire the Pandora stone, he could take his precious Sarah and leave unharmed."

The holographic figure growled. "Kill him, now!"

"But, Supreme Commander—"

"Argos, may I remind you that you are ten years late? I should execute you on the spot for this failure."

"I have not rested a single minute in the last ten years from my efforts to bring you back here from your dimensional prison. Surely that must count for something?"

"It does, and for your efforts, you will keep breathing. Now destroy that Alliance ship at once, or face the consequences. Arakan out."

The holographic transmission ended.

Argos rose and made a fist so tightly that blood spilled onto his ready-room carpet.

Ungrateful bastard. After everything I've done, how can he treat me this way?

He walked back to the bridge, blood still dripping from his hand.

"Target this ship . . ." Argos hesitated, his gaze fixed upon the *Iron Fire*. After a moment of silence, he completed the order. "And open fire."

~

RYONNA TOOK Sarah in her arms and held her tightly.

"I'm so glad to see you again, Sarah. We've all missed you."

Tears formed in Sarah's eyes. "Thank you, Ryonna, I'm glad to see you too."

Daniel approached Chase with doubts in his eyes. "Glad you're both back . . . But where is Aphroditis?"

"I had to leave her with Argos."

"What? And you're okay with that?"

"Far from it," said Chase with a grave look. "But for the time being, that's how it has to be."

"What's this planet that appeared out of nowhere?"

"It would seem this is Erevos, the home planet of the Furies."

This revelation sent an icy-cold wave upon the entire bridge.

Ryonna took a step forward. "Weren't the Furies defeated ten thousand years ago? What's going on, Chase?"

Tar'Lock clicked nervously.

"I thought so too, but apparently bringing them back was Argos' plan all along. When the Olympians defeated the Furies so long ago, with the help of the other ancient races, they decided to trap them in another dimension outside of space and time. Argos needed me to get hold of the Pandora stone as well as access to an Olympian to bring the planet back into our dimension."

"That's the stone we got from defeating the Titan, isn't it?" interjected Tar'Lock.

Chase nodded.

"Now what?" asked Fillio.

"Now we have to find a way to defeat the Furies all over again," answered Chase with confidence.

Keera's eyes widened. "I know I'm new here, but do you realize we're talking about the vilest and most dangerous beings that ever lived? How are we supposed to do that?"

"Keera, I wish I knew, but we'll find a way. We have to. We should get the hell out of here now that all these ships have appeared. It's not safe here. We'll have plenty of time to discuss all this later."

As if on cue the ship rocked as a volley of laser fire hit the plating of the *Iron Fire*.

Chase lost no time and jumped to the captain's chair, closed his eyes and took mental control of the ship. He raised the ship's shields and activated the hyperspace engines, but they didn't answer.

"Son of a . . ."

They all took their places at different stations and Sarah sat next to Chase.

"What's going on?"

"The hyperspace engines have been damaged. We can't jump out of here. Brace for impact."

A volley of torpedoes and more laser fire pounded the *Iron Fire*'s shields. Chase used all his concentration to avoid as much fire from the enemy fleet as he could with some pretty fancy evasive flying, but there were too many and the shields were lowering at an alarming rate.

"That snake bastard. He told us we could leave."

"And you believed him?" asked Ryonna.

Chase didn't answer, even though he knew Ryonna was right. "Tar'Lock, take Keera to engineering and try to repair the drive."

"I'll go with them," added Ryonna.

"You two," said Chase, looking at Daniel and Fillio, "take

your StarFuries and provide the fleet with alternative targets."

"You want us to do what?"

"At this rate the shields won't hold long enough for us to repair the hyperspace engines."

"Chase, what will two StarFuries do against a fleet of behemoth-class ships?"

Chase's mind raced. They were right. As good as they were, they were vastly outnumbered and this was one fight they would never win.

"We have to do something!" shouted Chase in frustration.

"Chase, can't we outrun them?" asked Daniel.

"The *Iron Fire* took too much damage from that first volley."

"Alright, we'll get to our fighters, but I doubt it will make a difference."

That gave Chase an idea. "No, you're right, it won't. I have a better idea."

Chase took mental control of the StarFuries and launched them at once.

"What are you doing?"

"Getting the hell out of here and buying us some time."

"But you just said we couldn't outrun them with sub-light speed."

"We'll jump out of here."

"Chase, you're not making any sense. We can't jump."

"The StarFuries can."

"So shouldn't we be on board them instead of having them out there?"

"They will open the hyperspace windows."

"Chase, the StarFuries are too small. The *Iron Fire* will never be able to ride inside the corridors they create."

The ship rocked and half the people on the bridge crashed to the floor.

"If you have a better idea I'm all ears, but right now I can't think of anything else."

"This is suicide."

"Perhaps not. I'll try using my powers to widen the corridors."

"Can you *do* that?"

"We're about to find out."

Chase heard Ares in his mind.

No, Chase, you must not use your powers in space.

I have to. If I don't we'll all die here and this was all for nothing.

I don't think Argos wants you dead. The fact that he disabled your engines and didn't go full power on his first attack is suspicious.

Nevertheless, we've seen firsthand how he treats his prisoners. I'm not surrendering. But I agree, something doesn't add up. I can feel it. I don't think he's acting of his own volition. But in the end it doesn't matter. We have to try something.

I hope you know what you're doing.

Chase didn't answer. Not only didn't he know what to say, but he had no idea if his plan was even within the realm of the possible. But it was the only way to escape the immediate threat.

He sent one StarFury to fly in front of the *Iron Fire*, while the other vectored toward the armada, trying to catch some aggro and to test a theory. As expected, Argos started firing on the starfighter, which made little sense since it was absolutely no threat. Was Argos acting against his will by attacking them? He felt no deception from him when he promised to let them go, so this sudden change made no sense. Perhaps it had something to do with the Furies.

Nevertheless, Chase had battled with Argos' forces for long enough to recognize that he wasn't using the full power of his fleet at the moment and his strategies seemed weak at best, as if he didn't want to destroy the *Iron Fire*.

"Shouldn't we be dead already?" asked Sarah.

"Yeah, something is up. I don't think Argos wants the *Iron Fire* destroyed. He must be putting on a show, trying to convince the Furies he is at least trying. So let's give him a good one."

"That makes no sense. Why would he fire on us but try to spare us?" asked Daniel.

"You know what, I think I'd better ask him."

"You're gonna do *what*?"

"I'm going to ask him."

Chase reached for Argos in his mind.

What do you want, Laiyos? said Argos when he felt his brother within his mind.

Why are you holding off? But, most importantly, why did you start shooting at us?

There was no answer.

They asked you to, didn't they? said Chase.

Yes. I hate when I need to break my word. I promised you would be able to take Sarah and your unborn child out of here. I owed you that much for your help today.

Glad you think so. So what's the plan here?

Why aren't you out of here already?

Your first volley took us by surprise. Our shields were down and it disabled our hyperspace engines.

Chase detected a little compassion behind the words of his brother and it really troubled him. Even though he understood the pride behind keeping one's word, it was Argos, after all. Why did he care so much? They were still archenemies, after all. Or were they?

Let me ask you something. You really wanted me by your side, didn't you?

I don't know what you're talking about, brother.

Don't play coy. We're the only ones talking here, so you don't need to appear tough for anyone else. I felt something when I left your ship. I thought it was fear but perhaps it was something else.

Get a grip, Laiyos, you mean nothing to me. Like I told you, I just don't like being told what to do, especially if that means breaking a promise I've made.

Chase knew he was talking with Argos' ego right now and there was no way he would admit that his decision could be based on anything else. Still, he could clearly sense Argos didn't want to destroy the *Iron Fire*.

Argos, I have a plan to get me and my friends out of here and make it look like I outsmarted you. But I'm gonna need your help.

Argos growled. *I'm listening.*

∿

THE STARFURY WAS NEARLY UPON ARGOS' fleet. Chase targeted the ship he was about to destroy, with Argos' help. He fired all four drones in shielded torpedo mode toward it. The fleet tried to destroy the drones but their shields held up and they exploded on the target's shield in quick succession, their quadrinium-enhanced core successfully draining the ship's shields. Not enough to fully disable them, but enough for the next part of his plan.

Chase overloaded the StarFury's engines and micro-jumped the ship toward the targeted Zarlack destroyer. The starfighter jumped into the capital ship and exploded at its center, creating a chain reaction of explosions that took the capital ship out, which in turn created a powerful shock-wave that damaged the surrounding ships. With that out of the way, Chase concentrated on the other StarFury and activated its jump engines. Just when it was about to create a hyperspace window the StarFury was hit with a powerful yellow plasma blast that came out of nowhere and destroyed it.

"Fuck! What was that?" shouted Chase in frustration.

"The shot came from the planet," said Sarah.

A few more shots hit the *Iron Fire* and sparks flew inside the bridge as the lights blinked for a few seconds.

Dammit, the Furies are taking things into their own hands.

As the *Iron Fire* received more pounding from the planet, its shields drained quickly. Chase's mind raced to find another plan, but he was quickly running out of options.

"Keera, I don't suppose you've managed to restore the jump engines already?"

"Not only haven't we managed to repair them, but the last impacts have destabilized half the ship's power conduits. The shield generators are fluctuating dangerously."

"What do we do now?" inquired Daniel, his voice trembling.

"Abandon ship. Everyone to the *Valken*. Once on board we'll jump out of here."

Chase hated the idea of losing the *Iron Fire*, but he could no longer see an outcome that could save his ship. He briefly thought about using the *Valken* to open a hyperspace window for the *Iron Fire* to ride, but surely the Furies would dispatch it before it could get into position, as they did the StarFury a moment ago. In fact, he wasn't even sure they would have time to board the *Valken* in their current predicament. Another shot impacted the starboard shields and one of the consoles on the bridge exploded, confirming his fears: the ship was seconds away from being blown to bits.

"Tar'Lock, bring your party to the *Valken* at superspeed."

"On our way. See you there."

Before anyone could say anything on the bridge, Chase grabbed Sarah, Fillio and Daniel, and erected a force field around them just before the next shot took out power in their section of the ship, effectively disabling the force field that was holding pressure within the bridge's viewport, thanks to Argos' punching through it earlier. Chase took his friends through that same hole, punching a bigger one on their way through and flew toward the cargo bay, dodging incoming fire from the planet on his way.

He ignored Fillio's screams, but understood how disorienting it must have been to be flying in outer space outside a ship.

They arrived at the *Valken* at the same time as Tar'Lock, Keera and Ryonna. They boarded the ship when all hell broke loose. Everything around the *Valken* exploded and the ship was rocked pretty hard. Keera fell and hit her head hard against the nearest bulkhead.

"We're not gonna make it," shouted Tar'Lock.

Chase expanded his mind, found the *Valken*'s computer with his thoughts and blindly jumped the ship at the exact moment the *Iron Fire* was obliterated in a fiery display of successive explosions.

3

A rgos stood with a blank expression on his face as the *Iron Fire* exploded into a million pieces. A sense of dread filled his soul and he was taken by surprise by the wave of emotion his brother's demise brought to the surface.

"Master, we've received a transmission from Erevos. They want you to report to the planet's surface at once," said his communications officer.

Argos exhaled deeply, knowing this would not be a pleasant meeting. Argos hadn't expected the Furies to fire from the surface. He would have to find a way to explain how so many Zarlack capital ships couldn't destroy a measly ship like the *Iron Fire.*

He left the bridge without another word, took the *Dark Star* and vectored toward the surface to the coordinates provided, well within the currently dark side of the planet. His ship rocked a little upon entering the inhospitable atmosphere of Erevos. Bright lightning ignited quick flashes of light inside the cockpit of the *Dark Star* while heavy rain relentlessly poured on the cockpit's viewport.

Memories of Argos' childhood with Laiyos came to him while he piloted his ship toward the planet's surface.

Was Laiyos really dead?

And if he was, why did it bother him so much? He tried to convince himself it was because he had given his word they would be spared. But deep inside he knew that was not the only reason. A lightning bolt nearly struck the front of his ship, illuminating the cockpit brightly for just a moment. Argos could see his reflection in the glass. Except he saw his brother's face instead.

You're still alive, aren't you? Good for you. You've always been annoyingly resourceful. At least you're consistent.

Argos smiled slightly to himself as he vectored his ship toward the landing pad atop one of the many tall buildings in the metropolis below. Even with the very harsh weather conditions he could see the massive and breathtaking city in every direction, as far as the eye could see. Many craft of different sizes and shapes were flying all around, providing a mesmerizing light show. The blurred lights emanating from buildings farther away gave the metropolis an ethereal quality. As he exited the *Dark Star* he was greeted with a nasty, rough sand-and-rain storm. It didn't take long for him to erect a force field around himself to deflect the offending weather elements. He walked the ramp separating his ship from the building's entrance. It was a very angular and massive structure that towered over the rest of the megapolis around it. Clearly some sort of headquarters, thought Argos as he stepped through a door that dematerialized upon approach and rematerialized once he was in. As he walked, some red lights appeared in midair, floating and lighting his way a few meters in front of him as well as behind, casting ominous red tones on the dark gray walls around him. He soon arrived at the end of the corridor where a shiny red circle was drawn on the floor.

Argos looked at it just long enough for a voice to be heard. "Please step on the platform for transport," said the synthesized voice.

Argos entered the circle and was teleported with a hum to somewhere else.

He stood in a large room with a very high ceiling. On each side lines of Fury soldiers extended for a few hundred yards, after which stairs lead to a throne platform, towering above the enormous room. As far from it as he was at the moment, Argos had no doubt Supreme Commander Arakan would be sitting on the throne. The soldiers all saluted synchronously as he walked down the path to the bottom of the stairs. As he passed by, soldiers on each side illuminated their red auras and their eyes shone red. Some sort of official military welcome, thought Argos. Even though they were his brethren, he felt uneasy with the display. At the top of the stairs he saw the throne room, and the soldiers disappeared, leaving him alone, looking up at the throne where Arakan sat and where Arakan looked down at Argos.

This entire room must be a giant holographic display.

"Come closer, Argos," said Arakan. His voice was low and throaty.

Argos arrived in front of the throne. Then he noticed another Fury standing behind the throne in the shadows. Argos wondered if the throne was real or also a projection.

The second Fury took a few steps into the light. He was an imposing man, taller than Argos, with short, orange hair and piercing yellow eyes.

"Kneel in front of your master," said the warrior.

Argos took a knee and lowered his head.

Arakan spoke. "I don't really know if I should congratulate you or kill you where you stand."

Argos' blood froze as fear engulfed him.

"Surely I have accomplished my mission, Master."

"A little on the late side, but I suppose you have, and that is why I'm considering letting you live."

Argos couldn't help but swear in his mind. He had devoted the last ten years of his life to freeing the Furies from their captivity and this was the thanks he got?

"Do you have anything to say on the matter, Argos?"

Argos needed to take a stand or things could get out of hand, so he rose and looked straight into the supreme commander's eyes.

"I have done as you asked. You're now free from the dimensional prison the Olympians had trapped our people in ten thousand years ago. I'd think you would grant me leniency for the small delay it took me to accomplish this goal."

"Spoken like a true Fury. I suppose you are correct, but then you didn't destroy the ship in orbit as ordered."

"My brother is a resilient Fury, his flying skills—"

"Enough! Don't try to find excuses."

Supreme Commander Arakan rose and waved a hand.

A giant holographic projection appeared in the middle of the hall. It showed the battle that had just happened between the Zarlack destroyers and the tiny *Iron Fire*. Argos turned around and looked at it.

"Mind explaining how a small ship like this could not be destroyed in less than a minute?"

Argos swallowed hard. He had to make a choice, either stand his ground or crawl in fear and hope he would be forgiven. Neither choice was appealing but he decided upon the former.

With a look of determination, he turned back to face Arakan's interrogating gaze. "I had given my word to my brother that he could leave this place alive! Perhaps it's a concept that is unknown to you, but I keep my promises. Your renewed presence in the universe should be proof of that."

"So you decided to disobey a direct order from your commander in chief?"

"You've destroyed the ship anyway, so what does it matter?"

"I don't like your tone, Argos. Tread carefully."

"I apologize for any disrespect, Master, but I have bled and fought to bring you back here, thanks in part to my brother's help in acquiring the Pandora stone and bringing me an Olympian to make the dimension portal work. In exchange for his help I promised him safe passage for him and his friends."

"Why would you do such a thing?"

"To bring you back as early as possible. Forgive me if I was mistaken, but I thought that was why you required my help in the first place. And if I may add—"

Argos was interrupted by the second Fury. "You may not!"

Arakan raised his hand again. "Let him speak, Miseo."

Miseo took a step back and apologized. "Sorry, Father."

"Continue," said Arakan coldly.

"My brother and his friends are inconsequential now that you're back. They will be defeated shortly. So whether they died today or in a few days or weeks, what's the difference? They cannot possibly hope to defeat us now, so I really don't see why keeping my word was such an offense."

Arakan walked from the throne and approached Argos. His corpulence was impressive, and his ornate body armor and black cape made him look larger than life. The multiple scars across his face increased his already overwhelming presence.

He raised a hand and a column of red light engulfed Argos. Instantly the gravity increased tenfold and Argos had trouble standing. The beam intensified even more and he felt a tremendous pressure inside his body, accompanied by excruciating waves of burning pain. Argos felt that each bone and internal organ was being pressured to the limit of shattering or exploding. The level of burning pain was so strong that he couldn't try to counteract the effects of that crushing wave.

"Listen very carefully, Argos. I can crush you anytime I want and there is nothing you can do about it. I do not like my orders to be defied, questioned or misinterpreted. If you didn't want to destroy the ship, you should have convinced me when you received the order, not accepted them and then defied me behind my back. This is the first and last time this ever happens; are we clear?"

When he thought his body couldn't take it any longer and would shatter under the pressure, the pain stopped.

Argos fell to the floor, panting heavily, blood spilling from his nose, ears and mouth. It took him a moment to muster the strength to speak. "Understood, Master, please forgive me."

"Because you have accomplished your primary mission, I will overlook this act of defiance. Bear in mind I will never be so lenient again."

Argos nodded as best he could as he tried to rise to his feet.

"Now, we need to discuss the next phase of our plans. We are running dangerously low on resources. We need to get enough quadrinium and a few other rare minerals to start building a fleet of ships. What's the status of your Zarlack fleets?"

"I have more than enough ships to get you as many resources as you require."

"Where can we find it in abundance?"

"Droxian space is the richest in quadrinium deposits, but I would avoid it, at least for the moment. They are a formidable enemy that thrives on war and they rejoined the Earth Alliance, so they would get help if they were attacked. While a victory could be achieved with the ships I have left, we would incur heavy losses and squander too many ships in the process. I propose we start by attacking smaller systems and draining their resources until we have enough materials, then Droxia will be a much easier target to deal with."

"Thank you for your assessment. My son will take over a ship currently in orbit and finish the job you couldn't."

"What do you mean, Master? The *Iron Fire* was destroyed."

Arakan pointed to the center of the hall and again a giant holographic projection appeared. It showed the yellow plasma fire impacting with the *Iron Fire* in slow motion. "Here," said Arakan, pointing toward the *Iron Fire*'s cargo bay. A quick blue flash could be seen just a fraction before flames engulfed the rest of the ship, blowing it into a million pieces.

"This is a hyperspace window. They've escaped!"

"Then let me track them for you. Let me redeem my earlier mistake, Master."

"No. My son will track them and eliminate them."

Arakan looked at his son. "Take a single ship and one of our starfighters and go now."

"Very well, Father. They will be dead by day's end."

Miseo pressed a touch control on his armor and teleported out of the throne hall.

"Laiyos is a very resourceful Fury. One ship might not be enough."

"Miseo is ten times the Fury you will ever be. I have faith he will complete his mission."

Argos wasn't accustomed to being treated with so much disdain and it made his blood boil.

"Yes, Master. What are my next orders?"

"You will make sure we get the resources we need to start building ships right away. Those are your orders."

"Will I still be allowed to command the first Fury fleet and crush Earth and its allies when the time comes?"

"You have deeply disappointed me today. You should feel lucky just being permitted to live one more day. As for the fleet, we shall see if you are given command. But if you even want the slightest chance of this happening, remember that nothing short of total obedience will be required of you."

Argos started to wonder if perhaps he should have listened to his brother when they were younger. Laiyos was always against this plan to help bring back the Furies. Until now Argos never understood why, but he was starting to question his beliefs. However, now was not the time to openly display doubts; so he brushed the thoughts away.

"Absolutely, Supreme Commander."

"Now leave and bring us the resources we so direly need to crush our enemies."

Argos bowed. "Thy will be done."

He quickly healed himself and walked down the stairs.

Not the hero's welcome I expected. How dare they treat me like a second rate citizen? They would still be trapped in another dimension if it wasn't for me.

Argos went back to the *Dark Star* and left Erevos' atmosphere with anger and hatred boiling in every fiber of his being.

WHEN THE *VALKEN* exited hyperspace sparks flew inside the ship. A wall console exploded and started a fire. Wailing alarms resonated within the ship.

Chase jumped up and extinguished the fire with a swift movement of his right hand. The cargo bay of the *Valken* had filled with smoke. Keera collapsed on the ground and Chase ran to her side. Blood gushed from a nasty wound in her scalp. He lost no time healing her and soon she was as good as new.

"Is everyone alright?" shouted Chase to be heard over the annoying alarms.

Sarah nodded.

"Well, we're in one piece so can't complain. What happened?" inquired Daniel.

"We've blindly jumped into hyperspace. Pretty much in the middle of the *Iron Fire*'s exploding."

"Can you shut down these alarms?" asked Daniel

"Let me give it a try." Chase closed his eyes and concentrated on the *Valken*'s computer, but the wailing alarms made it difficult. He pushed through, managed to tune them down in his own thoughts, and accessed the onboard computer. The alarms stopped.

"Thaaaaaaank you," said Tar'Lock, who had curled into a ball because of the pain strong noises caused him.

Keera opened her eyes slowly and tried to get up. "What happened? I thought I heard my ship's alarms going crazy, or was it just a nightmare?"

"I'm afraid not," answered Chase, his eyes filled with concern.

"What is it?"

"I turned them off with my thoughts but while I was inside the *Valken*'s computer I glanced at our status."

"Which is?" interjected Sarah.

"Not good. We've lost the jump engines, there's multiple damage all over the ship and life support is barely at fifteen percent."

"So you can also control computers mentally?" said Keera, raising an eyebrow.

Chase shrugged and attempted a smile.

"Any good news at all?" asked Fillio.

"Well, the communications array seems to be working so I've programmed the computer to broadcast a distress call, but we didn't jump nearly far enough from Erevos."

"That's just great. This day keeps getting better and better," said Tar'Lock with a series of fast-paced clicks.

Keera walked away from the group. "I'm gonna see if there's a planet nearby. At fifteen percent life support we won't last long in space."

Sarah followed her. "Wait up, I'm coming with you."

As the cargo doors closed behind her, Chase looked at his friends.

"There aren't any planets in range. I've checked."

Fillio held her neck and groaned. "Why didn't you tell them that?"

"Sarah's pretty shaken up. It will help keep her occupied for a while."

"What do we do now?" asked Daniel.

"I don't know. Let's see what we can repair on the ship."

"I'm on it," said Ryonna, already entering commands from the nearest terminal. Fillio and Tar'Lock joined her.

Daniel clearly had something on his mind. "What is it, my friend?"

"Are we gonna talk about what just happened?"

"You're gonna have to be more specific. A lot happened today."

"The part about the Fury world appearing out of nowhere and the implications."

Chase broke eye contact. He was still unsure how to deal with that at the moment. The sheer weight of the consequences that this new development could have for everyone in the universe was simply too much to contemplate. He'd already had his share of Armageddon-like close calls to deal with lately, and right now all he was worried about was getting his friends back home safely. He couldn't think about or address the bigger picture at the moment.

"I don't know what to tell you. Right now I don't really want to debate this, so the short version is: it's all my fault. But, like I promised Aphroditis, I'll do my best to fix this."

"I don't think it's your fault."

"We both know it is."

"How so?"

"Well, if I hadn't agreed to help Argos the Furies would still be trapped in another dimension. We have no idea what the fallout of this will be."

"Well if history is any indicator, we're looking at an extinction event, at least for any race other than the Furies currently living in this universe."

Chase clenched his teeth for a second. He was fully aware of this and it didn't help to hear it out loud. But defeating his fears and darkness in his vision had given him hope that there must be a way to deal with all that.

"We won't let it happen."

Daniel beamed a wide smile.

"What did I say?"

"You said 'we.'"

"So?"

"Well, it's about time you realized you're not alone in this."

"I guess I deserve that. I'm sorry for leaving the way I did back on Earth. I didn't want any of you to get hurt."

"That's a noble sentiment, but I think you've learned your lesson."

"I have. Without you guys we wouldn't have survived the fight against the Titan, but—"

"But if you hadn't, things might have turned out different. That's what you're thinking?"

"Yeah."

"That's nonsense. You had no idea what the price would be for getting Sarah back."

"I'm not sure I would have done anything differently had I known. Not if it meant sacrificing Sarah . . . again."

"This is all conjecture anyway. You didn't know, and what is happening now is done. So like you said, we'll find a way to get Aphroditis back and send the Furies back to where they just came from. Together."

"No."

Daniel's eyes widened. "What do you mean 'no'?"

"I mean trapping them in another dimension is not a viable option. This time we deal with them once and for all. The Furies must be wiped out, or they'll keep coming back. Let's make sure this is the last Fury war."

"Easy, tiger. We're talking about the Furies here. Up until now we thought you and Argos were the only two remaining Furies, and that had already caused serious havoc. We're talking about an entire planet of them bent on . . ." He let the words hang for a moment. "Well, I don't know what they're bent on, but I suppose being trapped for ten thousand years in another dimension hasn't softened their resolve for universal domination and destruction."

"It hasn't."

"Mind explaining how you know that? I was just assuming here."

"When the planet arrived I had another vision."

"Oh, I see. Pray tell?"

SARAH SAT next to Keera in the cockpit.

"We haven't been formerly introduced. My name is Sarah." She extended her hand to Keera.

"I know," she said, beaming her a smile. "You're all Chase talked about."

"He talked about me? Why?"

"When I met him he was dead set on finding his brother Argos and killing him. I don't know how much you know. Things went pretty fast in the last few hours. But Chase thought he had been forced to kill you."

"I . . . I have these memories. In fact, it's really troubling. I know they're not really mine, but I remember them as if they were. I know everything my clone has done." Sarah's expression darkened.

"Boy that must feel weird."

"It does. I'm sorry, you have better things to do. I just needed some time away . . ."

"It's okay. You can help me figure out our next move."

Sarah looked straight ahead at the stars while Keera fiddled with her controls for a while.

After a long silence, she looked back at Sarah. "It's none

of my business, but I've never seen someone so much in love as Chase."

Sarah attempted to smile but her expression changed almost instantly and tears flowed from her eyes.

"I'm sorry. You may not want to discuss this. Please excuse my big mouth."

Sarah put a hand on Keera's. "That's okay, you don't need to apologize. I'm just lost. I have trouble reconciling what happened, you know? There are a thousand thoughts overwhelming me at the moment. I . . . I don't really know how to deal with them."

"That's understandable. I know I'm a stranger, but if you need to talk, don't hesitate, okay?"

"That's very sweet of you, thanks. How . . .?" she stopped.

"How do I know Chase?"

Sarah nodded.

"We partnered to try and catch Argos. I'm a bounty hunter."

"I see."

"Look, I don't want you to get any ideas. I'm not interested in Chase."

"That's alright. Like I said, I'm very confused right now."

"Still, if you don't mind me saying, why aren't you back there with Chase? I'd think you'd want to be in his arms right now. In your position that's all I would think about."

"I have a really hard time forgiving him for what he did."

Keera's eye widened. "Forgiving? What does he have to be forgiven for?"

"Putting my wellbeing before that of every living being in the universe, for one."

"Chase had no idea that helping Argos would bring back the Furies. How could he? We all thought they were long gone."

"Still, he had to know that whatever Argos wanted him for would be nefarious."

"Look. Perhaps you should put yourself in his shoes for a little while. I've spent a good portion of time with him these last few days. When we met he was just a shell, his mind and heart broken. For just a second try to imagine if you were the one firing on his ship and killing him for the greater good. How would you feel?"

Sarah thought about it for quite a long time. "I guess . . ." was all she could answer.

"Look, it's none of my business but I'm gonna tell you what I think anyway."

"You seem like that type of person."

"What do you mean?"

"Well, you're direct, that's what I mean."

"Oh, yeah, I guess I am. Understand this. When I met Chase, he was just a way for me to cash in on the gigantic bounty that was on Argos' head. But before I knew it we became friends. He's an amazing guy, and I'm not just saying that because he saved me from being raped."

Sarah swallowed hard. "What?"

"Shortly after we met I had a—how to put it mildly—an unfortunate encounter with an old business partner. He tried to abuse me sexually. Thank the Olympian gods Chase arrived in the nick of time."

She smiled. "He does that a lot."

"What do you mean?"

"Save people at the eleventh hour."

"So doesn't that say a lot about him?"

"It does. And you've given me a lot to think about. Thank you, Keera."

"Anytime. Just remember, he did what he did because he

loves you. I'm not sure anything else really matters at the end of the day."

"It will if the universe pays the price for that love."

Keera stayed silent. Sarah was uncomfortable being the indirect reason why they were in their current situation.

"Any luck finding us a planet in range?"

"Nope. The *Valken*'s sensors are not working at their peak efficiency, but there doesn't seem to be anywhere in range we can land my ship."

"Can we repair it?"

"As far as I can tell, whatever can be done is being taken care of by your friends."

"As far as you can tell?"

"One of them is interfacing with the *Valken*'s system from the cargo bay's console. They're attempting to restore more power to life support and to restore the jump engines."

"Should we help?"

"Whoever is attempting repairs seems pretty skilled. Perhaps we could boost the sensors sensit—" She didn't finish her sentence before a rapid, repetitive alarm sounded from her console. "Oh crap."

"What is it?"

She activated the internal communications. "Chase, get up here stat!"

"What is it, Keera?" repeated Sarah.

"We've got company."

"Friend or foe?"

Keera's look toward Sarah said it better than any words could.

IN THE REAR of the *Valken*, Chase had finished explaining his vision to his friends. Fillio didn't seem to be feeling well and he took her to one side for a chat.

"You alright?"

"I'm not sure. I feel really tired of it all."

Chase recognized that mood. "Wanna talk about it?"

"Sure. I don't really know where to start, though."

"Perhaps you could tell me what has you worried."

"What doesn't these days? You know?"

Chase nodded.

"We've been fending off one attack after another since as long as I can remember now."

"I can relate to that."

"Yet the Furies getting back means it will be even more fighting, more death and destruction. When will it end, Chase?"

"I wish I could say soon. But I'm just realizing the real battle has yet to begin."

"I don't think I have the strength for that one. Perhaps I should resign."

"It's your right to do so and nobody will think less of you if you do. But I won't lie to you, we'd be losing one of our best wing commanders."

She attempted a smile. "Look at me rambling when you must feel responsible for the current situation."

This stung his heart. She noticed. "I'm so sorry. I shouldn't have said that. Please forgive me, Chase."

"You don't need to apologize. You haven't said anything I didn't know or acknowledge myself."

"Yet it was unfair saying it out loud."

"Think nothing of it. I'm more worried about how you feel at the moment."

"I'll be fine. Perhaps it's just the lack of sleep. I can't remember the last time I slept soundly for an entire night."

"I can help you with that."

"How?"

"Well, I can easily put you to sleep. The more my telekinetic and telepathic powers grow, the more I understand how the different regions of our brains work."

"That's handy. I might actually take you up on that once we get back to Earth, if you can spare the time."

"For you I'll make the time."

She shot him that same look of affection she had given him when they were closer back at the academy. But it made Chase slightly uncomfortable now.

"Thank you, Chase."

"Anytime, buddy."

"Buddy?"

"Well . . ."

"Say no more."

Chase bit his lip. That hadn't been very tactful. He knew from her call right after the fifth fleet had rejoined the Earth Alliance that she still had latent feelings for him.

Then again, his mind was filled with so many questions, so much anxiety about what was to come next, that he hadn't stopped once to think how others felt about the situation, or even the feelings they might have toward him. Was he being selfish? Clearly the last few months had taken a toll on his friend and he hadn't noticed.

Daniel was looking at the two of them strangely. That's when Chase realized that he liked Fillio.

He sent him a telepathic message. *Come and keep her company, will you? She really needs someone to talk to and I can think of nobody better than you.*

His expression changed and he smiled as he approached them.

"I've got to check on a few things," said Chase, aware how obvious he was being.

But it didn't seem to bother Fillio. "Alright, thanks for the talk, Chase."

"Anytime."

Daniel sat next to Fillio and a few minutes later he had managed to put a smile back on her face, and even to make her laugh.

Ryonna sat next to Chase. "I'm not the right person for fixing this jump engine."

"I'm sure you'll do fine, Ryonna. How are you? Besides the repairs, I mean?"

"Better than you, obviously."

"What do you mean?"

"Have you forgotten how empathic we Droxians are? You're broadcasting your emotions at the moment. They seem to be all over the place. Plus, after all this time I like to think I'm starting to get to know you."

"Right. I'm okay. Just overwhelmed by it all."

"I think that's the general consensus at the moment."

Ryonna gazed over at Daniel and Fillio when she saw Chase doing so.

"They're cute together. They'd make a nice couple."

"I agree. I can sense his love for her."

"Yeah, me too. I'm not sure how she feels about him, though."

Chase wasn't either. Did she still have residual feelings toward him, which could prevent her from seeing Daniel in the same light as he was seeing her?

His train of thought was interrupted when the speakers came to life. It was Keera. "Chase, get up here, stat!"

"Now what?" said Chase, running toward the cockpit.

4

Onboard the Zarlack destroyer, Miseo stood at the viewport on the bridge as the ship exited hyperspace.

"Scan the area for any energy signatures," said the Fury to nobody in particular.

"A medium-sized craft's signature has been detected on long-range sensors."

"Vector the ship toward it, and as soon as we're in range, fire with maximum firepower."

"Shouldn't we try to capture them?" said someone on the bridge.

Miseo looked at the crew. "Who said that?"

A Zarlack got up from his console and took a step forward. "I did . . . Master."

"Why do you think we should capture them?"

"From the sensor data we have on the ship, it seems badly damaged. They are basically disabled. Perhaps their passengers could be of more use to the Fury alive than dead."

"What's your name?"

"First Officer Zin'Dran, Master."

"Are you aware of the concept of an order, First Officer?"

"Of course, Master, and I apologize if I—"

He was cut short when he started levitating toward the Fury. He flailed his limbs, trying in vain to get back to the ground.

"Please, Master, I didn't mean any disrespect."

Miseo looked at the officer and his eyes glowed with an intense, bright-red hue.

"I don't know how Argos did things around here, but I think a little demonstration couldn't hurt."

A wave of energy shot upwards from Miseo's feet and sent his short hair dancing atop his scalp, as his aura shined brightly on the bridge, giving every console and bulkhead around him a red tinge.

The officer, realizing his life was about to end, flailed his limbs and tail even more, but soon he felt an invisible force applying pressure on every one of his muscles, restricting his every move. He tried to speak, to implore the Fury for mercy, but his windpipe refused to obey him. Soon his floating body was mere feet away from the Fury.

Another officer rose from his console and intervened. "Please, Master, spare his life!"

Miseo's ruby stare adjusted and looked at the second lizard man. He released his telekinetic grasp and First Officer Zin'Dran fell to the ground in front of Miseo.

"What is it to you?" asked Miseo, his hair still flowing upwards.

"Thank you, Master. Please don't kill my brother. He meant no disrespect."

"You're welcome," said Miseo with an evil smirk, as he waved his hand in multiple directions so quickly it blurred.

The newly standing officer's eyes froze in place as

multiple rays of thin, red light drew all over his body. Miseo closed his fist and each light-divided body part separated from the others and levitated in the air for a second, as if by magic, before falling one after the other on the ground with gruesome, splashy sounds.

"Nooooooo!" shouted First Officer Zin'Dran at the horrifying scene that claimed the life of his brother. Rage overtook him. Sharp claws erupted from his fingers and he launched himself toward Miseo.

But he never landed his blow. Miseo impacted his ribcage with an open palm and the Zarlack's body froze in midair, paralyzed.

Miseo started laughing. "Insects should never try to rebel against their masters. Every one of you, I suggest you look and learn."

Red light bled out of each of Zin'Dran's facial orifices. His skin burned and smoke rose from his body. His skin cracked and more red light bled through. Flames erupted from the hundred cracks in his body as he screeched in pain, while being burned alive from the inside out.

"As fun as this distraction has been . . ." added Miseo.

With a slight nudge of his mind he sent the still burning body flying over the bridge stations for every member of the crew to witness the gut-wrenching scene. Utter terror could be read in everyone's eyes. Soon first officer Zin'Dran's body had been burned to a crisp. Miseo then snapped his fingers and whatever was left of the Zarlack's body exploded, spilling hot ash everywhere on the bridge.

"Does anyone else have a suggestion? Now would be the time to speak."

After a few seconds of silence, Miseo turned his back to his slave crew and resumed looking at the stars through the bridge's viewport.

"Now, will someone please enter an intercept course."

"Course set, weapons to maximum," said another Zarlack officer, his voice trembling.

"About freaking time. Fire plasma cannons the second we're in range."

~

CHASE RUSHED INTO THE COCKPIT. "What is it?"

"We've got an incoming Zarlack destroyer on an approach vector."

"Evasive maneuvers?"

"Already pushing the sub-light engines beyond their limits. Not sure how long they'll keep up with this treatment in our current state. Any luck with the jump engines?"

"Ryonna said there're too many power nodes fried. She's trying to build a bypass but she needs more time."

"Time is the one resource we don't have right now."

"How long until the destroyer gets a firing solution?"

"Less than a minute."

"Dammit!"

"I don't see how we're getting out of this one."

Sarah, who had stayed silent until now, looked at Chase. "Chase, if we don't make it—"

"We're gonna make it. We didn't go through all of this to die here."

"Please, let me speak."

"I'm sorry."

"Thank you for coming to get me. That's all I wanted to say."

Chase didn't know how to answer; his mind was racing, trying to find a solution to their current predicament. He felt as if his mind was overheating from running multiple scenarios, none of which provided even a shadow of a solution.

"I have an idea. Turn the ship around. Face them head on."

"What?" exclaimed Keera. "Are you nuts? If we do that they'll have a firing solution on us in less than ten seconds."

"Whether we do that or wait another minute won't change anything, but I'd rather have a line of sight for what I'm gonna do next."

"Would you mind cueing us in?"

"No time. Please turn the ship about, now."

"I sure hope you know what you're doing."

"We're about to find out."

"Would you rather take the helm?"

"No, that's fine. Just plot an intercept course with the Zarlack destroyer. I'll take care of the rest."

Keera shot a dubious and fearful look toward Sarah, who just shrugged in response.

The *Valken*'s controls beeped frantically.

"They've targeted us," said Keera, "so whatever you're gonna do . . ."

"Not yet."

Keera didn't know what was more terrifying: the fact that they were mere seconds away from being obliterated by the incoming destroyer or the calm in Chase's voice.

Another set of more ominous beeps resonated in the *Valken*'s cockpit.

"They're firing plasma guns. Whatever shields we have left won't stop this attack. Not that my full shields would have anyway. Not if these readings are correct."

But Chase didn't answer. Instead he extended his hand forward.

"Chase, what are you doing?" asked Sarah.

Yes, what are you doing? asked Ares inside Chase's mind.

No choice, Ares, I've gotta do something, answered Chase telepathically.

This will not end up pretty.

That's kind of the idea here.

You could just as well destroy this ship with that move and you know it.

Don't really have any choice now, do I?

Two gigantic red plasma shots were approaching the ship fast. The enemy had not withheld anything; they had fired the most powerful weapon at their disposal. Whoever was on that ship clearly wanted them dead with the first volley.

But then something happened. The plasma shots compressed onto themselves and stopped advancing just a few hundred yards from the *Valken*, illuminating everything red in the cockpit. They kept compressing themselves, their length collapsing as they grew in size. Lightning burst around them. Soon both shots had merged into a giant plasma fireball with lightning bursting all around it.

"What the hell?" said Keera. "Are you doing this?"

She turned around to look at Chase when he didn't answer and saw him engulfed in a purple aura of flowing energy. Every muscle in his body flexed and trembled, his teeth clenched and a little blood teared from one of his eyes.

Her look turned from stunned to terrified. "Oh gods! I'll take that as a yes."

Chase unleashed a terrifying, animalistic growl that made both Keera and Sarah jump off their seats, just as the rest of the crew entered the cockpit to see the scene unfold.

"What is this?" asked Daniel, not believing or understanding what he was looking at.

Chase's growl intensified, his aura grew stronger and

brighter and his muscles grew in size. The ship trembled so much a whole new set of alarms resounded around them. Sparks flew from the ceiling when Chase's aura expanded to engulf almost half the cockpit.

Chase! shouted Ares. *Don't drain all your energy or you will die!*

I need more . . .

Stop this now, I beg you!

I c-c-can't. I'm almost there. Just . . . a . . . little . . . more . . .

The now huge plasma fireball shook heavily for a second and then shot back at impossible speed toward the Zarlack's destroyer. It created a powerful shockwave at its point of departure, which impacted the *Valken's* already feeble shields and they managed to diffuse most of the energy of the wave before giving out. The now going-in-reverse plasma fireball struck the Zarlack's destroyer, punching through its shields and plating as if they weren't there.

A powerful explosion exposed many of the ship's levels to space. Flames spewed. Metal debris was thrown into space, as were many crewmen from the decompressed levels. The Zarlack destroyer didn't explode but it was greatly damaged, most of its systems disabled on the spot.

"What *was* that?" asked Daniel, not believing his eyes.

Chase's aura vanished all at once.

"Wow, good job, Chase!" Daniel cheered.

Chase stood still, his arm still in front of him, but he didn't answer.

"Are you alright?" inquired Ryonna.

Chase fell to his knees, a blank stare in his eyes as more blood flowed from them. He collapsed to the ground face first.

"Oh my god, no! Chase!" shouted Sarah, who jumped

out of her chair and reached his side. She turned him over and shook him, trying to wake him up, but he had lost all color.

"Please, anyone, help! I don't think he's breathing."

Daniel jumped next to Sarah. He couldn't feel a pulse on Chase's jugular. His eyes filled with fear.

Keera went to the back of the cockpit and looked through her stuff, throwing everything from each drawer and cupboard she opened at a mad pace. "Keep him breathing while I look for my resuscitation kit."

Sarah gave Chase mouth to mouth while Daniel applied heart compressions. Tar'Lock clicked nervously and passed out. Ryonna and Fillio joined Keera in her search for the medical device.

"Dammit! Where is it?"

Sarah kept giving Chase mouth to mouth while her eyes filled with tears.

"Stay with us, buddy," said Daniel as he continued his cardiac compressions.

Then Sarah felt something burn inside her. Her round belly felt hot and the warmth expanded all over her body.

"Sarah!" shouted Ryonna, her eyes wide. "What's happening in your belly?"

She looked down and saw a shining, bright, golden aura bursting out of her. A bright, golden energy expanded from her belly and went toward Chase's inanimate body. It looked like a bright and shining golden umbilical cord. After a few seconds it detached from Sarah's body and was absorbed by Chase's.

Chase's eyes shot open and he gasped for air. Everyone exhaled heavily, relieved to see their friend come back to life.

Sarah grabbed Chase and held him tightly against her

still trembling body, her tears flowing like rivers on her delicate cheeks.

"You scared the shit out of me. Don't ever do that again!"

"Sorry, I . . . I had to do something."

She took his face in her hands and kissed him.

Ryonna let herself fall against the nearest bulkhead, while Fillio attended to Tar'Lock, slapping him gently awake.

Daniel's mouth was open and he was breathing rapidly, still shaken.

"Anyone have any explanation for what happened here?"

No one answered.

Then a golden sphere of energy appeared in the middle of the group and took human shape.

"Ares. I should have known," said Chase. "Thank you."

"That wasn't my doing. I was about to take control of Tar'Lock's body again to try to infuse some much needed life energy into you, but it looks like Chris beat me to it."

Chase's eyes grew. "How is that possible?"

"I don't know. I've never heard of anything like this before. Especially from an unborn baby."

Sarah stayed silent and put her arms around her slightly bulging belly. "But I'm only a few months pregnant. How is that even possible? And how do you know the name of my baby?"

"Chase told me you would name your child Chris."

"We didn't even have that conversation . . ." She looked at Chase, her face still streaming with tears.

"I saw him in a vision, and that was his name."

"This is just too much. So . . . we're having a boy then?"

"Looks that way."

"I'm exhausted." She turned toward Ares' golden aura. "Why is that?"

"I think Chris channeled some of your own energy as well. You should probably rest now."

"I'll rest when we're out of this. That ship isn't destroyed. We may want to finish the job first, and I don't mean you," said Sarah, pointing an accusing finger at Chase.

"I couldn't do anything at the moment even if I wanted to."

"Good!"

Ares took a step forward. "You may want to resume your posts and get the jump engine back online, because the shit is about to hit the fan," said Ares, pointing toward the cockpit.

Keera jumped back to her seat and Daniel joined her on the co-pilot seat.

Clearly disabled and unable to fire any of its main weapons, the Zarlack destroyer had sent a squadron of starfighters to intercept the *Valken*.

"Shit, we're in no shape to take on a squadron of ships," said Keera, while trying in vain to restore the shields. "Dammit, they'll be in firing range in less than a minute."

Ryonna pointed toward where Chase had blocked the plasma fire. "What's happening there?"

A dark sphere blacked out the stars. Purple lightning burst around the sphere as it grew.

"We should get the fuck out of here," said Ares. "This is a tear in space and time. It will most likely destroy this system within minutes."

Chase's face grew somber, but he didn't say a word. He didn't have to. He knew there was a good chance this would happen when he used his powers this way.

"We're out of here, then. I'm redirecting any ounce of juice to the sub-light engines," said Keera.

The *Valken* turned around and flew away from both the growing anomaly and the incoming wave of fighters.

The anomaly grew in size exponentially, and then it exploded on itself, creating a black hole that started sucking in everything around it. The incoming starfighters were the first to be affected by the gravitational pull, and for a moment it looked as though they were stuck in place. But then they started spinning uncontrollably and were sucked in toward the center of the still-growing black hole.

The *Valken*, which had traveled a sizeable distance away, started shaking and losing speed. Its engines moaned as the gravitational pull grew stronger.

"This is not good!" shouted Keera.

"No shit," answered Daniel. "What's that?" He pointed at a newly blinking control.

"That's an incoming communication. Patching it through."

"Starship *Valken*, this is the EAD *Destiny*, do you require assistance?"

"Commodore! Boy it's good to hear your voice, sir," answered Daniel.

"We've tried locating the *Iron Fire*, but its beacon stopped transmitting. We were scanning the surrounding systems when our long-range sensors detected the *Valken*'s signature. What's your status, Commander?"

"We need a lift, ASAP. We're about to get sucked into a black hole."

"On our way. We'll micro-jump near your coordinates."

"No!" interjected Chase. "Commodore, don't jump here."

"Chase, it's good to hear your voice. I'm listening."

"From the force of the gravitational pull I'd say it's too

dangerous for the *Destiny* to approach within tractor-beam distance."

Keera keyed in commands on her terminal at impressive speed.

"Chase is correct, sir, the *Destiny*'s mass is way too big. You'd be sucked in before you had time to approach us. Looks like the Zarlack destroyer is already drifting toward the black hole, even though it's farther from it than we are."

"Options anyone?" asked the commodore.

Chase's mind raced to find a solution. He was too weak to use his powers to push the ship away. Not to mention that that could create a second anomaly. He approached the co-pilot seat.

"Do you mind?" he asked Daniel.

"Sure, go ahead, buddy." Daniel gave him his chair.

"Gimme a sec, Commodore." He entered calculations on his console at lightning speed. "Alright. I'm sending you jumping coordinates now. That's a few thousand clicks from the *Destiny*'s point of no return. Whatever you do, don't advance beyond that point, and make sure the jump engines are ready to engage at a second's notice. However, there's no way we can reach these coordinates on our own at our current velocity. Soon the gravitational force will be too strong for the *Valken*'s engines."

"Then what good will it do? How do we get all of you home, son?"

"I've got an idea about that, but one thing at a time. Have a dozen StarFuries ready to launch. I'll remote control them."

"Roger that, Lieutenant Commander. *Destiny* jumping now. ETA is two minutes."

"Thank you, Commodore."

The communication ended.

Sarah looked worried. "Chase, is that wise? Your energy levels are low."

"I'll be fine. Chris gave me more than enough juice to do this."

"To do what exactly?" asked Ryonna.

"You'll have to trust me. It would take too much time to explain."

～

ABOARD THE DAMAGED ZARLACK DESTROYER, Miseo looked at the growing black hole as everyone from the bridge floated in the vacuum of space and was slowly sucked out of the bridge. Miseo had erected a force field around himself and stayed there, pensive, looking and reflecting upon what had just happened.

Impressive. This is no ordinary Fury.

He felt the gravitational pull exerted by the black hole slowly taking hold of the disabled destroyer. After a few moments observing the bodies of countless dead Zarlack's being slowly sucked toward the black hole, he turned around and flew toward the launching bays. He had to fly through the levels that had been obliterated by the plasma fireball. The damage was extensive, decks upon decks exposed to space, bodies and debris everywhere around him. The sheer scale of the damage was enough to send a shiver down his spine.

We're going to have to tread carefully when we next attack this particular foe.

He landed on one of the decks that was exposed to space on the other side of the ship. He entered his Fury starfighter and launched it into space. The sub-light engines moaned and his ship had trouble breaking free of the gravitational pull. He punched them at maximum and soon the pull lowered in intensity. When he was far enough from the black hole he keyed in the coordinates for Erevos and jumped into hyperspace.

WHEN THE *DESTINY* jumped out of hyperspace, Chase closed his eyes and took mental control of the dozen StarFuries. The first StarFury tractor beamed the nearest fighter, which in turn tractored the next, until each StarFury was a link in a chain. Chase extended their formation toward the *Valken*, approaching from the side in a pendulum trajectory, while the ships farthest away from the lead ship all faced backward at different angles, pushing their sub-light engines at the maximum in a coordinated effort to counter the gravitational pull of the black hole.

"I see what he's doing," said Keera.

"We all see," added Daniel, "and it's insane to think he can remote control all these ships with the required precision to carry out such a complicated and ingenious maneuver with only his mind."

"How do you feel, Chase?" inquired Sarah, putting her hand on his shoulder.

He flashed her a thumbs up as an answer.

Soon the nearest and last StarFury in the chain approached from the *Valken*'s aft side and tractored the *Valken*, which had positioned itself to be able to add its own engine power to the current swinging momentum of the starfighter chain. Once they were through half the maneuver, each StarFury reoriented its trajectory to help gain more velocity and augment the momentum and burst from the black hole's gravitational hold.

A minute later, at the end of the maneuver, every ship was far enough away from the black hole and already on its way back to the *Destiny*.

Once they were on the ship, Commodore Saroudis jumped the *Destiny* out of the system, as instructed by Chase.

~

DANIEL HAD stood outside Fillio's quarters for minutes now. His heart was beating fast and he still didn't know if he could ring the doorbell.

Why am I feeling this way? I'm not an adolescent anymore.

But when a crew member shot him a look from the other side of the hall, he felt compelled to act. He rang the bell.

"Come in," said Fillio as the door slid open.

Daniel walked in and found Fillio wrapped in a towel. He looked away.

"If it's not a good time I can come back later."

"Don't be silly. I just took a shower. I really needed one."

Daniel blushed a little.

"Anything you wanted to talk about?" she added.

"I . . . I just wanted to see how you were doing. I got the feeling you weren't yourself back on board the *Valken*."

She looked at him for a few seconds before answering. "That's sweet of you. Between you and me, I haven't been myself for a while now."

"Anything I can do about that?"

"That depends. What did you have in mind?"

Daniel's heart pounded in his chest.

"When we get back to Earth, I thought, you know . . . perhaps we could go for a bite, just the two of us?"

She smiled. "You took your sweet time to ask me out. You know that, right?"

Daniel scratched his head. "Yeah, not exactly comfortable in these situations."

"Situations?"

"I mean, I . . ."

She laughed like a little girl. "I'm sorry, Daniel, and yes I would definitely love to go on a date with you."

That filled him with renewed confidence. "Cool. I'm looking forward to it."

"So am I. Anything else you'd like to talk about."

"Just checking up on you. I was worried."

"You said that already."

"Right. I guess I should be going now."

He walked back toward the door when she grabbed his hand.

"Please, don't go yet."

When he turned around she undid her towel and let it fall to the floor. She approached him and they kissed passionately. Soon they were on her bed and she helped him get undressed.

5

Argos received an incoming transmission from Miseo.

Calling to gloat about destroying a measly cargo ship with one of my destroyers, no doubt.

"Argos here, what can I do for you— ? What shall I call you? Master?"

"None of that with me. My dad loves his titles. I have no time for nonsense like this. Miseo will do. I just had a very interesting encounter with your twin brother. He managed to disable and eventually doom the destroyer I had borrowed from you."

Borrowed, right!

"I tried telling you my brother was resourceful."

"Indeed, and I'm starting to think we should have listened to you. He displayed a level of power I was not expecting. I would like to discuss the issue with you in more detail."

And now you need my help, again. How typical.

"Sure, whatever you need."

"I'll be landing on your ship shortly."

"Looking forward to your arrival, Miseo."

"Miseo out."

If you think you and I are going to be friends, you've got another thing coming.

Argos felt anger rise in him. The Furies' return hadn't worked at all how he imagined it would. In his head, he had envisioned not only a hero's welcome but also an instant place of power within the Fury ranks. He was the only reason they weren't still prisoners outside space and time, after all. A fact that Supreme Commander Arakan, and his son, to a lesser degree perhaps, seemed to have conveniently forgotten.

Argos looked at the stars from his ready room on his flagship destroyer. He noticed the low-level hum emanating from the machine in which Aphroditis stood, barely breathing. The blank stare in her all-white eyes made her look like a ghost of her own self. Argos almost felt pity for her, though he quickly brushed that pathetic display of sentimentality aside. The Olympians deserved everything they got, and he looked forward to the day the Furies would rid them from the universe. He had no doubt that was Arakan's plan as well. After all, they had been instrumental in trapping the Furies in an alternate dimension. If they managed it once, they could most certainly do it again, a fact he was sure Arakan knew.

There were some beeps, and a tactical holo-screen popped up. It took Argos out of his pensive state. The fleet he had sent to the nearest world rich in quadrinium had arrived. He watched the battle unfold. This particular world was no match for the Zarlack's advanced technology. In less than twenty minutes the world's defenses had been taken care of. Argos grew bored and turned off the holo-screen. There was no challenge in the mission he had been assigned, but only the results mattered. If he dreamt to gain a position of power within the Fury ranks, he would have to do their grind work for a while. That last thought didn't help his feelings of anger one bit.

When Argos heard a hiss from the jar next to him, he opened the lid and let the Kyrian snake bite him on the arm. He closed his eyes as the venom ran through his veins, and soon all his worries faded away.

CHASE ENTERED the *Destiny*'s captain's ready room.

"Ahh, Chase, please come in."

"Commodore, it's good to see you. Impeccable timing as always."

"You can thank Ares for that. I fear that if he hadn't intervened I would have resigned my commission."

"Really? Why?"

"I simply couldn't take the rigidity of the admiral. She didn't want to see reason, past rules and regulations."

Chase couldn't help but crack a laugh.

"What's so funny, Chase?"

"Nothing. It's just I think I'm rubbing off on you."

Saroudis smiled. "You have that effect on people, but you can be a real pain in the butt too. I'm sure you know that."

"I know. And my impulsivity can also have dire consequences, as I'm learning right now."

"About that . . . After my debrief with Sarah, I got the feeling this wasn't the happy reunion you were hoping for."

"You can say that again, but I understand her."

"It's a double-edged sword, Chase. On the one hand your act was driven by love, and I'm sure deep down she knows that. But it's frightening to her to know how far you're willing to go for her. Personally I think Argos would have found a way to make it happen one way or the other. And if I had your powers and was given the opportunity to save my own family, I would have done the same as you did."

"Even if by doing so you'd be dooming the universe, and most likely your own lives in the process?"

"We can't make decisions based on what could happen, Chase. For one thing, the universe hasn't fallen yet. Sure, the Fury resurgence is going to make things a lot more difficult, but what's to say it's not necessary? The Olympians were unwise to trap them instead of annihilating them when they had the chance."

"You seem pretty caught up with the latest events."

"Ares also made a visit before I started my debriefs with the rest of the crew. He thought a little more context would help."

"I realize now how blinded I was by hatred and desire for revenge. All I wanted to do was kill Argos, and when I learned Sarah was still alive, saving her became my only target. I didn't stop once to think of the consequences, even when Aphroditis and Ares both tried to warn me."

"Yet in your place I think I would have done the same thing."

"It's good to hear. I wish Sarah would see it that way as well."

"You need to give her time. It's very different from her perspective. Had she been asked before, she would have rather sacrificed herself, which is understandable if the Furies lay siege and annihilate our universe. And that's what she fears most: to have been a pawn used to bring about the destruction of all life. That must be an unbearable load to deal with."

"I won't let it happen. I will stop the Furies."

"We will, Chase, all of us together."

"Right. If I've learned something in the last few days it's that I can count on all my friends."

"As we can count on you. It goes both ways."

"Thanks, Adonis."

"You're welcome, son. I'm sure Sarah will understand in time, but right now she's just been hit with the enormity of it all."

"Speaking of which, should we formulate a battle plan? I think we should go on the offensive while the Furies aren't fully armed and ready."

"Do we know they aren't?"

"If they had a fleet ready it would have been detected when we were in orbit. Too bad the *Iron Fire* has been destroyed. Its sensor logs could have given us a clearer picture of what's happening on the surface of Erevos."

"That's the name of their planet?"

Chase nodded. "It is indeed. As you know, the computer core memory of each AI computer on board Alliance ships is encased in a very resilient nanotube casing, doubled with a self-powered force field. There's a good chance it survived. Perhaps we can recover it. With a cloaked StarFury, that could be attempted. Should we go now?"

Saroudis looked pensive.

"Negative, Chase. While I agree the information could be very valuable, right now we need to get back to Earth. They need to know the Furies are back and we need to prepare accordingly."

"I agree, but how?"

"I don't really know. More defensive measures, trying to grow the Alliance by recruiting more currently independent races from every sector, look for the Olympians."

"You're not serious?"

"Why not?"

"From what I've gathered, Zeus wants nothing to do with us primitive beings."

"Aphroditis told me the same thing, but we have to try."

"What about finding other ancients?"

"I've tried asking her about that. She didn't say anything about it, but I felt she was evading my questions on the subject."

"Any idea why?"

"None, but my instinct tells me that other Earth mythologies must have a link with other ancient races out there. We should investigate that, at least."

"I agree. We need more allies."

"You seem tired, Chase."

"I am."

"Try to get some rest. We'll have plenty of time for planning our next moves when we get back to Earth."

"Right. Won't I be considered a traitor by the admiral, though?"

"I'm hoping not. At least, not if I have anything to say about it. But I think Ares' intervention might have softened Admiral Thassos' view of the situation."

"And yet the first thing you'll announce is that I helped bring the Furies, the cruelest and most dangerous foe this universe has ever known, back into play."

"Right, well, I will do my best to protect you from that. Perhaps she doesn't need to know it was your direct actions that led to that."

"Not sure lying to her is a good strategy either. Secrets tend to get into the open one way or another."

"I know. We'll cross that bridge when we get to it."

"Which will basically be tomorrow," said Chase with a wide smile.

"So let's agree not to worry today?"

"Deal."

"Now go get some rest, Lieutenant Commander. That's an order."

"Very well, Commodore, as you command."

Chase walked back toward his quarters on the *Destiny*. He wanted to go see Sarah but his instinct told him it was too soon. As the commodore had suggested, he should probably just give her some space and time to process it all. He felt knackered anyway, so when he arrived in his quarters he let himself drop into his bed. Except his head never touched his pillow.

CHASE LANDED ON SOME SOFT, blue grass in the middle of the night, on a planet he didn't recognize. That sent some light, cyan fluff flying all around and soon green, glowing fireflies came and grabbed the soft fluffy material his falling on the ground had sent flying upward.

"Now what!" said Chase out loud.

Then he saw a beautiful, blue-green ringed planet in the sky above him, with an asteroid field in front of it. Multiple light sources approached the planet. Soon what he could only surmise were ships started firing on the planet. First, small, orange-red dots appeared on its surface. Quickly they grew in size and number. Chase felt very uncomfortable witnessing the attack without being able to do anything about it. But he didn't even know where he was.

"You're on the third moon of planet Tyronis. It's under attack as we speak by Argos' Zarlack forces."

"Hello, Ares. You couldn't have just appeared in my quarters?"

"Wouldn't have had the same impact as showing it to you now, would it?"

"I guess not. What am I supposed to do about it though?"

"Nothing. This world is already lost. There's nothing we can do about it. Many other small and beautiful worlds and systems like this one will fall in the coming weeks. It's unavoidable."

"If you want to say I told you so, be my guest."

"That's not why I'm showing you this."

"Then why?"

"We need to be aware of what Argos is doing and see how we can stop him."

"He tried to spare me."

"What? When?"

"When we left Erevos."

"Yet the *Iron Fire* was destroyed."

"By the Furies' weapons on the surface, not by his destroyers."

"What are you trying to tell me, Chase?"

"I think there is doubt in him. I'm no longer convinced he is fully evil."

"I'm not sure I can give him the benefit of the doubt. With him having killed me and doomed my sister to eternal imprisonment."

"We'll get Aphroditis out of there, I promise you."

"Chase, please don't promise things you can't guarantee delivering."

"Okay, let me rephrase that: I will do whatever is in my power to save her. Better?"

"Yes. And I thank you for it. Still, Argos has to be dealt with, and I must say I'm surprised you are considering any other action but retribution."

"True. I still feel like killing him, but he could have finished us off easily, and he didn't."

"He had given you his word."

"Yes, and he tried to keep it."

"I still don't see what it changes in the larger scale of things."

"I don't know, but it bugs me. And my instinct is telling me that there is still good somewhere in him. I did feel a lot of fear emanating from him when we last met."

"Well, for the time being I think it's safe to say he remains our enemy."

"I have no doubts about that either, don't worry, Ares. What is it you wanted to talk about?"

"Argos' first target, Tyronis, is located near Erevos, and its asteroid field is rich in many valuable resources, including, but not only, quadrinium."

"So?"

"So, I think it's clear the Furies are in dire need of resources. They will need them to rebuild their fleet."

"Rebuild?"

"In the final days of the war, the coalition of worlds that defeated their armies destroyed their fleet. It had been a terrible battle that lasted for days. It took the combined forces of hundreds of worlds and thousands of ships to win that battle."

"So they are rebuilding it?"

"That would be my guess."

"That means we have a short time-window to make sure this never happens."

"I think so."

"If you have to guess, how long do we have?"

"Weeks I'd say. A few months at the most."

"Can I ask you something?"

"Sure. Anything."

"Are there any other ancients around?"

"I suppose so."

"Saroudis said he felt Aphroditis deflected the question when he asked her."

"Since the Fury War, Olympians have cut all ties with the other ancient races. Now I'm thinking their ill-advised decision to not finish them off is perhaps the reason behind this."

"That would make sense. Who are the most powerful ones you know of?"

There was silence.

"What is it, Ares? Why don't you want to answer?"

"I'm not sure it's even a good idea to mention any names."

"And yet you will. We are past the time for petty, ancient rivalry."

"There's one race that has a technological advantage we could use. But they are not keen on other races, and they definitely don't want to hear of the Olympians ever again."

"Will you tell me their names, already?"

"The Asgardians."

"Thank you. Wait, Asgard? Why does that name ring a bell?"

"Because Earth has them in their mythologies as well."

"The reason being?"

"After we left Earth and guided you to create the Alliance, they took over the protection of the planet briefly. There was a void to be filled, deity-wise, and so they filled it."

"You say that like it's a bad thing."

"No, not necessarily, but they are a warrior race. They live to do battle. They even teach that dying on the battlefield is a glorious thing. That they should feel proud to end up in Valhalla, their word for heaven."

"Ryonna would sure like them."

"Yes, I bet she would. The Droxians' strong sense of honor resembles that of the Asgardians."

"Where can we find them?"

"I have no idea, Chase. You'll have to answer that question on your own. But understand one thing."

"I'm listening."

"If you strike an alliance with them, you can forever say goodbye to allying yourself with the rest of the Olympians."

"I thought there was no way Zeus would even consider such a thing."

"Yesterday perhaps. Today I wouldn't completely strike it out."

"Why? What has changed?"

"The Furies are back, that's what has changed. I bet they haven't forgotten who trapped them outside time and space. You can bet your ass they will want to exterminate whatever is left of our ranks."

"Then we may have a way to convince Zeus?"

"Except, you're also the one responsible for bringing them back. So I guess it's not going to be an easy sell, no matter how you present it. But if you find the Asgardians and ally yourself with them, Zeus will not want to hear a word of what you have to say."

"Damn your godly pride. Now is the time to forget about these old feuds and rebuild the biggest alliance possible."

"You're preaching to the choir, Chase. I'm just warning you it won't be as simple as that."

"I'm beginning to get the gist of that. So basically I either choose to contact the Olympians or the Asgardians?"

"Yes."

"And you don't know where the latter are. Do you know where Olympians are?"

There was another silence.

"You do. Well, I guess a visit to Zeus should be in order soon."

"I'll guide you there when the time comes. For the moment you need to rest and try to mend your relationship with Sarah."

"What does Sarah have to do with any of it?"

"I'm sure that just like me you felt how powerful Chris already is. He may still have a role to play, and therefore Sarah, whether she wants it or not, is an important part of what's to come."

"I'm really getting tired of this destiny crap. My son will be too young to wage war, and I sure hope we defeat the Furies long before he can talk."

"I wish I could say this is possible, but the fact of the matter is I have no idea what the future holds, the only one who did is . . ."

"Yeah, I know, she is now Argos' prisoner, thanks to me. I did get a glimpse of her power when she gave me that amulet."

"And you also saw the future?"

"I saw something. It did feel like the future. Furies came to Earth."

"That's almost certainly happening at one point or another. Do you still have the amulet?"

"Nope. I had to break it in order save Argos' life when we fought the Titan."

"And save Sarah's in the process."

"Yes, otherwise I would have gladly let Argos be crushed."

"The things we do for love."

"You can say that again."

"Rest, Chase, we'll talk more in the coming days."

"Ares?"

"Yes."

"See if you can arrange a meeting with Zeus, will you?"

"I'll see what I can do. You should try to train more when you get back to Earth."

"I intend to train relentlessly, in fact. Something tells me that Argos is no longer the strongest enemy I will have to face."

"What makes you think that?"

"I don't know, and that worries me, but I can feel it in my bones."

MISEO WALKED INTO ARGOS' ready room without so much as an announcement.

"We need to talk."

"Evidently. What happened to my ship?"

"It's being digested by a black hole your brother created on the battlefield."

"How did *that* happen?"

"Somehow he mustered enough strength to not only block a full powered plasma shot from your destroyer but to send it back toward it. In doing so a black hole appeared in space."

Laiyos really is a formidable warrior. I don't think I could have done that.

"That's impressive."

"Too much for a low-class Fury. What are you two hiding?"

"I can't speak for my brother, but I'm not hiding anything."

"Aren't you two twins? Shouldn't you have the same powers; or at the very least similar strength?"

"We definitely don't share similar powers, and as difficult as it is for me to admit it, he's stronger than me. On two occasions he defeated me and had me at death's door."

"And yet you're still alive."

"That's only because I had the right bargaining chip."

"Which is?"

"Was. I had his lover hostage."

"And you let her go? You fool!"

"My letting her go is the reason you're breathing air in this universe now, no offense."

"In that case I might have spoken hastily."

"You must get that from your father."

"I suggest you watch your tone, Argos. While I'm more inclined to listen to what you have to offer than my father is, do not make the fatal mistake of disrespecting him in front of me a second time."

Showing your true colors.

"Duly noted. I'm sorry if I let my anger get the better of me."

"Why would you be angry?"

"You have to be joking, right? I've devoted most of my life to freeing my people from their prison and as a thank you I almost got killed for it today."

"My father had no intention of killing you. He doesn't respond well to insubordination, however, as you have witnessed. And neither do I."

"What insubordination?"

"Don't play coy with me, Argos. We asked you to destroy the *Iron Fire* and you put up a show, but we both know you could have eradicated that ship. Instead you let it escape. I would like to know why?"

"I don't think you'd understand."

"Try me."

"I gave my word to Laiyos I'd let him go in exchange for his help acquiring both the Pandora stone as well as providing an Olympian sacrifice to break the dimensional hold on Erevos."

Miseo looked at the machine in the corner of the room where Aphroditis stood.

"That's the one?"

"Yes. In exchange for his actions, and after carefully orchestrating a scenario where he could not refuse my help, I let his precious Sarah go and gave my word I would not destroy his ship."

"I understand."

What? Argos' expression changed.

"You seem surprised, Argos."

"I am."

"You value your word. It's an honorable quality and I respect that. But never forget the chain of command. Even if it clashes with your own values or, in this case, affects your own ego. If my father or I give you a direct order, you must obey it, no matter if it goes against your better judgment. Is that clear?"

"Like crystal."

"Still, under the circumstances I believe my father's reaction was perhaps hasty."

"Will you tell him that?"

"Not in so many words, but I will try to make sure you get treated better. We indeed owe you our freedom."

That must have been hard for you to spit out.

"Thank you, Miseo."

"You've mentioned different powers with respect to your brother Laiyos."

"Yes. He seems not to age, and when he is pushed to the limit his power increases tenfold. In that *Ultra*-Fury mode he is as powerful as he is unpredictable."

"Ultra Fury—" Miseo's expression became more serious.

"Did I say anything wrong?"

"No . . . It's just that your mention of Ultra Fury reminds me of an old legend amongst the Fury people."

"Which is?"

"Well, legend has it that once every fifty thousand years a warrior of superior strength is born. He is supposedly immortal and would be more powerful than every other Fury combined."

"This is nonsense. And I can tell you from my experience with your father that he is infinitely more powerful than Laiyos; and I bet he only showed me but a glimpse of his powers, am I correct?"

"Yes, Supreme Commander Arakan is the most powerful Fury there is. He thinks he is the Fury of legend, in fact."

"You don't seem to agree."

"My father is very powerful, but immortal he isn't; or, if he is, he still shows age."

"Unlike Laiyos."

"Yes. If your brother is that legendary warrior, he must be killed before he realizes the power he wields."

"I don't believe in this legend nonsense, but killing Laiyos is actually on my to-do list."

"Good. I'll help you if necessary."

"That will most likely be the case. Like I said, I lost in both our previous encounters."

"You're a good warrior. I can sense a strong energy from you, but you reek of fear."

What? What is he talking about? Laiyos said the same thing.

"I don't know what you're talking about."

"That's because it's rooted deep within your subconscious, but I can smell it on you."

Argos wanted to argue with Miseo but decided against it.

"If you say so. What's next?"

"How's the mission we gave you going?"

"My forces have invaded Tyronis. They're cleaning up the planet as we speak. We'll soon be able to leverage all the rich resources this planet and its belts have to offer."

"That's great news. Have your armada go to the next world for more resources the minute they're done."

"What's the rush?"

"We need to rebuild a fleet. We need to send a message that we are back and we won't do that with those pathetic Zarlack vessels."

"Pathetic?"

"They may look powerful, but they're nothing compared to our own ships. With the resources you'll secure from Tyronis we'll build the first one. Once it's done and you see it in action you'll understand."

"Looking forward to it."

"You will, soon enough."

"Very well. If that will be all?"

"For now. Thanks, Argos. I would appreciate that you don't repeat the words 'Ultra Fury' to my father, or to anyone for that matter."

"You do realize that I just invented the name?"

"Even so, invented or not I don't like the image it projects. Please keep that to yourself. We'll soon kill your brother anyway, together. I take it you don't have a problem with that?"

"None at all but I'd really like to be the one delivering the final blow."

"If at all convenient, I will gladly grant you this honor."

"Thank you, Miseo."

Miseo turned his back and left Argos' ready room as quickly and unceremoniously as he had entered it.

6

Whenmodore Saroudis entered the
admiral's ready room, she smiled at him.

"Hello, Adonis, please take a seat."

"Thank you, Ally."

"So, I've read your report. I must say I did not see that coming. So now on top of Argos and his Zarlack army, we can expect the Furies to come knocking on our doorstep. This is a nightmare."

Saroudis stayed silent, not sure how to answer, not even sure there was anything he could say under the circumstances.

"And this is thanks to your protégé Chase. He outdid himself this time."

"With all due respect, I don't think that's fair."

"Fair? That's what we get for trusting a Fury I guess."

"I'm not sure I like where this conversation is heading, Admiral."

"So you don't think he was in on it all along?"

"In on it? Of course not! Chase is an Earth Alliance officer. He fights on our side. There was no way he could have anticipated what has unfolded. Argos manipulated him from the very start."

"You don't have to protect him, Adonis. Not anymore. I think it's time we discuss his upcoming court martial and discuss imprisonment and perhaps even execution—"

"You can't be serious? He saved the *Destiny* battlegroup and Earth, twice over."

"How long are you gonna use this excuse to justify this insubordinate, hothead excuse for an officer."

Saroudis' blood boiled. "I don't believe what I'm hearing. The lieutenant commander is the only reason we're still breathing; we owe him our lives."

"I disagree. We would have prevailed with or without him. In fact, I now suspect he could very well be in league with his brother and might have manipulated you from the start. Think about it, Commodore. He was at the right place at the right time at every turn. He gained our trust, but who is to say this wasn't orchestrated from the start?"

"Admiral, Chase has served under my command for years. I know the man."

"Then perhaps Argos brainwashed him to do his bidding. He did that with Commander Kepler, after all. Perhaps he took control of the lieutenant commander as well at one point."

"I'm sorry, this is ludicrous. Chase was put in the most horrible position. We asked him to kill the love of his life to win the war, and he did it."

"She was a clone. Perhaps he knew that."

Saroudis felt a brooding headache building up.

"No, this is nuts. What the hell is with you, and this personal vendetta you seem to have against the lieutenant commander? What did he ever do to you? You know what? Don't answer that. But I want you to listen to me closely now. I've noticed a strange shift in your attitude lately and I'm really worried about you. I don't recognize the woman I have admired all these years. But you need to understand one thing. Yes, the Furies are back, and soon they'll become the most daunting enemy we have ever faced. To have a shadow of a chance of survival, we'll need Lieutenant Commander Athanatos on our side."

The admiral tapped her fingers on her wooden desk.

"I see. So am I supposed to just let all of this go?"

"All of what, Admiral?"

"The lieutenant commander assaulted some of my officers and put them out of commission, then he stole one of our ships, which he since lost. To make things worse, many of our officers followed him, stealing quadrinium from your ship in a clear act of mutiny. Then they helped him help Argos obtain a stone required to power a machine that actually freed the Furies from another dimension where the Olympians had locked them up during the last war. To top it *all*, an Olympian was voluntary sacrificed to make the machine work. Did I miss anything?"

Saroudis knew that from the outside it did look very bad.

"No you didn't. Aphroditis isn't sacrificed per se. She's just locked in the machine at the moment."

She shot him a seriously grave look.

"Alright, Admiral, I agree this sounds bad, but it's done now. I need my officers to prepare to repel the enemy when the time comes."

"And that includes the lieutenant commander?"

"Especially the lieutenant commander."

Something blinked on her desk for half a second. The admiral looked at it for a long time, as if lost doing so.

"Admiral?" inquired Saroudis, a little worried.

She rose from her desk and walked toward the viewport, looking into space.

"You're not making things easy for me, Commodore. But you've made your case. Very well, I'll let you deal with this. But that's the last time I give you any leeway in these matters. You're dismissed."

The commodore was relieved to hear her say that, but something didn't feel right. The entire conversation made it very clear she had intended to nail Chase to the wall, and then, all of a sudden, she dropped the matter entirely.

He rose and approached the admiral near the viewport but she raised a hand, which stopped him in his tracks.

Her next sentence was icy cold. "What part of dismissed don't you understand, Commodore?"

"Very well, Admiral, thank you."

Saroudis left her ready room, still unsure what had just happened.

THREE WEEKS HAD PASSED since Chase's return to Earth. It had been a difficult time. Sarah was still quite distant and Chase felt uneasy about how to mend the relationship. Argos' forces had started conquering resource-rich worlds and every request Chase had made to Admiral Thassos, either directly or through Commodore Saroudis, to go stop him had been flat-out rejected.

She wanted to make sure the Alliance was ready for their next attack and preferred to have a strong defense around Earth. He had argued against her decision for more than a week upon his return but it had all been in vain. Admiral Thassos had explained what had happened while Chase went on his revengeful path: the threat of the Gaia AI presence on Earth. She also wanted this to be resolved before going on the offensive.

Yet Gaia had given no signs of life since his return, so Chase thought her argument was unfounded and sounded more like an excuse.

But it had become clear to him that whatever frail relationship he had with the admiral before was now entirely gone. The only reason Chase was still a member of Earth Alliance was thanks to Commodore Saroudis, and perhaps the occasional appearance of Ares.

His request to at least go find the Olympians or the Asgardians had also been denied point blank, and he had to fight every one of his instincts to just go do these things on his own and the admiral be damned.

But he didn't want to leave Sarah and Chris behind. Since he had seen them in trouble in his vision, he feared that if he wasn't there when the next battle happened, they could get killed.

Yet the stars beckoned him. He wanted to get out there and fight the enemy, not wait and give them time to build ships with which they could destroy everything and everyone.

As almost every other day since his return, he was out training. He always chose a deserted place, to make sure he didn't hurt anyone.

Ares had been absent for a few days, and that made training much less efficient, but already Chase felt he could reach full power in much less time than before, though he didn't manage to enter the same fury mode that allowed him to defeat Argos twice.

It seemed only utter rage helped him reach this almost unlimited power. He did feel near, though, a couple of times during training, so he would keep training until he could unlock the secret to accessing this power consciously.

Chase had chosen to train in the Death Valley desert today. It was so hot that the landscape appeared blurry and wavy. Chase closed his eyes and grew his aura. Soon he felt a tremendous amount of power burning within him. When he re-opened his eyes, sand was dancing around him like a tornado as he stood in the eye of the storm that his purple aura had created.

Purple lightning ran over his muscles. He focused on a series of huge boulders he had brought from all around his training ground. He sent them flying high in the sky with his mind until they disappeared from sight. He then released his grip and sent a whirlwind shockwave in their direction as soon as he reacquired a visual. The shockwave randomly affected their trajectory and gave them a wild spin. He flew upwards at max speed, leaving a huge sand crater at the point of departure and sending large waves of sand all around. In less than a second he was approaching the large chunks of stones heading his way in the most chaotic fashion.

Chase split the first boulder in two with a flying kick. Before completing his kick the next boulder almost crushed him and he had to use all his reflexes to dodge it. Even so, the boulder still grazed his face and cut him under the left eye. His reaction was immediate and he blew the boulder up with a well-timed fireball. The resulting shockwave altered the other boulders' trajectory and created unexpected wind currents.

Chase destroyed the third boulder with his knee before getting rid of the fourth by exploding it from the inside out with a powerful kinetic shockwave. The last boulder, the biggest one yet, approached at impressive speed. He decided to try to block this one.

He extended his hands forward and braced for impact. The sheer velocity and giant mass of the boulder sent Chase flying with it down toward the surface, but soon he slowed its descent and was holding it with just one hand above his head. He lit up his hand with a powerful fireball and disintegrated it with little to no effort. He looked down at the debris from all the other boulders as it approached the sandy ground. He sent a rapid flurry of small fireballs and made sure to disintegrate every single chunk before it impacted with the sand. It drained a lot of his energy, and once the attack was over, he was panting heavily.

He let himself drop smoothly back to the sand as more dust from the destroyed boulders was deposited on the dunes around him.

Then something fast appeared in the sky. It was flying faster than any Earth plane, and for a second Chase feared it might be a Fury.

But soon a construction droid landed in front of him, spilling sand all around him.

"Hu-Hello? What can I do for you?"

"What are you doing here?"

Chase wondered why the droid was talking to him and why on Earth it cared. Then it hit him. "Gaia, I presume?"

"Yes, I can use this droid body to communicate with you."

"Nice to meet you, Gaia. And to answer your question, I'm training."

"I see. As for meeting you, I wish I could say the same."

"Oh, why's that?"

"You are dangerous, and I'm still deciding if I want you on my planet."

Your planet?

Then Chase remembered his conversation with Spiros, Cedric and Yanis. This did match what they had told him.

"You have nothing to fear from me, Gaia, I assure you. I'll give my life before I let Earth fall."

"That's what Spiros told me, and the only reason I didn't obliterate the shuttle you used to get down upon your return."

"Charming. Remind me to send Spiros a fruit basket to thank him for that," said Chase, grinning.

"I do not respond well to sarcasm."

"What do you respond well to, Gaia? Is saving this world twice over not enough to convince you I mean no harm to this world?"

"I wasn't born back then, but I did find evidence to support this and I thank you for it."

Funny way of showing it.

"You're welcome. I guess."

"But then there was Tokyo."

"Right, I'm not proud of myself, but—"

"You were mad, angry at the man who had forced you to kill the woman you loved. I witnessed that fight and heard everything Argos told you. I almost intervened, in fact."

"Not sure what you could have done, really. But yeah, that's pretty much what happened. There isn't a single day when I don't think of the damage and lives I might have taken during this fight. I'm not proud of myself, believe me."

"And hence my problem trusting you. On paper you seem like a good guy, but your emotions drive you, to the point where you sometimes lose control and let your rage guide your actions. What's to say you won't destroy this world if something happens to Sarah or your unborn child?"

"You are well informed, I'll grant you that."

"I see everything, Chase. I have linked with the planet on the biological level, every animal, every plant. I know everything there is to know about Earth. I speak for this world. Even those boulders you crushed a minute ago."

"Shouldn't I have done that?"

"No, that's fine, and I appreciate your diligence in training far away from any populated area. However, you did injure a hawk earlier on. You probably didn't feel it."

Chase closed his eyes and expanded his thoughts. He felt the bird about three miles away, its feathers warm from the contact with the burning sand.

"Be right back," said Chase, before flying toward the injured bird so fast it looked as if he teleported there.

It was a majestic creature, and indeed it had a stone-sized hole in one of its wings and was bleeding. When Chase approached, it screamed.

"Easy, my friend. I'm really sorry for hurting you, but let me fix you up."

Chase put his hand on the bird and in less than a second the hole in its wing had mended, and the hawk stopped bleeding. It flew upwards and screamed loudly in the sky, before flying back and landing on Chase's shoulder.

"Hey, buddy, feeling better?"

The hawk bumped his head affectionately against Chase's neck. He petted the bird from neck to tail.

The droid landed nearby.

"I'm sorry, Gaia, I will try to be more mindful in the future."

"Thank you for healing my brethren."

"I hurt that poor bird. It's only fair I healed him."

"I have a proposition for you."

"I'm listening."

"We want to help you train."

"We?"

"I've spoken with Spiros about this. He's the one who proposed we help you in your training endeavors. I was reticent at first, but he is very good at argumentation and he and your other friends hold you in the highest regards."

"Glad to hear it, Gaia. I hope I can win your trust as well one day."

"You're on the right path. I sensed nothing but love for life when you rushed away from me to attend to that wounded bird."

The hawk, still perched on Chase's shoulder, screamed as if to underline Gaia's comment.

"It was only natural. Wish I had something to feed you, though."

"Why don't you use the same technique you did to locate the bird to locate a treat for him?" inquired Gaia.

"That's an interesting thought. Let me try."

Chase closed his eyes, expanded his mind and located a flurry of insects under the surface of the sand. Two of them were dead, so he levitated them and brought them to the hawk, who ate them right away.

"I doubt that will be enough. He would probably need to find some live prey, but I don't have the heart to give him a live rodent."

"And so you shouldn't. Let nature balance itself. It's a complex equation, but one that knows what it's doing."

"Right. So about training, what did you have in mind? Don't take this the wrong way, Gaia, but I could probably dispatch that droid body of yours with a sneeze."

"We've already made some of them stronger, with stronger armor and powerful shields. We have a few ready and more are coming."

"How did you spin using these resources to help me train with Admiral Thassos?"

"She doesn't need to know. Spiros requested the resources for some R&D. In his eyes, making you stronger is the best way we can protect this world."

"Sneaky, but I appreciate the gesture. I don't know what's wrong with the admiral lately, but she doesn't seem to understand the danger we all face."

"I agree. Our thinking is that you'll progress faster fighting intelligent droids rather than squandering your energy exploding boulders."

"Can't argue with that logic. And I look forward to some more intensive training. How intelligent are we talking about here?"

"I'll pilot some of them myself for maximum efficiency, and I will learn fighting tactics while doing so. That will in turn make them stronger and more able to provide the challenge you need to progress faster."

"Impressive. When do we start?" Chase was unable to contain his excitement at the thought of tougher training.

"Let me show you what we've come up with. Follow me," said Gaia, flying upwards and veering at ninety degrees toward the northeast.

"Gotta go, buddy," said Chase to the hawk, who also took flight.

Chase was soon in the sky flying beside Gaia.

DANIEL AND FILLIO were walking along the beach at dawn after their dinner date, hand in hand.

"I had a really good time tonight, Daniel, thank you for the lovely evening."

"You're welcome. I had a great time too. You're a great gal."

She looked at him, raising an eyebrow.

"Gal?"

"Did I say anything wrong?"

"No, silly, I'm just teasing you. But while I appreciate these dates of ours and the fine time we're spending in the sack, I don't want to give you the wrong impression."

"What impression?"

"That I might be looking for something serious. Don't get me wrong, Daniel, you're a great guy. You're funny, sweet and a good lover, but I'm still trying to adjust to life on Earth. This doesn't feel right somehow."

"Oh . . ."

"Let me rephrase that. I don't want you to misunderstand what I'm trying to say. You and I, we're both officers. In the old days we would not be able to fraternize the way we do at the moment. Even on Earth they have regulations against it. I'm really happy for all the quality time we're having, but I . . . I have not been dealing well with the fall of the former Alliance. I— I lost everyone back home, my parents, my two sisters. The only one who survived is my little brother Yanis."

"I know. We've all lost everything and almost everyone we loved and cared about. I understand how you feel."

"And yet you seem to adapt to this new life of ours. I, on the other hand . . ."

He stopped and looked into her eyes. "What is it, Fillio?"

"Don't you ever ask yourself if any of this is worth it?"

"What do you mean? Any of what?"

"Everything. Life, the war, all this senseless fighting. I'm getting tired of it."

He took her in his arms for a very long time.

"Is there anything else bothering you, Fillio?"

She looked at the waves ending their relentless travel on the sandy shore. Their sound had a calming effect.

"I'm not sure."

Daniel sensed something bothering her on a deeper level. He wished he knew what it was so he could help her with it. "You know you can tell me anything?"

She gently caressed his cheek with the back of her hand. "You're so sweet. I apologize for crapping up the mood tonight. I think I'm just tired lately."

"Don't worry about it. I just want you to know I'm here for you. No matter what it is, you can always talk to me about it."

She smiled and they resumed their romantic walk along the beach.

RYONNA WAS pensive as she watched the interstellar news broadcast in Tar'Lock's flat. She hadn't seen Ronan in almost three weeks, ever since he had been transferred to the *Phoenix*. She was proud of him, of course, but she didn't like the fact that he was in Droxian space while she was on Earth.

What was she doing here? she wondered. The admiral's lack of aggression, letting Argos and his forces invade more worlds, really annoyed her. Perhaps even more than it did Chase. She hadn't seen him in three days. He was training more and more lately.

"You okay, Ryonna?" inquired Tar'Lock.

"What are we still doing here?"

"I don't know. I think the admiral was shaken by the last attack on Earth. She's playing it safe."

"Which is exactly the opposite of what she should be doing right now. I think it's time for new leadership."

"Easy there, tiger."

"Don't tell me you don't think so too."

"Sure, the admiral's conservative approach to planetary defense is worrisome."

"Conservative? Call it what it is. She's a coward."

"And yet we haven't been attacked, perhaps because the show of force around both Earth and Droxia was enough to give Argos pause. Have you thought of that?"

"Or that's exactly what he wants, so he can amass a vast stockpile of resources and let the Fury rebuild their ships in peace. This is a mistake! I can feel it with every fiber of my being."

"Have you tried contacting your connections on Droxia?"

"I've asked my brother-in-law Jonas to relay a message to high command."

"And?"

"And for the time being they are happy to abide by the admiral's current defensive posture."

"Droxia hasn't been attacked either since the first time the *Destiny* battlegroup and the admiral's fleet intervened to save your world. They must feel indebted to her."

"Perhaps. I just hate staying here doing nothing. Don't you?"

"Well, after years of imprisonment in Hellstar and the very eventful weeks that followed, I'm actually glad for some down time; but I'll grant you that days seem to pass slowly."

"You can say that again." Ryonna exhaled in frustration. "I have to go see Sarah. I'll be back later."

"Give her my best."

"Will do."

Ryonna arrived at Sarah's place a little before the agreed upon time. She rang her doorbell nonetheless.

"Hey, Ryonna, you're early. Please come in."

They sat on her living-room sofa.

"How are you doing, Ryonna?"

"I'm going nuts these days. There's nothing for me to do. I feel utterly useless."

"I actually enjoy having time to rest, even though I do miss the thrills of fighting with the StarFuries. I go on patrols from time to time but it's not the same."

"At least you do fly."

"You're quite grumpy. Can't you go train with Chase?"

"He doesn't think it's a good idea."

"What do *you* think?"

"That I wish he didn't see me as a porcelain doll. I don't care how strong he is, I can still teach him a thing or two about combat!"

"He is overprotective at times, but he means well."

"And yet you two are not really on good terms. Why?"

"I'd rather we talked about something else. Why did you want to see me?"

"To see how you were doing and try to understand the tension between the two of you. But since you don't want to talk about that I guess I should be on my way," said Ryonna, getting up from the sofa.

"Hey easy, sit down."

"But you just said . . ."

"I know, but perhaps we can talk about it anyway. That's why you came and I'm happy to see you. So please stay."

Ryonna sat back down and attempted a smile. "I know it's none of my business but I'm having difficulty understanding what the problem is between you two."

"The problem is that Chase was willing to sacrifice the

future for me. I would never have accepted that if given the choice. I was perfectly fine dying, if that meant the Furies stayed trapped where they belong."

"Let's get one thing straight: the Furies deserve to be dead, no one is arguing that. I don't know what the Olympians were thinking, trapping them instead, but one way or another they would have escaped. It seems to be incumbent on our generation to deal with them."

"And all of that because of me . . ."

"You can't be serious?"

"I'm deadly serious."

"Then you're a fool, Sarah, no offense."

"None taken, but please enlighten me."

"You're blaming Chase for something he did, but had no knowledge of. He didn't know helping Argos would mean the resurgence of the Furies. And for the love of Olympian gods, put yourself in his shoes for just a minute! He thought he'd killed you. When faced with the impossible choice of saving you or the universe he chose the way you wanted him to choose. It nearly destroyed him too. He sank really low and wanted to kill himself the moment Argos had paid for putting him in this position. But then he learned you and Chris were still alive. How could *anyone* ask him to make that same choice a second time? Ask yourself this: would you have been able to?"

Sarah looked down as tears fell from her eyes.

"You should consider yourself lucky you have someone like Chase who loves you the way he does, and is willing to risk everything to save you."

"But I don't want him to, that's the problem."

"And I think he got the message. Perhaps you should forgive him."

"I have forgiven him."

Ryonna raised an eyebrow.

"Alright, I'm trying to forgive him. I realize how much love he has for me and the baby. That also scares me. He is a Fury, after all."

Ryonna slapped Sarah.

"What the hell!?"

"I'm sorry, Sarah, but don't you dare think of Chase as a Fury. Everything he has done until now was to save others. He has put his life on the line to save us all, you, me, my son, this planet, Droxia . . . He is the bravest man I have ever met. And even if his genes are Fury, he shares none of their psychopathic and aggressive tendencies."

Sarah held her slightly reddish cheek.

"Okay, perhaps I deserved that slap."

"There's no perhaps and you know it."

She smiled and nodded. "I will talk with him."

"Good. This nonsense has dragged on long enough. I firmly believe the only way we survive what's coming next is if Chase has his head in the game, and right now the two of you keeping your distance with a child on the way is a bad idea."

"I miss him, that's true. And as weird as it sounds, I think Chris does too."

"How so?"

"Every time I think about breaking up with Chase for good I get these horrible cramps, like Chris is voicing his disagreement. It's a little creepy, really."

"I think after seeing him resurrecting Chase we can safely assume he will be something else, and not just a human baby."

"That's the problem, Ryonna. This scares the shit out of me too. I love Chase, and I love my baby, but they both scare me sometimes."

"You're a military commander, Sarah, or have you forgotten? The Sarah I met was not scared of anything. Get a grip!"

"You're right. It must be these damn hormones. I was warned about them, but the side effects of pregnancy seem much stronger than expected."

"And let's not discount that you may have some Fury DNA in you as well now."

"Say what?"

"There is an exchange of DNA between a baby and a mother. You clearly have a Fury baby with amazing abilities growing in you. This might also place stress on you and unbalance your system. I'm no doctor, but I think this could also explain your mood swings, your fears and perhaps also some of the feelings of anger you harbor toward Chase."

"That's an interesting point of view. I'll keep it in mind. Thank you, Ryonna."

"You're welcome, Sarah. I'm sorry for slapping you."

"That's okay. I needed that."

Ryonna smiled.

7

Chase and the Gaia droid landed at the outskirts of the Death Valley desert.

"Why have we stopped?" asked Chase.

"We've arrived."

"I don't see anything here."

The ground shook in front of them, and as sand moved to the side, a metallic trap door slid open and revealed stairs.

"Neat," said Chase as he started climbing down the stairway. Lights turned on as he advanced.

At the bottom, Spiros Malayianis was waiting for them near a giant steel door.

"Hey, Spiros, nice to see you again."

"Likewise, Chase. Welcome to your tailored training facility."

"Thanks. I can't wait to test it, though I doubt AI controlled droids will provide a challenge for long. And I'm afraid you're gonna waste a lot of resources."

"You're expecting them to get destroyed by the dozens, are you?"

"Yeah, won't they?"

"I'm looking forward to seeing how you survive your first training session."

Chase raised an eyebrow. "Survive? You can't be serious."

Spiros keyed a few commands near the giant door, which slid open slowly. It was the thickest door Chase had ever seen. The engine that powered the sucker must have been draining quite some power. The moment the door was fully open, lights turned on, revealing the room beyond. The place was huge, the size of a football field at least. Chase could see droids standing there, three of them around the middle of the room. They looked de-activated.

"Three droids?" said Chase, smirking widely. "At least give me a challenge."

"Get in, Chase. Good luck."

"Yeah right."

Chase walked toward the center of the giant room. He stopped in front of the first droid. Two more stood behind it, forming a triangle. They looked really sleek: humanoid shaped, smooth; and their chrome finish reflected the light.

Chase approached the droid and knocked its head twice. "Anyone there?"

Its eyes flashed green. Chase was briefly startled and took a step back. A light turned on at his right and revealed a large control room behind a large window. Chase saw Spiros and the Gaia droid standing there.

"Are you ready, Chase?"

"Sure."

"I'll just activate one droid so you can get a feeling of its power. Don't pull any punches."

"If I don't it might be scrap metal very fast."

"I think you'll be surprised."

"Alright."

The first droid launched itself at Chase and threw a series of punches and kicks at a surprisingly fast rate, but it was still way too slow to be any danger to Chase. Several of them together could be another story.

"Fight back, Chase," said Spiros over the speakers.

Chase blocked the next two attacks and punched the droid straight in the face. A blue shield blocked the impact. The droid was thrown back a few feet but was soon back on the offensive.

"That's cool. Activate the other two, Spiros."

Now all three droids attacked Chase and it required a lot more concentration to not get hit, but with enough focus he repelled their attacks easily, often throwing them away temporarily with well-placed punches and kicks. Chase's blood boiled with joy as he fought the droids. He noticed they started to anticipate some of his attacks.

"These things are cool. I'll take twenty please."

"That won't be necessary, Chase."

Then something happened. The entire arena hummed and trembled for a second and Chase felt heavier. His speed was cut in half.

"What the—"

But then one of the droids caught him off guard with a strong uppercut that sent him flying. When he crashed against the floor it hurt more than it ought to.

"What just happened?"

"I've artificially doubled the gravity inside the chamber. Do you still want twenty of them at this setting?"

Chase got up, wiped a little blood off the corner of his mouth, looked at Spiros and smiled. "This is awesome. Thank you! How far can the gravity go?"

"Oh, right now it's maximum setting would crush you, most likely, but in time, as your body acclimates to it, you should be able to develop your speed, reflexes and overall power."

Bring it on! "Cool."

"There's more."

A panel opened on the high ceiling and a turret dropped down and started firing plasma at Chase. He jumped out of the way, but the droids were already upon him. He somersaulted over them, sending one flying against the nearest wall with full force. It lost no time getting back up and running back toward the brawl. Chase blocked a spin kick from another droid and sent the third to the ground by sweeping its feet from under it with a crouched kick.

The fact that the droids didn't seem to get damaged, thanks to their shields, made for very focused training on Chase's part. At this level of gravity, he already had to give most of himself to stay ahead of the game, and could already feel his tiredness growing.

"Can I blow some of them up?"

"You can try."

Chase opened his palm and a blue fireball shot toward a droid, which deflected it with the back of its hand, to Chase's surprise. Its shield lit up in the process. The droid didn't stop and was now on top of Chase and launched a series of attacks. It anticipated Chase's counterattacks with more ease. Then Chase was hit from behind. Having placed all his focus on that one droid he hadn't heard the other coming. He was thrown forward, where the third droid stopped his momentum by smashing him to the ground with a powerful right hook.

Anger started to fill Chase's body. He loved the challenge, but didn't really appreciate being beaten by tin cans.

He jumped back to his feet just in time to feel something coming from behind. One of the droids sent lasers his way. Chase deflected them and sent a flurry of fireballs toward his attacker. Two of them were deflected but the next few hit their targets. The droid was thrown in every direction with each new impact and fell to the ground. Smoke rose from it.

The other two droids fired toward Chase as well. He flew upwards and created a giant fireball the size of a car and sent it toward the droids. They jumped out of the way, but the impact with the ground and resulting explosion and shockwave sent them flying uncontrollably. Chase flew toward one of them and landed a series of punches, kicks and knees, sending that particular droid flying even further.

The turret above fired three more shots toward Chase, who back flipped three times to dodge the incoming attacks, but was rewarded with a metallic knee in the thorax in the middle of his evasive action. Some of his ribs broke and he spat blood. He crashed to the ground a few yards away. He took to his knees but was panting heavily.

The turret rose back into the ceiling and the two droids still standing ran back to the center of the room and deactivated.

"What's happening?"

"The computer says you've injured yourself."

"It's just a couple of broken ribs. Nothing I can't handle."

"I read three broken."

"Alright, give me a sec to heal myself."

Chase healed his wounds and did an internal power check. He was running on fumes.

"Perhaps I need to take a little break. I exhausted too much energy destroying boulders before. What's with the third droid? Did I destroy it?"

"It's self-repairing. It will be back on its feet in a few minutes, don't worry."

"I might destroy a few at each session."

"Yes, we're aware of that, but at the same time you have to push yourself to your limits with the gravity being doubled. That way you can emulate fighting stronger and faster foes."

"That's very ingenious, Spiros, thank you so much."

"My pleasure. Gaia helped."

"I'm sure she did. Thanks."

The arena hummed again and the gravity returned to normal. Chase seemed so light he felt compelled to throw a quick succession of punches and kicks into the air.

"Wow, this is cool. I think I already feel a little faster."

"That's the idea. You should get some rest now. There's a mess hall and even sleeping quarters here. Anything you need, really."

Chase smiled.

I'm gonna enjoy spending most of my time here.

WHEN DANIEL CAME to Chase's quarters, he looked worried.

"What is it, bro? What can I do for you?"

"I wanted to talk to you about Fillio, if you have the time."

"Sure. Everything alright?"

"We . . . we've been spending quite some time together and most of it is great, but there seems to be something wrong and I can't put my finger on it."

"What do you mean 'wrong'?"

"I wish I knew. We're having a lot of fun together and, to tell you the truth, I'm falling for her."

Chase smiled. "That's great, isn't it?"

"Yeah I thought so too, but lately she's been a little distant."

"Distant how?"

"Something seems to be really eating at her soul, but every time I try to raise the subject, she changes it."

"These constant battles and risking our lives every few weeks takes a toll on most of us."

"You seem fine."

"Well, I'm not. Perhaps I'm just better at hiding it than Fillio."

"Can I ask you something?"

"Sure."

"Did the two of you . . .?"

"What?"

"You know. When the fifth fleet helped us defend Droxia, the way she talked with you, it seemed the two of you were good friends, perhaps even something more."

"We were close at one point, but we never went all the way."

"Any reason why?"

"I'm not sure. When we first met after the academy, she had just lost most of her family. She felt lost and very depressed. At that time she was also mad at the world around her. Her anger and thirst for payback was her driving force, but it was also taking a toll on her. We quickly became friends and I felt she wanted more. It almost happened a few times, in fact, but I sensed something wasn't right. I think she hadn't processed her grief properly, and all that affection seemed misplaced at the time. I wanted to be a good friend but I didn't want to start a relationship under the circumstances. Don't get me wrong, she's a lovely girl, but we were both pilots. We weren't supposed to fraternize and get attached to one another that way."

"Since when did Chase Athanatos give a crap about rules and regulations?"

"Touché. But this was not just about regulations. I once found her in my quarters with my sidearm in her hands after we had spent the night together. And by spend the night I just mean sleep in the same bed. We never had sex, but she needed a presence sometimes and I was happy to provide it for her. But when I saw her with that gun, I had the definite feeling that she was seriously considering using it on herself. I felt that if we ever embraced a physical and emotional relationship, it could be a liability on the battle-field. She was already carrying so much pain with her in that cockpit when we flew on missions. I thought if we got close and something happened to me, it might actually push her over the edge. I didn't want to be responsible for that. Perhaps that was selfish of me—I don't know—but it didn't feel right."

"That's heavy. And I don't think that's selfish. On the contrary."

"Daniel, it's possible she still carries a lot of that weight around with her. And perhaps you can help her, in time, to unburden herself. But I suggest you avoid telling her about this conversation. If she wants to tell you, you should let her do it on her own terms."

"You're probably right. I appreciate you sharing this with me, though. I hope it wasn't nosy of me asking you. It's just I worry about her."

"No worries. I completely understand. I think the two of you having a relationship is great, for the both of you. I can't think of a nicer guy for her to put her trust in."

"I'm not sure she wants something serious, you know …"

"My advice to you is to give her time. And be there for her when she needs you."

Daniel took Chase in his arms and patted his back. "Thanks, bro."

"Anytime."

"How are things with you and Sarah?"

"We've been better. Hopefully time will heal these wounds."

"Jeez! It's not easy understanding women, is it? I mean, you risked everything to save her and now you're being blamed for it."

"To tell you the truth, Daniel, I don't disagree with her point of view. I did a selfish act. I wanted to save her, and to hell with the consequences. And I risked way more than I was aware of at the time. I was blinded by my obsession to rescue her."

"That's only human and you know it."

"Perhaps. And yet now we're going to have to face the most dangerous race that ever walked amongst the stars, thanks to me."

"Still, I don't think it's your fault. The commodore doesn't think it either, so why do you?"

"I appreciate the vote of confidence, Daniel, but it *is* my fault. Did I mean for all this? Of course not. But that doesn't change the facts, you know."

"Wanna talk about it some more?"

"What is there to talk about? I just have to train and make sure I can do everything in my power to defeat them."

"That *we* defeat them, Chase. We're all in this together. You should share that heavy load of yours with the rest of us."

"Right."

Chase smiled back at his brother-in-arms, but no matter what anyone told him, he felt responsible. For the countless deaths on Earth and the inevitable future victims the Furies would add to the already unbearable body count. But also for Aphroditis' imprisonment inside the dimensional machine, as well as Ares' death.

ANOTHER FOUR WEEKS had passed and, as per his routine that day, like every day, Chase returned to the training facility in the wee hours of the morning. It was definitely more fun than transforming boulders to dust. He was already training at 4 Gs and felt more and more powerful with every passing day.

Today he was battling against five droids and like every morning when he had amped the difficulty, either in number of droids or level of artificial gravity, he had trouble holding his own at first. The first two weeks of training he had either damaged or destroyed more than half the available droids, and he was now trying to train without letting his instincts take over to the point where he couldn't control his strikes and transformed his metal sparring partners into another useless pile of scrap.

But that meant holding off, sometimes, and that often cost him more damage than he would have otherwise incurred. He was fine with that, as he felt that his overall resistance to blows was growing as well over time.

In the control center, Spiros entered with his morning coffee and sat on his chair, watching Chase's life signs and monitoring that all went well. They'd all had a scare the week before when one of the droids malfunctioned and blew up in Chase's face. Some of the shrapnel had been propelled too close to Chase's heart. His fast healing abilities had, of course, come in handy but Spiros was determined to make the entire training facility foolproof.

He was exhausted that morning. Like many nights before he had pulled an all-nighter working on designing the next gen of battle droids. Not only could they help Chase train more efficiently, but they could become a really efficient foot army in case of an invasion.

He poured a cocktail of drugs into his coffee.

"You should ease up on the stims," said the Gaia droid.

Spiros stumbled from his chair and almost spilled his coffee. He held his heart.

"You almost gave me a heart attack. I didn't see you there."

"I was recharging."

"Right. The new power modules will help you recharge faster, but if you don't want me to take stims you should let me sleep every once in a while."

"I believe you are incorrect in your assumption that I am keeping you from getting rest."

As much as he wanted to tell her otherwise, she was correct. Spiros was the one who decided to work all day monitoring Chase while he fought and then work most of the nights with Gaia.

"I really look forward to testing the new droid body. I want a new avatar. This one is too inefficient. We'll need to design one with a much larger memory capacity so I can at least copy some of my matrix into it. But we'll also need secondary memory banks to store all the data we've been learning from observing Chase fight."

"Speaking of which, how can you even function inside

this body? Isn't the memory way too small to accommodate most of your basic AI?"

"It is, but I've installed an ultra-fast wireless connection that allows me to access my functions remotely. There is a slight delay though, and it is not efficient."

"We can't have that now, can we?"

"Sarcasm, I take it."

Spiros smiled but then felt a sting in his heart. It had skipped a beat or two. While a good part of his vital functions had been replaced or enhanced by nanites and other augments over the years, Spiros still had a good-old beating heart.

"Are you alright? I am detecting some strange vitals."

"I bet you are. I'll be fine, but you're right. I can't continue replacing sleep with stims and stay up all night with you for much longer."

"Not to mention you are snoring heavily when you fall asleep without realizing it lately."

Spiros smiled. "Snoring is a normal bodily function."

"Not according to my medical files."

"Right. Trying to argue with the world's largest encyclopedia! What was I thinking?"

"Is there a reason you vocalize when being sarcastic? Since I'm not very receptive to it, as you undoubtedly know by now, wouldn't it be simpler to just think it?"

She certainly didn't have the warmest of personalities at times, but Spiros did find Gaia quite endearing nonetheless.

"I suppose so, but what's the fun in that? Plus, I haven't lost hope that your algorithm might improve the more you are subjected to it."

"Or is it you just like hearing yourself talk?"

Spiros chuckled.

They had come a long way since their rocky start, and

Spiros had put his complete trust in her. Cedric and Yanis were still secretly working on means to disable her, if that was ever needed, even though he no longer thought it was necessary. The admiral, on the other hand, preferred being prepared.

Which reminded him. His last talk with the admiral had been odd. Not only did she seem more aggressive than before, but some of her latest decisions didn't seem to make much sense.

A droid impacted with the control room's shielded glass and exploded.

This time Spiros spilled coffee all over himself.

"Oops, I'm really sorry about that," said Chase, while continuing to spar with the remaining four droids.

Spiros made a face. "I need to go change. Can you please monitor him for me while I do that?"

"Of course, Spiros. While you're at it, why don't you sleep for a few hours. I am perfectly able to do this, you know."

Spiros wanted to complain but he felt another sting in his chest.

"You know what? That's actually not the worst idea."

CHASE WENT to see Sarah and check on the baby before going to train for the day. He rang at her apartment and a bunch of repressed feelings came to the surface. He had visited her at least twice a week lately and it did seem she was slightly warmer with him over time. But there was still an invisible but palpable tension that prevented them from going back to how things had once been between them.

"Who is it?"

"It's me, Chase."

"Oh, I wished you'd called before."

"I can come another time."

She opened the door. "Don't be silly, come in."

She looked pale.

"Is everything alright?"

"You look great too, thank you."

"Did I say anything wrong?" Chase sensed a colder than usual tone in her voice.

"No, it's just this damn morning sickness I get sometimes. Your son can't get here soon enough."

"My son?"

"Sorry, our son. I was just trying to emphasize that bringing a half-Fury baby into the world seems extra everything. I've had all the symptoms my mom told me she had to go through with me, multiplied by at least four."

"I'm really sorry for the discomfort."

"It's okay, Chase, I just got up on the wrong side of the bed this morning. It will pass."

"I really don't mind coming another time."

"It's fine. You're here and I'm glad to see you. Please sit." She indicated the couch.

She sat near him today. That was a good sign.

"How's your training going?"

"Very well. Yesterday I was able to spar with six droids while the gravity was at a full 5 Gs."

"You feel stronger?"

"I feel stronger than ever before. In fact, I have to control myself all the time, otherwise I could destroy not only my metal sparring partners but probably the entire facility."

She smiled. "I hope it will be enough in our upcoming fight with the Furies."

"So do I. We still don't know what their technological

firepower will be like. That's got me worried. I can keep training until I'm strong enough to defeat my enemies during close encounters, but most of the bigger battles will be fought in space."

"And we can't have you destroying entire systems. I get it."

Chase's expression turned grave.

"I'm sorry, that sounded worse than I wanted it to."

"That's alright. I had been warned by Ares not to do this, and he was right."

"I don't think you had any choice. The important thing is that we managed to escape."

Chase wanted to take her in his arms and kiss her with passion but he knew it was probably still too early for that. Perhaps when the baby was born things would work themselves out.

"What's that look?"

"What look?"

"Just now you wanted to say or do something, and then your face changed while you thought about it."

"I'd rather not say."

"And I'd rather you did. Spit it out, Chase. I promise I won't bite."

Chase took a deep breath. "I was just thinking how great it would be to kiss you right now."

"Then why don't you?"

He raised an eyebrow.

"Well if you won't . . ." She grabbed his head and kissed him.

His entire body filled with a warmth he had almost forgotten.

They made out most of that morning, and for the first time in weeks, Chase arrived late at the training facility.

~

CHASE WAS NOW TRAINING against twenty droids at once at 10
Gs. While Spiros initially thought he could get the artificial
gravity all the way to 50 Gs, the moment they had tried to
climb to 15, they had overloaded and damaged half of the
facility's power conduits. There was a design flaw that he
needed to address, but until he found a fix, that meant
Chase had to amp up the number of sparring partners.

Chase felt incredibly fast today. He moved with such
ease that the twenty droids and every single plasma cannon
hit mostly air all day long. But then the droids all stopped
and the cannons retreated back into the ceiling.

"Huh, Spiros? What's up?"

"Nothing is up. Gaia would like to spar with you."

"Alright, but shouldn't she just add herself to the mix?"

"Why don't you ask her?"

The artificial gravity lowered back to normal so the force
field around the training area could be lowered. The doors
slid open and a new droid entered. It's paint job—dark red
with silver highlights—made it look more imposing. Its
shape was very close to that of the other droids, but Chase
noted a few differences. Chase thought it looked slicker.

"Gaia?"

"Yes, this is my new avatar body. Unlike my previous
one, this one can leave the planet and take part of my AI
matrix along."

"And that is important why?"

"So that I can accompany you on missions, with the rest
of the droid army, and remote control them. I got the idea
from you, in fact, the way you remote piloted the squadrons
of Manticore starfighters when you came ahead of your fleet
to save this world. I have also documented your fighting

techniques into secondary memory banks, so I can help the droids fight more like you."

"I thought they already did."

"With some technical limitations. However, this new avatar body isn't subject to them."

"What about letting me *recycle* the older ones?" said Chase enthusiastically.

"When this revision has been thoroughly tested and validated. And once we have built enough of them, then, yes, perhaps. For now this is a prototype."

"I should go easy on you, then?"

"Within reason. You'd be surprised how much more resistant, fast and powerful this iteration is."

"What are we waiting for then?"

The doors closed back down, the force field rose and the artificial gravity was cranked back up by a factor of ten.

Chase took an offensive posture and so did Gaia.

When Gaia launched herself at Chase, he was surprised how much faster her droid body was compared to those he had been sparring with until now. He had just enough time to dodge her first set of hooks and parried her roundhouse kick with both elbows.

Chase countered by pushing her away with a kinetic shockwave and immediately launched a spinning hook kick to her head.

She dodged it, grabbed his leg and sent him crashing against the nearest wall with great force.

Chase recovered immediately and sent a fireball her way. She let it hit her shields that lit up green for just a second.

"Why didn't you try to dodge it?"

"I want to test the shields' efficiency."

"And? How much did they drain from this impact?"

"Less than five percent."

"That's pretty good, isn't it? When I send three of these fireballs at the other droids the third one tends to destroy them."

"Yes, these shields are much more powerful, thanks to the new, efficient power supply we've designed for it. They also recharge much faster. They are already back at one hundred percent."

"Cool."

Chase and Gaia resumed their training for hours that day, testing her new avatar droid, and Chase was bested a few times. He was careful not to deploy all his energy to avoid damaging the prototype, though.

Over the next few days both Chase and Gaia progressed on different levels. Gaia was able to anticipate Chase's attacks better the more she observed his technique and Chase was getting faster and stronger as well.

IT HAD NOW BEEN ALMOST three months since they had returned from Erevos. Chase and Spiros entered the *Destiny*'s conference room at the same time. Already sitting around the table were Sarah, Ryonna, Daniel and the commodore.

"Please sit down, we have an emergency to discuss."

Chase noticed the face of Admiral Thassos on the nearest holo-display.

Saroudis stood and addressed everyone.

"At 19:35 today a probe we sent to Alpha Prime received a distress call."

Chase's expression changed completely. "There are survivors?"

"Apparently so. We think pockets of resistance went

underground after the Zarlack invaded the system and destroyed most of the infrastructure there. It took them until now to manage an assault on a communications tower to send the distress call. However, the transmission hasn't been authenticated."

"When are we leaving, Commodore?"

"Not so fast, Lieutenant Commander," interrupted the admiral.

"What do you mean, not so fast? If there are survivors on Alpha Prime we have a duty to rescue them. In fact, we should reclaim the entire sector while we're at it."

"I agree we need to go to Alpha Prime," added Daniel.

"I'm not ready to commit a large scale force at this point."

Chase made fists and clenched his teeth. He couldn't hide his frustration. He shot an angry look at Commodore Saroudis. "We have to do something!" Chase insisted.

"Lieutenant Commander, you're only here as a courtesy to the commodore, but don't think your past acts of treason have been forgotten."

Treason?

Saroudis waved a hand to make sure Chase didn't escalate the tension any further. This was a very volatile situation and the commodore knew it when he addressed the admiral next.

"Admiral, I believe we must send at least a few ships. The Zarlack forces must be spread thinly in their conquest of resource-rich worlds at the moment, so three or four ships, including the *Destiny*, is probably all we need to retake the system."

"It could be a trap."

"Nevertheless, Lieutenant Commander Athanatos is correct, we're duty bound to render assistance."

"I don't care what the lieutenant commander thinks."

Daniel got up. "Admiral, if I may?"

"You may not, Commander, take back your seat."

Daniel swallowed hard. "Yes, Admiral."

He sat back, but not before giving Chase a worried look.

Chase reached the commodore with his mind.

Adonis, you have to do something. I don't know what the hell is wrong with the admiral these days but you need to seize command of the fleet, now!

Saroudis shot him a surprised look, but then realized only he had heard Chase telepathically.

Your family could still be alive amongst the survivors. Do you want to take the risk that they are killed while we sit on our asses waiting? Now that the resistance has sent a message, they've clearly put a target on their backs. Let me lead a full-force assault to Alpha Prime. Perhaps it's not too late.

Saroudis swallowed hard. Chase could see the conflict in him.

"Admiral," said Saroudis, treading carefully. "I believe we should vote on this issue."

"Vote? I'm sorry, that's not how things work around here. I've let your band of rebels off the hook more than enough in the past, but they'll either follow my orders or they'll be court-martialed. And that goes for you as well, Commodore."

She's losing it, added Chase telepathically. *Do something before it's too late.*

"Admiral, as second-in-command of the fleet I'm afraid you leave me no choice but to declare you unfit for duty. I'm relieving you of your command, effective immediately."

"In your dreams, Commodore! I don't recognize your authority in these matters. You're the one who's relieved of—"

The admiral reached for her throat, unable to breathe or speak.

Saroudis understood what was going on immediately.

"Chase! What are you doing? Stop this at once."

"Don't worry, Commodore, I'm just making sure she doesn't finish that illegal order. I understand she's scared after what happened on Earth—even though she was not here to protect it during the last attack—but enough is enough. Your relieving her of command was done by the book, under the circumstances. I for one have had enough of staying on the sidelines while Argos conquers one world after another. Soon we'll have Fury ships on our doorsteps if this continues. We all know this is the right thing to do."

Ryonna stood up. "I agree with Chase. The admiral is a coward and needed to be relieved of command. Unless I don't understand the regulations of the Earth Alliance, you've just done that. It matters not what she says now and I'm glad Chase silenced her."

Chase looked at Sarah. "Do you want to add anything?"

"I think you're all correct, but please let her go. You're scaring her even more." There was genuine concern in Sarah's eyes.

Chase released his grip and the admiral breathed heavily. "You'll all pay for—"

"Sleep!" said Chase, and the admiral fell to the floor.

He turned to Saroudis. "I think you need to address the fleet and let them know of the changes in the command structure. You should also have her sorry ass escorted to the brig."

"Chase! She is my friend. You shouldn't have intervened."

"Do you want us to go see if your family is amongst the

survivors on Alpha Prime or do you want to stay here and debate my lack of protocol?"

"I should throw you in the brig with her."

"Do what you must, Commodore, but I'm through waiting for the Furies to build up their strength unchallenged, with the help of my brother, while the admiral pisses her pants not knowing what to do about it."

"Chase," said Sarah, putting her hand on his.

"What?" That was when he saw the eyes of everyone staring at him. Everyone but Ryonna had a little fear in their eyes.

"Chase," said the commodore. "Nobody is challenging your intentions, but you need to learn to voice them properly."

"We— don't— have— time— for— this."

"Everyone, please give us the room."

When they had left the conference room Saroudis looked straight in Chase's eyes.

"You're not in command here, Lieutenant Commander! There are things I'm willing to tolerate from you, but today you went too far."

"At the risk of repeating myself, we don't have time for this, Adonis."

"Commodore!"

"Right, my apologies. Commodore, I know you know I'm right. We need to go to Alpha Prime, now!"

"I agree with you, but I'm sick and tired of your repetitive displays of insubordination. Effective immediately, I demote you back to the rank of lieutenant."

Chase was so angry—not at being demoted but at the sermon, which meant losing more time—that he wanted to smash the conference table.

But then a golden light appeared between them.

"If I may?" said Ares in his energy form.

"Hello, Ares," said Chase.

"Ares, this is an internal dispute. While I appreciate your past help, this particular conversation doesn't concern you."

"And with all due respect, Commodore, I think you need to hear me out."

"Very well."

"While Chase's impulsive reaction is questionable at best, he is correct. Not only was relieving the admiral necessary, it was a long time coming. You both know how erratic she's been the past few months. Friend or not the stakes are too high. Do I have to remind you that the Furies are back? They are just too powerful, and the most ruthless conqueror race that ever lived in this universe. If we don't act now they will annihilate us."

"I am well aware of this, Ares."

"Then let's stop this useless display of testosterone between the two of you. Chase, apologize for your usual lack of tact. Commodore, you've demoted Chase for his questionable attitude. Now can we please move on and address the real threats that we will all be facing soon?"

The commodore exhaled deeply. "Very well."

"I'm sorry, Commodore," said Chase.

"We all know you're not, but Ares is right, we need to start preparing for the shit storm the return of the Furies will bring along with them."

"On that we can all agree."

"And Chase?" added Saroudis.

"Yes, sir?"

"Please don't give me false hope again or use my family as an excuse to force my decisions the way you just did back then."

"You do realize some of them might have survived?"

"And they may not have. I don't need to think about this right now. We're going to Alpha Prime to reclaim the planet and render assistance to any survivors in the process, whether or not my family is amongst them."

"Understood."

ARGOS WENT to the brig on his ship and stood in front of Admiral Thassos.

"What do you want?" she asked with defiance burning in her eyes.

"Well, it seems your doppelgänger has been removed from command."

"I'm glad to hear it. About time, too."

"It doesn't matter anyway. Thanks to her we've managed to expand unchallenged these past few weeks. She has fulfilled her primary mission."

"You have no intention of ever letting me out of here alive, do you?"

"That depends. Would you reconsider our previous talk about giving me the command codes for the planetary shield?"

"I can't do that. I won't!"

He sensed that she meant it with every fiber of her being. Argos wondered if perhaps breaking her was worth it. But since the admiral's clone had reported that the AI now protecting Earth could retake control of the planetary shield at any time she pleased, it seemed futile to invest time and effort getting the codes anyway. He would have to find another way to work around this shield when the time came to crush Earth once and for all.

"What about Commodore Saroudis? Any way I can exploit a weakness there? I hear the two of you are close."

"Go fuck yourself!"

I guess not.

"Well then, this is goodbye."

"What? Wait!"

But Argos didn't. He closed his fist and the admiral exploded, painting the room red.

C hase sat on the bridge of the *Hope*. He was a little surprised to have still been given command of the strongest battleship in the fleet. But that made sense in a strategic way. While his superior and friend Saroudis was annoyed with him, he was no fool and still recognized what Chase had to offer on the battlefield. They had made the jump toward Alpha Prime that morning. Chase's blood was pumping. The attempt to find survivors on their home world, as well as reclaim it, was a long time coming. The Droxians had sent four battleships and the Obsidian another three. Chase was confident that twelve battleships were more than enough to accomplish their mission.

"Yanis to the captain."

"Go ahead, Yanis, what can I do for you?"

"Can you please come down to engineering. I need to show you something."

"On my way."

In engineering, Yanis had a holo-display of the StarFury specs rotating on its vertical axis.

"What is it, my friend?"

"To counter the Zarlack's kamikaze tactics I've made modifications to the StarFuries."

"I'm listening."

"I've found a way to flash charge the jump-engine chambers to seventy percent. And it only takes twenty seconds to do so."

"Are you telling me we can jump the ship every twenty seconds?"

"Yep, and that was not easy. I almost blew myself up a few times in the process. Our current capacitors' designs were never meant to be charged so fast. I must have destroyed at least one hundred of them until I found the right way to do this. I just didn't have time to implement a macro that would allow the StarFury to make a much larger jump than before using this upgrade. Since it will emerge from hyperspace on a regular basis, it's still a far cry from jumping with a destroyer or a jumpgate, and the range is still limited by the total amount of quadrinium in your chambers. I will see if there's a way to equip the StarFury with a larger quadrinium chamber to increase its range in the future."

"This is great news. As always, great job, pal," said Chase, clapping his friend on the shoulder.

"Yes, but I must warn you that I stumbled onto an interesting side effect in the process."

"Oh really? And what's that?"

"The key to flash charging the capacitors without blowing up the ship in the process was to feed multiple smaller power streams to it, rather than a single overload pulse."

"And?"

"Well, then it came to me. Since I would have to redesign

a good portion of the power distribution circuits in the Star-Furies anyway, what if I could channel more power to other parts of the ship."

"What are you telling me?"

"I've placed power converters all around the ship's external armor. When your shields are taxed, a small part of that power is syphoned back into the ship."

"Does that mean the more we get hit the more power we get?"

"That's the idea, yes. Each impact with the shield will convert a little of that spent energy to recharge the engines, the weapons and a few other systems, making the StarFury even more resilient."

"Are all the StarFuries already modified?"

"No, I only managed the stable modification of the new power distribution system and overhaul of the power circuits about ten days ago. But a good third of our fighters on board have been overhauled."

"That's already a lot of ships."

"There's a little catch, though."

"Why don't I like the sound of that?"

"Well, you see if your shields receive a hit that drains them entirely in one shot—say, for example, from a Zarlack destroyer's fully powered plasma shot—the ship may overload."

"That's not good."

"I know, and I will try to find a way around it, but my analysis of battle logs shows this is a very rare scenario in large-scale battles. The destroyers usually pound other destroyers with these types of weapons. They let their smaller fighters deal with our StarFuries."

"Then we'd better hope they don't change their tactics."

"Don't worry, pal, I'll have that fixed on my next iteration. I just need to work on it more and could use Spiros' help too, but he's been too busy working on your training facilities back on Earth lately. I think he has a thing for Gaia."

Chase raised an eyebrow.

"You do realize she's artificial, an AI? Sure, she has a personality and she is clearly a self-aware being, but . . ."

"Yeah, well, lately he doesn't even call to say hi anymore."

"Are you jealous?" said Chase with a playful smile.

Yanis punched him on the shoulder. "Don't be dumb. I'm just saying, we haven't seen him here much lately."

Yanis grimaced and held his fist in his other hand.

"You okay?"

"I'm fine, but what are you made of? Steel?"

Chase chuckled. "I understand you miss having Spiros around, but I for one am very grateful for the job he did on the training facility. That place will help me unlock more of my abilities. These past few weeks I've felt stronger than I ever thought possible."

"I'm glad to hear it. We'll sure need that."

"Yeah, but for once I feel ready instead of overwhelmed. But enough about me. How are you doing these days?"

"I'm okay. I just hate being away from Earth all the time."

"Why's that?"

"Finally scored a girlfriend. She's an engineer working on the admiral's ship. We really clicked."

"I'm glad to hear it, buddy. Don't worry, we'll be back on Earth in no time."

"Chase?"

"Yes."

"Sorry you got demoted."

"Don't worry, pal, you know I don't really care for rank."

"Still, I think it was harsh, after everything you've done. I'd expect you'd be captain instead of back to lieutenant."

"Doesn't matter, Yanis. Do we have enough StarFuries for me to remote fly a few when we arrive on Alpha Prime?"

"There're a few in reserve just for you, but is it wise to try and captain the *Hope* and fly these remotely?"

"My brain seems to handle it fine, but don't worry, I'll be careful."

"And if you could make sure my sister is safe."

"She's an officer in the Earth Alliance. She doesn't need patronizing, and she is more than equipped to take care of herself."

"You know what I mean, Chase."

"Yeah, I'll keep her safe."

"Thank you."

"I should get back to my quarters. Sarah is waiting for me."

"How are the two of you doing? I got the feeling it was rocky between the two of you lately."

"Just before we left for this mission she asked that we talk and things are getting better."

"You must feel relieved."

"Indeed, with Chris only a few months from being born, the last thing I want is tension between us. But I understand why she felt the way she did."

"Speaking of which, how come she came on this mission? Wouldn't it have been safer for her to stay on Earth in her condition."

"She'd tell you she's pregnant, not disabled, and I wouldn't mention it to her either if I were you. That is, if you value the use of your fingers."

"She wouldn't?"

"No, but you'd get a mouthful nonetheless. I think her

mood swings with her pregnancy are stronger than the average human."

"No doubt because she's carrying a Fury hybrid."

"Yeah, that seems to be the consensus amongst the docs as well."

"Say hello for me, then."

"Will do. Thanks, Yanis."

WHEN CHASE ARRIVED before his quarters he paused for a second. His heart was beating fast. He felt a little like he did when he had first met Sarah, shy and worried about his next move. Their last kissing session removed some of the tension, but he still felt uneasy. Still, if the commodore could focus on the mission without putting his own family in the equation, perhaps there was something he could learn from it. He too should set aside his personal life struggles while on a mission. And for a brief instant he contemplated going for a run instead. But that wasn't putting his emotions on the side; that was running away and not facing his fears. So he decided against it.

When the door opened he saw Sarah sleeping with her back toward the bulkhead. When the door closed she opened her eyes and yawned.

"You okay?" said Chase, still not sure what to say to her.

She yawned again.

"This son of yours is draining the life out of me. I have to eat three times as much as before."

Chase smiled. "He's your son, too."

"You know what I mean. Come, sit."

Chase sat next to her on the bed.

"Look, Sarah—"

She put her finger to his mouth. "Shhhh, no talking."

She embraced him vigorously and they kissed.

They made passionate love, and all of Chase's worries and uneasiness vanished for a little while.

An hour later they lay on the bed, looking at the ceiling.

"That was pretty good, sailor."

He smiled.

"I missed your smile so much," said Sarah as she gently brushed the back of her hand against his cheek.

"I've missed you too. Before I learned you were still alive I never thought I would get the chance to see you again. Experiencing this every day was the hardest part."

"It must have been very hard. I'm sorry for giving you so much flak about it. But you understand how I felt, right?"

"I do. It still stung a little, but you had every right to be mad at me."

"You have to understand one thing, Chase. I was mad, yes; a little scared; but also overwhelmed by it all. I witnessed everything my clone did. I know you two also made love when I was being held prisoner. That was not easy to accept, even though I can't blame you for that. She was my exact duplicate, after all. In fact, seeing it unfold felt like a good dream sometimes. But then it turned to nightmares when she got up in the middle of the night and started plotting against the Earth Alliance. She almost destroyed my planet singlehandedly."

"The important thing is she didn't. I'm so sorry you had to go through all this."

"Not your fault. If anything you're the reason it's all over now. Except . . ."

"Except I put everyone's lives in jeopardy."

"You know what, it was unfair of me to go there again. I don't want any tension between us. We're soon to be parents.

We must put this behind us. If not for ourselves, then for Chris."

"I agree. But the fact remains, I've helped Argos bring back the Furies. But we'll defeat them. We have to."

"We do. But aren't you worried you're outnumbered now? It was already difficult fighting Argos, but now we have a planet full of them to deal with."

"We'll find a way. When the current crisis is over, I'll go speak to Zeus."

"I thought he wanted nothing to do with us."

"Ares believes that with the Furies back in the picture, we might be able to strike a deal with the Olympians."

"That seems like a long shot, but I guess we don't really have any choice."

"We might, actually. If the Olympians refuse to help we'll try to locate the Asgardians."

"As in the Norse gods of Asgard? Thor and his bunch?"

"You've heard of them?"

"Yes, the Nordic mythology is well known on Earth, almost as well as the Greek one, in fact. More in northern Europe, though."

"What can you tell me about it?"

"Legend has it Thor is very attractive," said Sarah with a playful yet lusty smile.

"Very funny!"

She laughed, but then proceeded to describe the myths and legends she knew about the Norse gods for a good half an hour. Her tales captivated Chase.

"They might be as powerful as the Olympians. Ares thinks their advanced technology could be of great use to us."

"Would be great if we got both Olympians and the Asgard gods—what did you call them? Asgardians?"

"Yes."

"Well, if we can get them both on our side, perhaps we do stand a chance."

"Ares believes it's unlikely. The rivalry between the two runs too deep."

"In the face of extinction, perhaps this will get resolved."

"Perhaps. In any case, we'll need new powerful allies. But that will have to wait. Right now the target is to reclaim my home world."

"You must be ecstatic at the thought of seeing survivors. Who knows, perhaps even some friends."

"Most of my friends were in the *Destiny*'s battlegroup, except Fillio and a handful of other fighter pilots. It would sure be great if some of them survived, but like Saroudis said, this is not a personal mission, for either of us."

"I understand, and he's right. The mission is to get your world back and rescue the survivors, whoever they turn out to be."

"How do you want to play this when we arrive? I'd rather you didn't climb in a StarFury."

She shot him a look.

"We've talked about this before. Actually, you talked with my clone about it. As confusing as it all is, I agree with the sermon she gave you. I'm not made of glass."

"And you know I agree."

"But don't worry, thanks to your pestering Yanis about remote controlling fighters, I can simply fly one from the bridge, right?"

"Yep. So the only thing you need to worry about is making sure the *Hope* doesn't get destroyed."

"Yeah, should be simple enough, right?"

They both laughed.

"More seriously, though, perhaps you'd like to be the

Hope's wing commander. I was about to say 'again' but then realized..."

"That the first time it was my clone. You really don't have to tiptoe around that. It will take some time to get used to the fact that she replaced me for a while. I have accepted it. As for being wing commander, that's sweet, Chase, but a wing commander should be in her ship when her wing-mates go into battle, so I'd rather you let Fillio assume that role."

"Very well, it's settled then."

They resumed kissing.

ARGOS ENTERED the supreme commander's throne room. It felt really empty without the hundreds of warriors who all witnessed him getting his punishment last time, even if they were just present holographically. When he arrived at the top of the stairs, Supreme Commander Arakan gestured him to come close.

"Supreme Commander, I'm reporting for duty as ordered," said Argos after taking a knee.

"Rise, Argos. I had a chat with Miseo. He told me your intel and strategy has been incredibly useful for our expansion."

"I'm glad to serve my people."

"Good. And I'm glad our initial talk cleared any misunderstandings."

If that's your version of an apology, I'll take it.

"It did, Supreme Commander."

"What have you to report?"

"The Alliance has taken the bait and are going back to their home world as we speak."

"I take it you've prepared a little surprise for them once they arrive?"

"I did, but I'm sure my brother will manage to regain control of their sector."

"Then why not simply send more forces there? What are you trying to pull, Argos?"

"Supreme Commander, if I may, this is just a diversion. While they're fighting to regain control of Alpha Prime, we can safely attack and destroy Droxia."

"They have a huge contingent of ships protecting that world, and it only takes three hours for the humans to travel to their rescue with their jumpgate. Are you certain your plan is sound? We can't risk losing too many of the Zarlack fleet until our own ships are fully operational."

"And we won't. I have made sure of it, Supreme Commander. I would only require that you give me a few of your best fighters, so they can destroy Droxia from within while we divert their fleet away from orbit. I have a little surprise for them."

"Wouldn't you and Miseo suffice for that task?"

"While Droxians are no match for any of us individually, we're still talking about destroying multiple cities and nearly five billion Droxians in just a few hours."

"Clearly you haven't seen my son Miseo fight yet. But fine, I'll send one of my strongest generals with you as well. You, however, will stay with the fleet. Your plan seems to require precise planning. It may be wise for you to be directing the ships while General Arkoolis and Miseo wipe the Droxians off the face of their world."

"Very well, Supreme Commander. We'll be jumping to Droxia within the hour."

"Very good. You're dismissed, Argos."

"If I may, Supreme Commander. If I succeed with this

mission, will I be given command of the Fury attack fleet and a seat at your generals' table?"

"I wish I could say yes, but it will take more than one successful mission for you to redeem your earlier act of defiance. For the time being I would be happy to just be breathing, Argos, if I were you. We'll re-assess all this once you've completed your mission."

Son of a bitch! This is not what we agreed upon when I sacrificed everything to bring you back from the void.

"I can sense your anger, Argos. You'd be wise to not push this issue any further for the moment."

"Very well, Supreme Commander. Thy will be done."

Argos left the throne room.

Anger didn't even begin to describe how Argos felt. He had singlehandedly rescued his brethren. Since their return he had secured no less than seven systems rich in resources that had allowed them to start building ships, and still he was being treated as though it never happened. Had he made a mistake? Should he have tried to conquer the universe on his own instead of relinquishing all the power to that fool Arakan? He felt cheated and humiliated.

We're not done with this, Arakan, even if I have to rip your spine out of your body myself one day.

CHASE WAS BACK in the *Hope*'s captain's chair when the fleet jumped out of hyperspace near Alpha Prime. It felt a little unreal being back in orbit, almost a year after the fall of the Star Alliance. Sarah sat by his side, holding his hand.

"Captain, we've detected five behemoth-class Zarlack ships coming our way. They've launched multiple squadrons of fighters," said one of his crewmen.

"Launch the StarFuries. Instruct the rest of the fleet to deploy fighters and remind them to keep their distance as much as possible in close combat. They'll most certainly try to ram us like they did back on Earth."

"Orders relayed, Captain."

"Here, Sarah," said Chase, handing her the neuronal interface devices. "You can use these to pilot your StarFury."

"What about you?"

"I don't need these anymore."

"Show off."

Chase smiled as she took the cylindrical devices and put them on her temples.

"Let's see how this feels for real this time."

Soon she was flying with Fillio's wing. They engaged the first waves of fighters and it felt so good flying a starfighter, even remotely. She deployed the StarFury drones and was dispatching Zarlack fighters with great ease. Even though she only had memories of flying a StarFury remotely, it felt as if she knew it already. She nearly got hit by a kamikaze fighter when it blew just yards from her empty canopy, illuminating her shields a radiant blue.

"Watch out for these. They no longer try to just fight us off; and remember, your StarFury is equipped with the multiple jump capability, so every time one of these punks tries to ram you, just micro-jump out of the way."

"Roger that, Daddy. Thanks for the assist."

She didn't need to open her eyes to know Chase was probably smiling at her remark.

Fillio had ordered a change of formation and that meant separating from Chase's wing. She still didn't understand how he was able to pilot five StarFuries and command the *Hope* simultaneously with his mind. But it mattered not, even though she had to admit she was a little jealous. Would

Chris be able to do the same one day? That sent a shiver down her spine and she felt warmth in her belly.

Four Zarlack fighters had locked onto her ship and were approaching at ramming speed. Of course, there was no fear since she wasn't physically inside the craft, but she didn't intend to let her StarFury get destroyed. She deployed one of her drones and set it as a mine and the next instant she micro-jumped ahead of the incoming fighters. She felt the explosion that took the quadruplet of fighters.

"Take that, suckers."

"Enjoying the StarFury's technological superiority?" asked Chase.

"I am. It's a worthy successor of the Thunderbolt."

"So much has happened lately I almost forgot that particular ship even existed."

"Says the man who was so proud of having helped design it."

"Touché."

Chase's wing's flying patterns were out of this world. He was literally dispatching a full Zarlack squadron every minute or so, always changing his patterns and strategies to never let them adapt.

Sarah got her head back into the battle when her shields were illuminated by sizzling laser fire coming from her aft side. She went evasive and locked onto the craft responsible for the tickle on her shield. She pounded it with rapid laser fire, and when its shields were down to twenty percent she sent it to hell with a well-placed missile down its engine pipe. The battle was going well, but soon the behemoth destroyers would enter firing range.

"Everyone beware. For those of you with second iteration StarFuries, if you get hit by long-range fire, you risk your ship overloading or even exploding," Chase informed all the StarFury squadrons.

"Whose brilliant idea was that?" inquired Fillio.

"Your brother's."

"That figures. I'm gonna have a talk with him later."

"Enjoy almost unlimited micro-jump capabilities in the meantime."

"Can't argue with that now, can we?"

CHASE OPENED a channel toward the planet.

"Can anyone hear me? This is Lieutenant Comma— Lieutenant Athanatos to Alpha Prime, we've received your distress call. If you receive us, please ping us so we can locate you on the surface. We'll send a rescue crew the minute the battle is over up here."

There was no response.

Chase had an idea and opened a channel to the *Destiny*.

"Yes, Lieutenant."

"Commodore, I think we can easily handle things here. You should jump the *Destiny* to the far side of the planet and send an away team down to the surface."

"You may still need the *Destiny*'s firepower. It's been upgraded and is now a match to the *Hope*'s."

"I think we can handle five behemoth-class destroyers even without the *Destiny*, sir."

"We both know Argos is smarter than to show his hand openly. I'm sure more ships await somewhere."

"And if needed you can always rejoin the fight, sir. I think the sooner we send ground troops to the surface the better."

"As much as it pains me to admit it, I have grown accustomed to trusting your instincts. Rejoin the *Destiny* once the battle is over. You have the fleet, Lieutenant."

"Good luck, Commodore."

"Likewise, Lieutenant."

The rank calling bothered Chase a little, but he understood why Saroudis was doing it. They had grown complaisant enough in their friendship to ignore it, but their last argument probably required it. For a while anyway. The first plasma fire exploding not far from the *Hope*'s shields was Chase's cue to get his head into the battle instead of letting it wander.

He brought the *Hope* about and fired a full salvo of torpedoes at the nearest Zarlack destroyer. He switched to the main guns and waited until the first torpedoes impacted with their targets.

Now!

He fired the *Hope*'s main guns and split the Zarlack destroyer in two, before both parts exploded in a bright, fiery display.

But then he heard a voice.

Jump the ship, Dad, now!

It sent a shiver down his spine.

Chris?

There's no more time, jump!

Chase decided to trust the voice and micro-jumped the *Hope*.

What happened next was terrifying. Three additional ships de-cloaked out of nowhere, and all jumped within the remainder of the fleet. The resulting explosion illuminated space so brightly that for a few seconds it looked like a star forming. When the dust settled, Chase couldn't believe his eyes. More than half the fleet had been incinerated. Only a handful of ships remained, and most were heavily damaged. One of the original Zarlack destroyers had been destroyed in the blast as well.

"Holy crap, what is this? I've lost contact with my Star-Fury," exclaimed Sarah.

"Open your eyes and see."

Sarah looked in horror at the flying graveyard scene that unfolded in front of her eyes.

"What happened?"

"Three additional Zarlack destroyers were hidden, cloaked—however that's possible—and they simultaneously jumped into the center of the battle theater. They must have either overloaded their engines or exploded them when they collided with each other upon their exit from hyperspace."

"Dear gods. This is new."

"Yes, it seems Argos has found yet another way to inflict incommensurable damage by sacrificing ships."

"How did you know to jump out of there?"

"You wouldn't believe me if I told you."

"Try me."

"Chris told me."

"What?"

"He reached into my thoughts and told me to jump. Given the tone of his . . . voice, I just obeyed."

"You're right, I'm having serious problems believing my unborn child can already speak to you telepathically."

"I know," said Chase with a grave tone.

"The *Destiny*?"

"I sent them away a minute ago."

"Thank god. What about Fillio, though?"

"Chase to Commander Steriopoulou, do you copy? Please respond?"

Chase looked at Sarah with genuine concern when he saw her expression change.

He looked forward and saw them too. The remaining three Zarlack destroyers were coming about and vectored toward the *Hope* at full burn.

~

WHEN THE ZARLACK battlegroup exited hyperspace near Droxia, Miseo came to the bridge.

"Anything I can do for you, Miseo?" inquired Argos.

"No, don't mind me. I'm just curious to witness your strategic prowess. I am curious to see how you intend to defeat a world as well guarded as Droxia."

"It's all in the planning, as you'll see."

"Like I said, don't mind me."

"Very well. Commander Orx'son, report."

"As requested we've exited hyperspace as far as possible from orbit, but just within sensor range. We've been detected and the entire Droxian fleet and Earth Alliance support ships are already vectoring toward our position."

"How many ships?"

"Thirty-five destroyers."

"Very well. We wait until they approach firing range."

"It will take less than three minutes for the ships to enter range."

Miseo locked both his arms across his chest.

"Would you like me to explain the next part of my plan?" inquired Argos.

"That won't be necessary. I'm just here to observe until it's time for General Arkoolis and myself to go to the surface to wipe the Droxians out of existence."

"Understood. Where's the general?"

"In his quarters, resting for the battle to come."

Argos hated being on the bridge. He preferred to dispatch orders from his ready room.

"If you don't mind, I'll go into my ready room for the next part."

"Yes, Argos, don't feel obliged to stay because of my presence."

"You can come with me if you like?"

"That won't be necessary. Go."

Still too condescending for my taste, but I don't have time to worry about that now.

Argos left the bridge and was soon sitting on his throne in his dark, flame-lit ready room.

He brought up his tactical holo-display, from which he would orchestrate the entire strategic deployment. The Droxian and Alliance ships approached the range of his surprise weapon. Argos sent the order to deploy the five graviton devices and activated their cloaking generators. Argos redistributed the power of every ship in the armada to boost the shielding by eighty percent by redirecting power from weapons and life support.

The incoming destroyers entered firing range, and laser fire and torpedoes were launched.

His comms activated. It was Miseo.

"You are aware of the hundreds-plus torpedoes and lasers currently on their way to impact with our ships, I presume?"

"All part of the plan."

"Looking forward to seeing your next move. Miseo out."

You won't be disappointed, Miseo. This Droxian and Alliance fleet won't know what hit them, that's for sure.

The ships started getting hit by both lasers and torpedoes, but the already far superior Zarlack shield held firm, even when pounded with more than twenty torpedoes.

Argos entered the command for phase two of his plan and his fleet micro-jumped to the jumpgate at the exact same time as the graviton devices deployed their fields. The countdown to their uncloaking appeared on his holo-instrument. The devices would remain cloaked for another one hundred and twenty minutes, more than enough time to end them all.

Argos walked back to the bridge. Miseo turned his head.

"Mind explaining what just happened? How come these ships aren't pursuing?"

"The graviton devices act as countermeasures to their engines. The more they push them, the more damage they incur. Some of the Droxian ships haven't figured it out yet, and these will soon destroy themselves."

"Ingenious."

"I'm glad you agree."

Argos turned his attention toward Commander Orx'son.

"Commander, please make this jumpgate go away."

"Firing now, Master."

"Master, huh?" underlined Miseo.

Got a problem with how I have my crew address me?

"They're used to calling me that."

"I wonder why."

Argos decided to let it go. His actions would speak louder than words today. The Zarlack armada opened fire and it wasn't long before the jumpgate's shields failed. Soon parts of the gate detached, and in less than a minute it exploded. A few smaller ships came from the surface but they were no match for the firepower of Argos' ship and were dispatched before they even entered their own firing range.

"Pretty good tactic, I must say."

"Glad you agree, Miseo."

"What's next?"

"We send all destroyers back to those paralyzed ships to finish them off one by one. I'll stay on this one, orbiting the planet and giving you support if needed."

"We won't need it. It's been a long time since we've fought. Unless you receive my direct order, do not fire on this planet."

"Very well. You have at least seven hours before the nearest Earth Alliance reinforcements come, now that the jumpgate has been destroyed on this side."

"That should be plenty of time. Let the destruction begin!"

On board the Droxian destroyer *Phoenix*, Ronan was thrown off his feet when flames spewed from a nearby bulkhead and nearly incinerated him.

"What the hell is happening?" he said out loud.

The ship rocked some more, and Ronan ran toward the nearest viewport. What he saw froze his blood. The Droxian armada was being attacked by two behemoth Zarlack ships. The Droxian fleet wasn't moving, so something must have been going terribly wrong.

"Cadet Ronan Isch'ys to the bridge, please respond?"

There was no answer. That didn't bode well. Electricity arced between two bulkheads and just missed Ronan.

"Okay, better get out of here."

Ronan ran to engineering. The door to the engineering room moaned but didn't open. Electricity again arced nearby. Ronan activated the manual release. The doors opened a few inches and he used all his strength to pry them open enough so he could enter the room.

Inside he found a lot of either dead or injured bodies

lying on the deck. He looked for his friend and superior Arknon. Of the first three bodies he checked, two were dead and the third one looked critical. There were small fires in the room and Ronan took care of them before they became more of a problem. Upon extinguishing the last of them he stumbled upon Commander Arknon, whose body was lying face down. Ronan dropped his extinguisher onto the deck and fell to his knees next to his friend.

"Arknon, are you hurt?" There was no response.

He dreaded turning the body of his friend and mentor. Ever since he was assigned to the *Phoenix*, he had been part colleague, part father figure. They had become best friends and, in the absence of his mother, Arknon had become the person in whom he could confide.

Ronan gently grabbed Arknon by the shoulder and turned his body onto his back. He was deeply relieved to find a pulse, albeit a faint one.

Arknon's face was cut in multiple places and bruised all over. Ronan shook him gently.

"Wake up. Please wake up, Arknon."

But he did not. Ronan carried his friend to the nearest med-bay and administered first aid, patching his obvious wounds as per the training he had received.

The ship rocked more and more. Ronan really needed to see what was happening, but was too consumed with trying to revive his friend.

He put him inside a regen tank and activated it. A pale, bluish-gray liquid filled the tank and control lights came to life. The tank hummed.

Another impact rocked the ship and Ronan fell on his ass.

He got back up and brought up a tactical holo-display. While he was still a cadet in the Droxian army, he had been learning everything there was to know about Droxian ships and strategies. The readouts made little sense at first. Every one of the Droxian and Earth ships were standing still, while Zarlack destroyers kept their distance just outside the fleet's firing range, using their own weaponry, with slightly superior range, to shoot and destroy the fleet little by little. The bastards were taking their sweet time and making sure they never entered range. Those three destroyers normally wouldn't stand a chance in hell against the bulk of the now-immobilized fleet.

Ronan punched the console.

"Cowards! This is not an honorable way to fight!"

He checked the sensor logs to try to figure out what prevented the fleet from moving. A powerful magnetic field interfered with the ship's engines. He tried locating the source, but it seemed to come from all around them, and he had trouble pinpointing a single source. Furthermore, no physical ship or object appeared on the scopes. It was as if the devices that generated that powerful field were not there.

"They're cloaked," realized Ronan.

He needed to do something. While the *Phoenix* was at the center of the fleet and mostly spared from the cowardly, vulture attack pattern of the Zarlack destroyers, soon the *Phoenix* would become a target itself. When that time came, Ronan had no doubt that his life would end, with that of everyone else aboard the ship.

He brought up the communication controls and tried to send a distress call on every band, but the computer indicated that the signal was being heavily jammed. His mind raced, trying to find a way. Then he remembered the device his mother had given him. Chase once gave her this device to activate in case she was in trouble during her mission to break him out of Hellstar. Upon their return, she had given it to him and told him to use it if he ever was in trouble. Today clearly qualified.

Since it was Alliance technology it would probably be jammed like the rest of the fleet's signals though, unless he found a way to put distance between it and the fleet.

An escape pod!

If he could release one with the devices on board it might work. The ejection system didn't rely on an engine and should not be affected by the field. At least, he hoped so. It wasn't as if he had any other options at the moment, so Ronan brought up the schematics of the ship, determined the safest vector away from enemy fire, and located the best deck from which to launch the escape pod.

Three minutes later, he reached the fifth deck, entered the first escape pod and activated the device. He wondered if he should go with it, but decided against it. He wouldn't abandon Arknon. First he had to make sure he woke up, and they could escape in a pod of their own. He exited the pod and sent it on its way. The hydraulic ejection system sent the pod away from the ship slowly.

When Ronan returned to the med-bay, he checked on Arknon, as the ship rocked more. The regen program was still running, but already many of his friend's wounds had been healed. Hopefully he could revive his friend in the next few minutes. He returned to the nearest console to get a status report. The readings weren't encouraging. Already a third of the vessels had either been fully disabled or destroyed.

He brushed his anger away for the moment. It wouldn't help him achieve anything now. He looked at his holo-instruments and checked the status of the escape pod carrying the transmitter. It was still there, which was good, but it wasn't advancing fast enough. It would take nearly two hours for it to exit the jamming range.

Ronan swore.

Nothing he could do about that now. Time to try and revive Arknon. He entered the command to stop the healing cycle and purge the regen liquid from the tank. A minute later he had removed his friend's body from the regen tank and laid him on the nearest med-bed. He injected him with a stimulant and slapped his face a couple of times.

Arknon jumped and startled Ronan in the process.

"Thank god you're okay."

"What's happening? Why am I in med-bay?"

"We're being attacked by a Zarlack fleet and our ships are immobilized."

"That would explain why the engines overloaded earlier when the captain ordered me to punch them to one hundred twenty percent. I don't remember anything after that."

"The fleet is being held in place by a powerful magnetic field. We need to find a way to either break the field or get the hell out of here before the *Phoenix* is destroyed."

Arknon held his head between his hands.

"You alright?"

"I'm okay, don't worry. I just have the mother of all headaches, that's all."

"Let me give you a painkiller."

"No, it might slow me down. We need to hurry. Any idea how long we have?"

As if in answer, the ship rocked strongly and Ronan had to prevent Arknon from falling from the bed.

"Not very long if I had to take a wild guess."

∾

WHEN MISEO and General Arkoolis exited the shuttle on the surface of Droxia, just outside one of the biggest cities on the planet, many armored vehicles came their way, both by land and air.

"Ah, good," said the general. "A welcoming party."

He cracked both his knuckles and neck.

Miseo just passed his hand through his hair and smiled.

The airborne Droxian attack craft were the first to reach their position. They fired a flurry of missiles.

The multiple concussive explosions sent rocks and flames flying high in the air. When the smoke settled, though, neither the general nor Miseo had moved an inch, and a circular area of a hundred yards around them seemed totally unscathed by the missile attack.

Miseo brushed some dust from his armor and took a step forward.

"My turn."

He shot in the air so quickly that the shockwave behind him uprooted every tree in a five-mile radius around his point of departure. He passed through the first Droxian craft as if it was made of paper. It exploded and debris fell back toward the surface. The other seven craft turned about and adjusted their vector toward Miseo, who floated in the air, waiting for them.

They opened fire with lasers. Each laser ricocheted off Miseo a few inches before reaching him. He raised both his hands with open palms. He closed both fists and all seven craft exploded simultaneously, igniting like fireworks as they painted the sky orange for a brief moment.

Then black patches of smoke appeared all around Miseo's position. *Ground artillery.* Miseo saw the far away tanks firing upon him in the sky and started laughing.

"They think they'll kill a Fury with this primitive

weaponry? I'm disappointed, given the Droxians' warrior reputation."

Miseo waved his right hand in the air and the area where the tanks were exploded, churning red hot pieces of metal and large rocks into the air.

Another squadron of aerial craft approached Miseo's position.

Before they could enter firing range Miseo waved two fingers in the air in every direction, very quickly. The result was highly destructive. The approaching craft were cut to pieces and exploded in midair.

Five drop ships landed ground troops less than a mile away.

"Finally, some fun. Let's see how strong these Droxians really are."

Miseo returned to the ground and walked toward the incoming ground forces. Soon laser fire rained down on him. It ricocheted away from him, inches before impact. After a while the troops stopped firing and charged toward Miseo with their bare hands.

Their speed was pathetic and Miseo had no trouble dodging every single punch and kick, even when they were all around him. After a few seconds he unleashed a shockwave that sent the foot soldiers flying for hundreds of yards. He smiled.

"I thought Droxians were formidable foes. I guess you guys don't live up to your reputation."

"How dare you?" said someone from behind him.

Miseo turned and saw a very tall and muscular Droxian, covered in scars, approaching him. The ground shook a little with every step he took. He was twice the size of Miseo and when he arrived next to him, he blocked the sunlight and plunged Miseo into the shadows.

"Let's hope you're stronger than your comrades."

"You're about to find out."

The Droxian sent a powerful punch right into Miseo's face. Upon impact dust and small rocks flew backward, but Miseo didn't budge an inch.

The Droxian took a step back.

"How can this be?"

"As expected, you're only slightly more powerful than these fools."

The Droxian spat on the ground and launched a combo of powerful hooks and kicks, each impacting Miseo; but again he didn't budge. The Droxian screamed as he gave it all he had.

"This is pointless. Your race will die today. We will kill you all."

The Droxian was panting heavily from his efforts, which had no effect whatsoever.

"My turn," said Miseo with a smirk.

Miseo extended two fingers upwards and the Droxian levitated off the ground, a look of utter terror on its face.

Miseo jumped toward him and slashed him in two with a single, flying kick, sending blood and guts into the air. Both parts of the already dead Droxian fell to the ground.

Miseo landed back on the ground and shook his head from side to side to express his disappointment.

The ground shook as three mechs landed near his position. They were fifty feet tall, a Droxian piloting each of them near the center of its steel torso. Each extended one arm and fired an extremely powerful plasma shot toward him.

Upon impact a large explosion engulfed Miseo. He emerged from the flames unscathed and flew at impossible speed toward the first mech, with his right arm extended, and punched though the torso of the mech warrior, exploding the pilot into pieces. The mech exploded soon after.

The other two mechs directed more plasma attacks toward Miseo's position in the air. None of them found their targets. Miseo appeared as though he teleported in and out of thin air, dodging every shot with ease. The previously dispatched soldiers were returning, and added their blasters' firepower to the mix, but to no avail. Not a single shot touched the Fury.

"This is getting boring," he said before unleashing an animalistic roar that froze everyone's blood.

A dark-red aura grew around him as he crossed both his arms across his chest, fire burning in his eyes. When he slashed both his arms away from his thorax it released two giant shockwaves that sliced both mechs in two, and split the ground beneath them. Two-mile-long crevasses were created and half the soldiers fell to their deaths in them. Those few remaining tried to run for it.

"Not so fast!" said Miseo, a look of pure evil in his eyes.

He extended his fist forward and they ran into an invisible wall. As he raised his fist slightly they all levitated into the air, flailing their limbs in vain.

"You're all just a pathetic bunch of helpless bugs, and bugs need to crushed."

Miseo then opened his fist and every one of the flying soldiers exploded from the inside out, providing a disgusting fireworks display of purple blood, guts and broken bones.

Miseo levitated back next to General Arkoolis.

"Looks like there isn't going to be any challenge today," said the general with disappointment in his voice.

"I'm afraid not. It will just be a matter of flattening these cities and annihilating these fools. Would you like to do the honors with this city, general?"

"Gladly. Thank you, Miseo."

Arkoolis extended his left arm forward with his palm open. He held his left bicep with his right hand while a wavy, bright-red aura engulfed him. A purple, spherical fireball grew quickly in front of his palm. It soon grew to six feet in diameter. Black lightning bolts crackled all around its surface. The general unleashed a war cry as he sent the fireball toward the city. It only took an instant for the attack to travel above the center of the city.

The general closed his palm and the attack detonated. The resulting explosion was devastating. It lit up the landscape with bright, white light first. Then everything around —trees, mountains, even clouds—was sucked into the center of the city. Buildings broke into a million pieces. Everything was sucked into the center of the attack, which acted like a localized black hole. After only a couple of seconds it all exploded with a powerful shockwave that went for thousands of miles. Both the explosion and resulting shockwave could be seen from orbit. A minute later a giant, smoky mushroom rose above what once was a very lively and busy city.

Nothing remained, no trace of civilization as far as the eye could see.

"Tell me something, Miseo, why don't we just explode the core of this planet and go?"

"Well, besides the fun of this approach, it sends a better message if we destroy these cities one by one, but let the planet stand as a reminder of our superiority. When the rest of the Alliance gets here they'll witness what only two Furies did in so little time. It should infuse the fear of their pathetic gods into all their hearts."

"Speaking of which, when do we settle the score with the Olympians?"

"One thing at the time. The Olympians are not an immediate threat, the Alliance is."

"Doesn't seem so from where I'm standing."

"Perhaps I should rephrase that. Argos' brother needs to be dealt with. He is one of us and could be a problem."

"Is he that powerful?"

Miseo knew how close the general and his father were so he needed to be careful what information he gave him.

"No, most likely not. Perhaps a good, low-class Fighter; but we'd better deal with him nonetheless. The other races are no threat to us."

"The Asgardians could be."

"And yet they are nowhere to be seen. I think it's safe to assume they're not interested in joining this pathetic Alliance."

"Who could blame them? These races are utterly powerless; the sooner we cleanse them from the universe the better for everyone."

Miseo smiled. "We should split up and get the show on the road. Don't worry about killing people outside of big cities. It's good to let a few survivors witness what we do to their world."

"Very well. I would tell you to be careful but . . ."

"Clearly not needed."

ONBOARD THE *VALKEN*, Keera had just exited from hyperspace at the outskirts of the Droxian system to investigate the weird readings she was getting from her navigational computer. She looked at her scopes with horror. Droxia was under a full-scale attack. She engaged her stealth systems and tried to hail the Droxian ships, but the signal was jammed. She wondered if she should activate the new cloak that Yanis had installed on her ship as a thank you for helping Chase and his friends, but at that distance she was pretty sure the Zarlacks wouldn't find her with her stealth systems on. It looked as though they had other things on their minds anyway.

"So much for my uneventful delivery run . . ."

She engaged her top-of-the-line anti-jamming communication array. It took a while for the computer to bypass the jamming frequency, but after a few minutes she opened a channel.

"This is Keera Hawking of the *Valken*. Anybody, please respond?"

A boyish voice answered. "This is Ronan, son of Ryonna and Jax Isch'ys."

"Ronan? Wait, as in Ryonna's boy? I know your mother!"

"Is she with you? Please tell me you have her on board."

"Afraid not, Ronan, she's deep in Alliance territory helping Chase regain Alpha Prime, last I heard."

"Understood. How did you manage to get a signal inside the jamming field?"

"I have specific tech designed to break or transmit through jamming fields. Very expensive tech; not exactly legal either."

"I'm glad to hear that. We need your help. Can you please let the Earth Alliance and my mother know what is transpiring here? Soon the fleet will be wiped out."

"I can see that. Sneaky tactic they've used."

"These Zarlacks have no honor. This is not how warfare is fought!"

Keera could sense the anger in Ronan's tone.

"Having had the displeasure of meeting Argos briefly I can tell you he will do whatever is necessary to achieve his goals. I don't think he cares one bit about being honorable."

"Can you send that distress call?"

"Hang on, I'm contacting Earth now. Okay, I've relayed the message, but it will take three hours for them to travel to Droxia with the jumpgate."

"The jumpgate has been destroyed already."

"Of course it has. Then the nearest help is at least seven hours away."

"We'll be long dead by then."

Keera wanted to find words to reassure Ronan, but she didn't know what she could tell him to make him feel better.

"You need to get out of there, Ronan."

"We know, but aside from the escape pods I don't see how. We'd be sitting ducks the moment we launched them."

"I might be able to do something about that."

"First things first. I've launched an escape pod transmitting a distress call to my mother a while back. Do you see it?"

"Let me check. I see a small and slow-moving object traveling away from the fleet on my scopes, yes."

"Is there any way you can use whatever tech you're using to talk with us to replicate and amplify this signal through the jamming fields?"

"I think so. Give me a minute ... and, done."

"Good, that should let my mother know we need help here."

"Look, Ronan, if you escape using an escape pod I could tractor you out."

"You'd risk becoming a target yourself."

"I have a cloak. It only lasts a few minutes but that's all I would need."

"I'm afraid the magnetic field trapping us would trap your ship as well, unless your tractor beam has at least a fifty-thousand-mile range?"

"Not even close, I'm afraid."

"Then don't even risk it. Enough people are going to die today. No need to add yourself to the list in a futile attempt to get us out of here."

"There has to be something I can do. I can't just stand here and let you and thousands of others die."

"If only we could pinpoint the devices that generate the fields, we could fire on them."

"I'm getting garbled readings. Let me try some more and get back to you shortly, okay?"

"Understood. Thanks for your help, Keera!"

"Sure thing. Hang on, Ronan, I'll do everything I can to get you out of here."

Keera tried different algorithms to try and detect the source of the fields but came up empty each time.

"Dammit!"

"Perhaps I can be of assistance," said a male voice behind her.

Keera thought she'd have a heart attack. She jumped out of her chair when a sphere of golden light appeared in the cockpit and soon took human shape.

"Ares! You need to stop doing that, man."

"Sorry, I was in Olympus when I felt a strong disturbance. Millions have just died on Droxia. I can feel Argos nearby."

"You can sense him?"

"Yes. But it's not his presence that has me worried, but the two other Furies currently on the surface of Droxia. They're infinitely more powerful than him."

"More powerful than Argos?" said Keera with a look of

terror.

Ares nodded gravely.

She struggled with the concept, and then brushed the thought away, not sure she even wanted to know what it could mean.

"Well, one problem at the time. Can you help me locate the fields that are holding the defense fleet immobilized?"

"That I can do. In fact, I can sense every single one of the artificial magnetic fields being generated. Let me tag them for you."

"Them? How many are there?"

"I sense five different sources."

"Thorough bastards."

Ares waved his hand above Keera's console and five golden dots were overlaid on her scopes. She tagged them and sent their coordinates to Ronan.

"Anything you can do to get Ronan out of there?"

"In order to delay Argos and his Fury friends I have to go now, before it's too late."

Keera's eyes widened. "What do you mean you have to go?"

But Ares was already gone.

"I guess not, then. Thanks anyway."

She re-established communication with Ronan.

"I've just sent you the coordinates of the magnetic fields generators. Can you take them out?"

"Two of them are in range of our turrets so we'll try. The bridge isn't responding, though. We'll get there and deal with these two one way or the other, but we can't dispatch the other three. Other ships nearer their location probably could, if they still have firing capabilities. Can you send the coordinates to the *Manticora* and the *Sphinx*?"

"Relaying now."

The three Zarlack destroyers were almost within firing range of the *Hope* when Ryonna stormed onto the bridge.

"What is it, Ryonna?"

She handed him the distress call device he had given her after their return to Hellstar.

"Please tell me this doesn't mean what I think it does?"

Chase wished he could tell her otherwise but it seemed Ronan was in trouble.

"It does."

Sarah looked puzzled. "What *does* it mean?"

"It means Ronan is in trouble. Chase, can you please try to establish contact with Droxia."

"Hang on."

The shipped rocked when the first wave of plasma fire ignited the *Hope*'s shield. Chase piloted the *Hope* into a series of evasive actions while he opened the channel to Droxia, but he never got a signal.

"This isn't good," said Chase.

"What's happening?" Ryonna was unable to contain the worry in her voice.

"I'm not getting through. And I can feel something is terribly wrong."

"I have to get out of here and back to Droxia!"

"It's too far, Ryonna. Even with a StarFury it would take you the better part of a week to reach Droxia."

"I can hijack a jump-capable ship on my way there."

"Most of what was once Alliance space is empty or under Zarlack occupation. That's a foolish plan at best."

"Chase! He is my son! I need to do something about it."

The ship rocked after being hit several more times. Chase shot a look at Sarah. She understood he needed to take care of this fight now.

"Look, Ryonna," said Sarah, "the moment we're done dealing with these ships we'll go back to Droxia with you. That's the fastest way to reach him anyway."

"I could use your help with targeting the laser batteries, Ryonna," said Chase, his eyes closed and already fully in combat mode, retaliating against their attackers with the *Hope's* laser batteries and torpedoes.

Of course, he didn't need Ryonna's help. He was perfectly able to remote control them with his mind, like every other part of the ship. But she needed to keep herself busy for the time being. So did Chase.

Argos, why am I sure you're behind all this again?

Chase pushed his own rhetorical thought away and returned his full attention to the fight.

You're right, he is behind it, heard Chase in his thoughts.

Ares. What's happening?

Droxia is under attack. The fleet has been immobilized and Argos is kicking the shit out of them at a distance, not taking any risks.

I have no love for him, but I didn't peg him for such a coward.

Well, he's not alone and might not be calling the shots anymore. Two of his Fury friends are destroying Droxia's cities one by one. You need to jump to Droxia as soon as possible.

We're at least twelve hours away, Ares, even if we left now. We're in the middle of a battle here, in case you didn't notice.

You're right. I need to find a way to delay them. I'll get back to you soon. Hurry up and dispatch your current enemies. I'll need your help to save Droxia soon.

How do you propose we do that? Last I checked there's nothing faster than hyperspace travel.

Well, I can travel faster, and I think you probably could as well.

What? Mind explaining that?

No time to explain now. Got to go put a wrench in your brother's well-oiled destructive machine. I'll get back to you soon.

The shipped rocked when more torpedoes impacted with the shields. It was time for Chase to get rid of his current opposition.

Today would be a very long day.

RONAN AND ARKNON arrived on the bridge and were shocked by the damage. Paneling and supporting bulkhead structures had fallen from the ceiling and wreaked havoc with most of the consoles. A few bodies lay around, some dead, some still breathing. A strong, steel support beam took the place of the captain's torso in the captain's chair.

"At least now we know why the bridge wasn't answering," said Ronan.

"We need to gain access to firing controls."

"Isn't that the tactical console?" asked Ronan, pointing at a destroyed console that was still shooting sparks.

"It was. I'll divert its main functions to the other working console. You need to do the same with navigational controls."

"I don't get it. The ship is not as badly damaged as the others nearer to the Zarlacks. How did this happen?"

Arknon was madly inputting commands to one of the few working terminals in his area.

"I think this happened when I was ordered to push the engines past their limits. It must have torn the ship apart. According to these readings, many decks have been exposed to space, and structural integrity is dangerously low. We have minimal shielding and life support is erratic at best."

"Will the ship fire, let alone fly?"

"We're about to find out. We at least need to find a way to fire either lasers or torpedoes so we can destroy these two field-generating devices."

"I sure hope the crew of the *Manticora* and *Sphinx* are in better shape, or we're not getting anywhere anytime soon."

"Many of the ships have been badly damaged. Even if we break free from the fields it's not going to be easy repelling those behemoth destroyers now."

"We have to try. I'm not dying any other way than fighting!" exclaimed Ronan.

"Your mother would be proud, as am I. But in the likely case we don't survive . . ."

"I'll have none of that, Arknon. Let's focus on what needs to be done. We're not giving up."

"Very well. I've managed to divert navigational controls to your console."

"I see them."

"The minute we're free from the field you need to put as

much distance between us and these Zarlack destroyers as you can."

"What? No! We're not fleeing."

"Who said anything about fleeing? But we need to regain shields to have the slightest chance to retaliate."

"That makes sense."

"It's alright to be scared, Ronan. Your training till now never prepared you for contingencies like this."

Ronan nodded.

"Looks like I'm the acting captain now, by the way," said Arknon.

"Captain Arknon. I like it."

"Which makes you my first officer, Ensign Isch'ys."

"Ensign?"

"I can't have a cadet for my first officer," said Arknon, smiling.

Another explosion rocked the ship.

"We'd better focus on getting back firing controls or both our new field promotions won't count for squat."

"Hang on, Ronan, I think I got it. Lasers are only at forty percent but I have half a dozen torpedoes ready to be launched. Targeting the coordinates we've received."

"Wish we could contact the other ships and check their status."

"Can't your friend out there manage to set this up?"

"Right, if anyone can do this it's her. I'm gonna ask her now."

Ronan opened a channel. "Keera? Do you read me?"

There was an uncomfortably long silence before she answered. "Yes, Ronan, what is it?"

"Any way to jury-rig us a channel with the other ships? The same way you are able to communicate with us."

"I think it's possible yes . . . Give me a minute to reconfigure my own communications to act as a hub for all the fleet's communication."

"Thank you, Keera."

"How is the destroying of these devices going? I see the *Manticora* is powering weapons."

"We're getting there."

"Alright, I'll leave you to it while I fulfill your last request."

"Thanks."

"Be careful, and good luck with dispatching these field generators."

"Roger that."

A nearby Alliance ship exploded and filled the bridge with a yellow-orange light for a brief instant. The ship shook when the shockwave hit whatever was left of the *Phoenix*'s shield.

"We don't have much time left," said Ronan.

"I've targeted the nearest field generator, Ronan. We're about to find out if this plan will work."

"It has to."

BACK ON EARTH inside the training facility, Spiros and Gaia were working together on improving the training battle droids when Ares appeared in the room in his humanoid, golden-aura form.

"What is this? Who . . . What are you?" asked Spiros.

"My name is Ares."

"Right, I've heard of you. You're the Olympian who trained Chase. This," said Spiros, pointing at the maintenance droid currently AI controlled, "is Gaia. Well, sort of."

"Never mind this, Spiros, I'm here for your battle droids. How many have you managed to produce?"

"A little rude, but okay. We have close to a hundred already. We're in the process of upgrading their memory banks with the latest data we've gathered from Chase's training these past months."

"I've also added tactics gathered from observing the fight between Argos and Chase that took place in Tokyo a while back," added the Gaia droid.

"Good, that will help. How efficient will these be against a very strong Fury?"

"On their own they don't stand a chance; these are for training purposes only. They are only efficient for that task when we've artificially altered the gravity inside the training chamber. We have a newer, more efficient model on its way, but we've just finished validating the prototype, so we'll need at least two days to start producing them."

"The old ones will have to do for now. How efficient would they be on Droxia?"

"Why Droxia?" inquired Spiros.

"It's under attack right now by two incredibly powerful Furies. I need to distract them until Chase can come and help."

"Well, since Droxian gravity is close to Earth's, in one-on-one combat they stand zero chance of providing any resistance to someone as powerful as Chase."

"That's what I was afraid of, except the Furies I want to use the droids against are significantly more powerful than he is."

"What? More powerful than Chase? He has progressed tremendously lately."

"Let's just hope he has made enough progress to fend

them off. What if I use all the droids at once against a single Fury?"

"I don't know what to tell you. Without observing these Furies in combat situations it's difficult to evaluate this. But even so, there would be the problem of transporting them there. Droxia is three hours away by jumpgate travel."

"The Droxian jumpgate has been destroyed, but don't worry, I'll take care of transport."

"What? How?"

"Never mind how, Spiros. How effective would nearly one hundred of them be?"

"It all depends, really. Gaia? What do you think?"

"If the target Furies use all their powers at once they won't last long, but they may at least provide a distraction for a time. It depends what tactics the Furies use against the droids. If, like Chase, they enjoy the challenge, then it could be a viable diversion, but I suspect the minute they were tired of it they could destroy all the droids quickly; except mine, which is a much better design. And by 'mine' I don't mean the one you're looking at now. My prototype avatar droid is currently recharging and finishing uploading the last changes we've build into it."

"Let's hope that buys us enough time. Any way to make them more efficient?"

"These droids have self-generating, anti-dampening fields to prevent being affected by the gravity variations as much as living beings would, so if you could change the gravity around them while they fight the Furies, they might actually overcome them."

"Interesting. I'll have to try that."

"Yes, but this is academic at best. Unless you could transport this entire facility to Droxia with you and lure them in here."

"I don't think I could move something so big, but perhaps I can locally affect the gravity once I'm there. I'm not yet sure of everything I can and cannot do in this new form. It's definitely something worth trying, though. Perhaps artificially altering gravity in a small, localized area might be doable."

"I'm not even gonna pretend to understand how that is even possible without technology."

"I wouldn't have time to explain anyway."

"Then perhaps you have a way to buy some time. But please note, Chase has been training at 10 Gs for quite a while now and his overall speed, reaction times and strength have all increased dramatically when he returns to Earth's normal gravity. It may be that the Furies will also see an increase in power if you force them to fight under gravity constraints."

"That's good to know, but it would only be for a few minutes. I doubt they'd gain much power in that time. Can you please have all the battle droids assembled in the center of that room?"

Spiros entered a few commands into the nearest console. "They're on their way. They should arrive in less than a minute."

"Thank you, Spiros. You may want to start building new ones for Chase to train with later. These you can mark as scrap metal already."

"Yeah, I got that. We'll crank up production on the newer units right away. Mind telling me how you'll transport them to Droxia? I'm really curious."

"It's complicated. I can affect time and space in this form, but it comes pretty much instinctively to me. I just think what I want to accomplish and voilà. I'm not really supposed to do these things, but today there's no choice."

"What do you mean you're not supposed to?"

"We're not supposed to use our evolved powers in non-corporeal form, but I don't see any other way out of this mess."

"What could happen if you do?"

"My father Zeus could probably find a way to banish me from this plane of existence. If that happens, I won't be able to help Chase anymore."

"Are you sure you want to risk doing it, then? From what I hear you've been extremely useful to us since . . . Well, since you died."

"I can't just let Furies destroy Droxia while there's a chance to do something about it. The blow it would strike to this still new Earth Alliance would be too severe. Plus, I've already been using my powers to help Chase and his friends, and managed to stay under my father's radar. I don't think I'm enough of a nuisance to him just yet. Let's hope it stays that way."

"Very well, as long as you know what you're doing," said Spiros. The droids entered the training room. "Your diversion army is here. Good luck, Ares."

"Ares?" said the Gaia droid.

"Yes? Gaia, is it?"

"It is. I'll be coming with you with my prototype avatar droid. My observations of Fury combat and my more advanced neuro-net should make one of the droids much stronger. Plus I could actually remote control them much more efficiently on the battlefield, rather than letting them fight using their basic sparring sub-routines."

"That sounds great, thank you, but wouldn't it be more efficient to copy yourself to every one of the droids?"

"These models haven't been designed to hold my complex AI matrix. They won't do. The newer model, however, is made of a much more durable alloy, with a stronger power source, shields and more advanced weaponry."

The current Gaia droid's lights turned off in its eyes and the droid fell to the ground, startling Spiros.

"Gaia! What happened?" he exclaimed.

"Over here!" said the only red-and-silver droid in the training room. It looked slicker and more advanced than the others.

"I guess that's my cue to go as well. Thanks, Spiros."

Before Spiros could say anything Ares' golden aura vanished from the control room and a golden light engulfed the battle-droid army inside the training room. They all vanished.

Chase had brought the *Hope* about and commenced firing upon the nearest Zarlack destroyer with a full salvo of torpedoes, but the ship micro-jumped at the last second before the torpedoes could impact its shield.

"Dammit! They've learned since last time. This will make everything more difficult."

"Chase," said Sarah, "any way I can help you?"

"You can assist Ryonna with targeting the laser batteries," said Chase, at the same time charging the *Hope*'s main weapon to max power.

"Roger that. I'll give her a hand."

"Be ready to open fire with every battery shortly."

It was time to test a theory. If it failed this would make this fight infinitely more difficult than Chase initially thought.

He jumped the *Hope* right next to the destroyer that had

jumped away a few seconds earlier. The second the *Hope* exited hyperspace Chase unleashed the *Hope*'s main guns toward the Zarlack destroyer's starboard side. As Chase suspected, the Zarlacks either didn't have time to jump again or were simply unable to, needing time to recharge their hyperdrive engines. The powerful plasma cannon drained most of the destroyer's shields, but they were still up. Ryonna and Sarah unleashed a barrier of laser fire from the *Hope*'s batteries, which drained what was left of its shields little by little. Chase redirected every ounce of power from life support to their shields and engines and pushed them to the maximum, attaining a very fast ramming velocity as he adjusted his course.

"Chase! What in god's name are you doing?" shouted Sarah.

"Hang on and trust me!"

The *Hope* impacted the Zarlack destroyer and broke it in half. The *Hope*'s shields were heavily taxed and dropped to less than ten percent in the process. The ship rocked heavily as fire and bright light engulfed the bridge's viewport. Sparks shot from bulkheads and the ceiling all around them, and a nearby console exploded and started a fire. Ryonna, who was nearest, jumped to get an extinguisher and dealt with it quickly.

"You're insane, you know that!" spat Sarah.

"We need insane today." There was determination in his eyes.

"I think it's not just today, but that's a conversation for another day."

He shot her a quick look and smiled.

But then the two remaining Zarlack destroyers jumped to either side of the *Hope* and pounded the ship's shields, as well as vectoring toward it.

"Now what, Chase? Please tell me you can jump again?"

"Not for another minute, I'm afraid."

"We don't have a minute!"

"I know."

The Zarlack ships were closing in.

"Are these ships gonna ram us?"

"Looks that way. It's their new way of fighting anyway."

"How long do we have?"

"About forty seconds I'd say, if our shields hold for that long, that is."

Chase felt the pressure rise inside him. Adrenaline shot throughout his body and his mind raced to find a solution.

He opened a channel to engineering.

"Chase! What the hell are you doing to my ship!" exclaimed Yanis, unable to contain his anger.

"Sorry, no time to talk. Please tell me you have a nuke on board."

"We do have one, yes, as per your request. You know how I feel about this, though."

"Not now, Yanis! Can we teleport it through one of the Zarlack's shields?"

"While Gaia provided us with the technology to beam objects safely now, we still haven't tested it. And to answer your question, no."

"Alright, prepare to beam the nuke the moment I send you coordinates. Do not hesitate!"

"Boy, I sure hope you know what you're doing—"

Chase turned off the communication.

"I'll be right back," he said to Sarah, before punching a hole in the nearest bulkhead and flying off the bridge.

Sarah's eye widened and met Ryonna's gaze.

"He's nuts!" said Sarah.

"He hasn't let us down yet. We should trust him."

Chase exited the ship from the nearest airlock with a shield protecting him from the void of space and providing him with an oxygen bubble. He flew toward the nearest ship in less than a second. He extended both his hands and joined his index fingers and thumbs together, forming a diamond shape. He mentally sent the coordinates to Yanis at the exact moment he shot a tempered shockwave toward the Zarlack's ship. He didn't use any more power than was needed to accomplish his goal, remembering very well what happened last time he used too much of his power in outer space. The moment it struck the destroyer's shields, it destabilized them for a brief instant. That was when he sent a telepathic message to Yanis.

Now!

Chase saw the nuke materialize inside the Zarlack's shields, and flew back toward the *Hope* as it detonated. Most of the blast was sent inwards and obliterated the destroyer. The shield provided enough containment to prevent damage to the *Hope*.

Chase mentally redirected every ounce of the *Hope*'s power to the engines, disabling the batteries instantly. They stopped firing. He needed to get the *Hope* out of the Zarlack's ramming trajectory, but there simply wasn't enough power to do so in time. That was when he heard a single word in his mind. *Push.*

He didn't even try to understand the provenance, and grabbed the *Hope*, helping it out of the way. He made sure not to use all of his power once again. If he did he knew that not only would their mission to reclaim Alpha Prime fail, but he could actually destroy the entire system if he created another anomaly so near the planet.

Then he felt another force join his. It was warm, but Chase didn't recognize it. It certainly wasn't Ares. It must be his unborn child helping him once again by adding his own energy to his. The *Hope*'s escape velocity grew and it dodged the incoming Zarlack ship by only a few yards. Both ships' shields ignited from the close encounter.

HAVING REGAINED WEAPONS CONTROL, Ronan and Arknon fired upon the cloaked magnetic-field generators in their firing range. It took a good minute to lower their shields before they finally managed to take them out. Less than a minute later the *Manticora* and *Sphinx* had dispatched the remaining three devices, and the few ships that had survived the relentless, cowardly bombing by the Zarlack forces all started moving again. They launched fighters and started firing back at the Zarlack destroyers.

The eleven ships still operational besides the *Phoenix* were in bad shape, but their added firepower gave pause to the Zarlacks, who went on the defensive and entered evasive patterns as they launched their own waves of starfighters to deal with the incoming Alliance wings.

Someone hailed them. "This is Admiral Zendonis to the *Phoenix*."

Ronan looked at Arknon. "Wanna answer that call?"

"This is Commander Arknon Ritalis onboard the *Phoenix*. What can I do for you, Admiral?"

"Where's your captain, Commander?"

"He didn't make it, I'm afraid."

"Are you the ones we have to thank for being able to use our engines again?"

"My colleague Ronan and I, yes, but we also had outside help."

"In any case, thank you. We thought we were toast. Our

engineering team was unable to find a solution. We don't know how you've managed that, but well done. Is the *Phoenix* battle ready?"

"Barely, but we will still join the fight shortly."

"Try and stay in our shadows. My readings show that your shields are low and your structural integrity is critical."

"Very well. Thank you, Admiral."

The communication ended.

"We're not out of this yet," said Arknon.

"No, but at least we stand a fighting chance now."

"I'll pilot the *Phoenix* while you mend the main gun batteries."

"Aye aye, Captain."

Arknon smiled as he vectored the *Phoenix* to trail in the *Manticora*'s shadow. "For the time being we use the *Manticora*'s shields while ours recharge. When they're at fifty percent I'll vector us away so we can have a clear line of fire."

Another hail came in. "You may want to take that call, Ronan, it's your friend, Keera."

"Hello, Ronan, you seem to be free of the magnetic fields."

"We are, thanks to you."

"You're welcome. Your ship seems badly damaged. Perhaps you should vector away from danger?"

"We can't let the other ships down. They're also quite damaged. Every gun counts. And this is the Droxian way. We don't shy away from battle, no matter the cost."

"Please be careful. If anything happens to you your mother will rip me a new one."

"She doesn't have to know you were ever here if anything happens."

"Still, she's my friend as well. I would rather not lie to her."

"I gotta go, Keera, we'll soon enter firing range."

"I'll stay at a safe distance and cloak if necessary. If you need to evacuate the *Phoenix*, I'll swing by to get you out, okay?"

"Sounds good. Thank you for your help, Keera, you may have saved my entire world."

"Don't want to be a party pooper, but two very powerful Furies are attacking your planet on the ground as we speak. Cities are being leveled at an alarming rate."

"Still, now we have a chance to do something about it. Ronan out."

The moment the communication ended, he brought the long-range sensors online and saw what Keera was talking about.

"This is very bad."

"What is it, Ronan?"

"Look at these readings, Arknon. At this rate every city on the surface of Droxia will be entirely destroyed within the hour."

"I'm not sure we can do anything about it."

"But if there's a way we should consider it. Keera said the damage is being done by only two Furies."

"How can anyone have that much power?"

"I've witnessed Chase, a friend of my mom, fight on Hellstar. Suffice it to say these Furies are very powerful."

"I might have a way to rid us of one of them, but you're not gonna like it."

"I think I know what your idea is. You want to crash the *Phoenix* into one of these Furies."

"How did you know?"

"'Cause that's the only thing that makes sense and has even the slightest chance of stopping these monsters."

"We could exit the ship using escape pods once we enter the atmosphere."

"What about the other people on the *Phoenix*? If there's anyone else still alive on board they'll be killed."

"Never said this would be a perfect plan. We're fighting for the survival of our entire race. We may not have a choice."

Ronan felt frustrated, but knew that Arknon was correct. There was little choice in the matter. They needed to do whatever it took to defend their world.

C hase flew back inside the *Hope* and returned to
the bridge.
"Well, that was stupid!" said Sarah.
"It worked."

"And if a black hole forms from your little stunt?"

"I was careful about that."

"You're reckless, and you know it."

"What do you say we table this argument for later. We
still have a destroyer to take care of."

Chase checked his instruments. The destroyer had
passed through the rest of its destroyed counterpart and was
already vectoring back toward the *Hope*.

It was gaining on them, and Chase swore before opening
a channel to engineering.

"Yanis, why can't we lose that ship at sub-light?"

"We can't go any faster because your last stunt has blown
three more power conduits. We're literally hemorrhaging
power."

"Anything you can do about that?"

Chase wanted to tell Yanis that he had no idea if his

sister had survived the suicidal blast that had started this fight, but he needed Yanis frosty. So against his better judgment he kept silent.

"You're impossible! You push my ships past their limits and then who's got to fix them for you when you break them?"

"Yanis, can you do it or not?"

"I'll try to reroute power as fast as I can."

"Thanks, Yanis. Chase out."

Multiple torpedoes impacted the already weak aft shields. *This is not going to end well.*

Checking power levels, Chase decided to micro-jump the *Hope* back near where the ambush had happened. Perhaps the Zarlacks' hyperspace engines needed more time than the Alliance's to recharge. He was about to find out. The ship wouldn't take this treatment for much longer. Perhaps he could try to locate Fillio at the same time.

The *Hope* micro-jumped once more. The sight of the devastation the ambush had caused the entire battlegroup grabbed Chase by the heart. So many had died, and they might have been added to the list if Chris hadn't told him to jump out of here. The *Hope*'s shields were recharging, but just when Chase thought he had bought a little reprieve from the enemy, the Zarlack jumped to less than three thousand miles on the *Hope*'s port side. It unleashed a flurry of torpedoes and a barrage of laser fire.

Chase tried to boost the shields but there was no more power. Now was as good a time as any to call the *Destiny* back into the fold. Chase reached for long-range communications and tried to send a message, but the array had been damaged.

Crap!

He called engineering.

"Yanis, status on these power modifications of yours?"

"You're shitting me, right? Your last jump disabled yet another conduit. Whatever time I needed before has just tripled."

"Chase out."

Chase realized he had been terribly rude with his friend, but the fact that he didn't even know if his friend's sister was alive or dead made matters even worse.

Three ceiling bulkhead panels fell down when the next set of torpedoes impacted the *Hope*'s shields. They almost fell on Sarah and Ryonna, but Chase stopped them with his mind and threw them to the side.

"Thanks," said Sarah.

"Anytime," added Chase.

The next laser-fire impact went through the shields that were no longer up on the port side. Part of deck three exploded and metal and other debris was sucked out into space.

Chase erected a force field on that deck.

Not going to end well at all.

Chase turned the *Hope* on its axis to present the starboard shields in an attempt to delay the inevitable but, while rotating, the ship moaned and the lights inside the bridge turned off.

Not now!

A laser pierced the bridge viewport. Chase tried to intercept it with his mind but was too late.

When it was about to incinerate both Sarah and Ryonna, a shield rose around both of them and absorbed the blast. It also protected them from the explosive decompression that followed.

Chase didn't know if he should be in awe of his yet-to-be-born child's powers or scared of them. For the time being that save had been a godsend, but he was wary of what that could mean in the future.

The decompression sucked a lot of equipment from the bridge out into space before the automatic force fields kicked in.

The blue-tinged field flashed multiple times. The power within the ship was too low and soon it would fail.

"We have to abandon ship," said Chase out loud.

"Chase!" exclaimed Sarah pointing in front of her.

That's when Chase saw it. The Zarlack ship blocked the light coming from the system's blue star and plunged the bridge into total darkness.

The enemy's destroyer charged its main plasma guns and opened fire.

～

WHEN ARES ARRIVED on the surface of Droxia with the battle droids, a city exploded in the distance. The shock-wave traveled in their direction really quickly.

"Brace yourselves!" shouted Ares to the droid army.

The Gaia droid took a defensive stance and all the other droids took the same stance a fraction of a second later.

The shockwave hit them full force and most of them skidded a few yards back until it had passed. Ares hadn't moved an inch, his non-corporeal form unaffected.

"We need to act fast. There's no way Chase can defeat both of these Furies. We need to get one of them out of commission, or at the very least wound him, before I can bring him here to finish him off. Perhaps that would give the other one pause."

"I've located the nearest Fury about fifty miles to the

north of here. We're going to intercept him right away. Perhaps you should go get Chase?"

"I will come with you to see if I can be of assistance."

"As you wish," said Gaia as she flew into the air.

The other droids followed as she flew north. After fifty miles they started their descent. They landed one after the other in front of General Arkoolis.

"What do we have here?" he said with a smirk. "I don't remember seeing these guys before. Too bad you're just a bunch of tin cans."

The general extended his right hand and sent a fireball toward the droids. The targeted droid deflected the fireball with its hand as its shield lit up. The fireball flew into the sky.

"Interesting. *Finally* some challenge. This might not be a boring day after all."

At least fifteen droids launched toward the general and delivered highly complex combos of punches, knees and kicks. The general blocked each of the attacks but had to take a few steps back in the process. He grew his aura and unleashed a war cry that sent a powerful shockwave all around him, flooring all fifteen droids. But the next wave was already on its way.

The general blocked the incoming attacks with ease. He sent three droids to the ground and decapitated a fourth with a powerful hook kick. Sparks shot from the droid's neck. The general was so distracted fighting another ten droids that he was surprised when the decapitated droid grabbed him from behind.

"What the hell?" The droid immobilized Arkoolis with all four limbs. "I thought I had killed that thing already."

The droid electrified itself and a large jolt of electricity passed through the general.

The other droids all unleashed plasma shots toward the general. The area around Arkoolis exploded repeatedly. The rest of the droids flew into the air to improve their angle of attack and add their own firepower to the mix. Five droids fired a blue ray of energy toward the Gaia droid and it siphoned the energy from them. It then created a huge, blue fireball between its hands. It shot it into the mix, and the already fiery battlefield exploded even more. The ground all around the point of impact split in multiple places. Stones, sand and water shot upwards through the cracks. The water extinguished the fire and generated a lot of smoke, which engulfed most of the droid army.

When the dust settled and the smoke dissipated, the general was still standing in the center of it all. He was covered with burns and bruises, but the droid that had delivered the electrical jolt throughout his body was gone. His teeth were clenched and he looked seriously pissed.

Without warning he shot two columns of powerful red energy in front of him that incinerated ten of the droids upon impact. Burning hot metal scrap and wiring hit the ground.

All remaining droids but Gaia's launched themselves at the Fury. But they all hit air. Some knocked into each other in their momentum. The Fury re-appeared high in the sky and prepared a giant fireball above his head and he threw it toward the tightly packed group of droids.

Gaia's droid intercepted the attack, extending both its open palms and siphoning every last bit of its energy.

"Impressive," said Arkoolis, "but ultimately futile."

He disappeared and reappeared right next to the Gaia droid and sent it flying miles away with a powerful knee blow to the droid's thorax. The droid impacted the ground far from its point of departure and a sandy cloud rose on the horizon.

"Now where were we?" Arkoolis reacquired visual contact with the droids he had tried blowing up a few moments before.

The droids split up and flew into the air, forming a sphere around him.

He didn't wait for them to make their move but started attacking one droid after the other. He moved at such incredible speeds it looked as if he was teleporting between each of the vicious punches and kicks he delivered to the droid army. While their shielding protected them from the blunt-force impact of Arkoolis' blows, they were still sent away, flying miles in every direction.

Ares appeared next to Gaia's droid as she was getting back up.

"How's it going?"

"Not well. That Fury is toying with the droid army. I think he enjoys the fight, just like Chase enjoyed fighting against the three units at 2 Gs when we first showed him the training facility."

"How much more powerful do you think this Fury is compared to Chase?"

"It's difficult to say. He seems slightly faster than Chase —at least most of the time—but it's possible he hasn't yet revealed all of his potential."

"What do you mean 'most of the time'?"

"When Chase enters that mode in which he is enraged, he is considerably faster than what I've seen from this Fury today."

"That's good to know."

"I'm not so sure. It took Chase the thought of losing Sarah to enter that mode. What if he cannot enter it anymore? He didn't reach that level of power while training, no matter how much stronger he has become."

"I'm sure he'll prevail. He has to."

"You do realize you're putting an entire world in the balance?"

"Not really. If I don't get Chase here soon this world is forfeited anyway."

"That's a correct assessment, based on the data I've observed."

"That's a very droid thing to say."

"Remember that I only have a partial version of my matrix in this body. Most of my emotional sub-routines won't fit this avatar's memory banks."

"Right. What's next?"

"Either you have a way to even the odds a little, or this Fury could wipe us out the moment he gets bored of the tickling we are inflicting on him."

"Tickling, huh?"

"Pretty much."

"Alright, let's get back in there. I'll see what I can do to level the playing field."

"Whatever you want to do, I suggest you do it fast."

"Understood."

The Gaia's droid flew back toward General Arkoolis and unleashed a flurry of plasma shots at him upon approach.

Arkoolis deflected the first five shots and blocked the last one with his right palm, making it vanish by closing his fist.

Then the ground around Arkoolis started glowing with a slight, golden hue. Stones and sand grains shook and vibrated.

The general felt the gravity increase.

"That's a neat trick."

The next wave of droids unleashed a series of terrible blows toward Arkoolis, who managed to dodge and block almost every attack. But every once in a while a punch, a kick, or even a plasma shot, scored him. In these rare instances, his purple metallic armor took most of the force and deflected the plasma with no sign of serious damage.

Ares' tactic of artificially augmenting the gravity in a localized area around the Fury seemed to be working. The more the droids attacked the general, the more he was hit. But he fought with all his might and lowered the number of enemies with well-timed and perfectly aimed fireballs.

The Gaia droid entered the mix and scored a full series of combo attacks that sent the general to the ground for the first time.

He spat blood on the ground and got up. He wiped his mouth with the back of his hand and looked at his own blood.

THE *PHOENIX* HAD RECHARGED MORE than half its shields when it emerged from the *Manticora*'s shadow and entered the fight against the Zarlack ships. The fourth destroyer which was orbiting Droxia rejoined the other three and its added firepower gave the Zarlacks the upper hand again as they went back on the offensive.

Six jump points formed near the battlefield, and for a moment Ronan and Arknon thought the Zarlacks had brought in reinforcements, but their instruments displayed a friendly signature. The ships were Obsidian.

"This is Emperor Raxin to Earth Alliance ships. We were in the area when we intercepted a distress call sent toward Earth. Engaging the enemy now."

The added firepower of the Obsidian ships, though far less advanced than both Droxian and Earth Alliance destroyers, brought balance again between the opposing fleets.

The *Phoenix* concentrated her fire on the nearest Zarlack destroyer, pounding it with battery laser fire and torpedoes. But the destroyer's shields were so strong it had only a limited impact. No matter how many ships fired upon those behemoth destroyers, their shields never seemed to waver. But then one of the newer design Alliance ships flew in front of the *Phoenix* and hit the Zarlacks with their powerful new plasma guns. It took a good portion of their target's shields. In response the Zarlack sent a full volley of torpedoes toward their target, already maneuvering away.

Three torpedoes that were meant for the Earth Alliance destroyer struck the port shields of the *Phoenix* and brought them down to fifteen percent.

The *Phoenix*'s batteries stopped firing.

"Ronan? What happened?"

"That last salvo took out our weapons."

"Most of our shields as well," said Arknon.

"I think we'd better try to take out one of the Furies on the surface. While the destruction in the northern hemisphere seems to have paused, the destruction in the south is still continuing at an alarming rate. Another five major cities have been obliterated. We need to make it stop."

"How do you propose we do that?"

"Just like we've discussed earlier: we crash the ship right on top of that Fury. I don't care how powerful these beings are, that *has* to kill them."

"We'll kill whomever is in the area of the crash, that's for sure."

"They'll die anyway if we don't do anything."

"Right. Let me clear it with the admiral first."

Arknon opened a channel to the *Manticora*.

"Admiral, requesting permission to leave the fleet. We're almost out of shields. We've just lost weapons as well and we believe we can do a better job trying to eradicate one of the Furies on the planet."

"Is that what is destroying our cities one by one? Furies?"

"From the intel we've received there are two Furies down on the surface at the moment."

"What? Only two individuals are responsible for inflicting so much damage?"

"I know it's hard to believe. We'll try to remove one from the equation until reinforcements arrive."

"How so? If they are so powerful I doubt our weaponry will do the trick."

"We're thinking of ramming the *Phoenix* into one of them."

There was silence.

"Any other day I would plain refuse this course of action, but today . . . today is Armageddon, and we stand on the brink of total annihilation."

"Does that mean we have a go?"

"Yes, Captain. How do you intend to get off the ship yourselves?"

"Escape pods."

"That's a risky proposition at best."

"We know, but we must try."

"I agree. Good luck. May the prophets of Droxia be with you."

"Thank you, Admiral. May they be with you as well."

Arknon vectored the *Phoenix* toward Droxia and pushed the sub-light engines to maximum.

"Ronan, see if you can lock onto the coordinates of the Fury in the southern hemisphere. Time to see if crashing a destroyer on its face will kill a Fury."

"I've located his position. Crap!"

"What is it, Ronan?"

"He's near the city where my uncle Jonas lives."

"Can we try to hail him?"

"Already opening that channel." There were a few seconds of silence. "There's no answer."

"Perhaps he fled the area. I take it there's utter panic on Droxia at the moment."

"I sure hope he got away."

"It was your idea to crash the ship. If you want to reconsider . . ."

"No, don't worry. The admiral was right. Today we face extinction, and sacrifices have to be made. We're about to doom anyone still alive on this ship anyway. I don't have the right to put my uncle before any of them."

"Spoken like a true Droxian."

Not far from Arknon a female Droxian regained consciousness.

"Are you alright, Lieutenant?"

She held her head in her hands. "I-I think so. Where's the captain?"

"I'm afraid he didn't make it. I'm in command now."

"Anything I can do to help?"

"In fact there is. We're about to crash this ship on the planet's surface. I need you to locate survivors throughout the ship, then you and whomever you find should get to the escape pods and abandon ship."

Her eyes grew wide.

"Do you need me to repeat that order, Lieutenant?"

She straightened up and saluted. "No, Captain, as you command."

She took a portable scanner and left the bridge.

"Do you think there are many people alive on board?" asked Ronan.

"The life-signs sensors are damaged, but I think we would have encountered more crewmen by now if there were any who had regained consciousness. None tried contacting the bridge either, so either internal communications are down or only a handful survived."

"Then why did you give her that assignment?"

"To keep her occupied while we approach Droxia. Who knows, maybe she'll save a life or two in the process."

IT FELT as if time had slowed down to a crawl when Chase looked at the incoming plasma fire from the Zarlack destroyer. Could he stop it with his mind? He could try, but the risk of creating an anomaly was very real. Would the ship survive the impact in their currently low-powered state?

But then something happened.

The *Destiny* exited hyperspace and positioned itself to protect the *Hope* and take the hit instead.

Chase exhaled deeply as time resumed a normal pace, his rapid heartbeat a reminder of how precious it was to be alive.

"That was too close for comfort," said Sarah.

The *Hope* received a hail. "Everyone alright over there?" asked Commodore Saroudis.

"Better than the rest of the fleet, thanks to you. We've lost a lot of ships."

"Well, thanks to your insisting on getting the *Destiny* away from the battlegroup, you were able to spare one more."

"Believe me, I had no idea what would happen."

"And yet your instinct was right once again."

"I'm unsure about that. We've lost a lot of good people today, Commodore."

"Don't second-guess yourself, Chase. What's done is done. Let's keep fighting. We'll have time to worry about this later."

Chase realized it was the first time the commodore had addressed him by his first name for a while. It felt good.

"I guess so. Thank you, Commodore, we could really use the assist."

"You should retreat and effect the necessary repairs. I'll get that last bogie out of the sky for you."

"Roger that. Commodore, we'll also try to see if anybody survived the initial blast that took out most of our fleet."

"Very well. The *Destiny* will join the search once I'm done here."

"Sarah, please scan for survivors in the debris field. Let's see if we can render assistance to the disabled ships as well."

"I'm on it."

Ryonna sat next to Chase.

"We have to jump back to Droxia now."

"I understand how you feel, Ryonna. We will go soon, I promise. But please give me just a few moments to try to locate Fillio first."

Ryonna seemed annoyed, but she knew better than to push Chase.

"I also suspect Ares has a way for me to reach Droxia faster than by jumping there."

"How is that even possible?"

"He has clearly acquired a new set of powers since Argos killed him. Tar'Lock told me how Ares took control of his body to bring the arena's force field down when we were fighting the Titan."

"He has told me that story as well."

"Where is he, by the way?"

"I slipped him a sedative in his food earlier on. He was getting on my nerves."

Chase smiled.

"Then we should let him sleep this one off. I doubt he could be of any use to us anyway."

Chase reached with his mind to try to locate a working StarFury. He was unsuccessful with the first three but the fourth one his mind probed seemed to be in flying order, even though it was heavily damaged.

He scanned the area with the *Hope*'s sensors, trying to locate Fillio's craft. It took a while but he located her fighter. It was in really bad shape. One of its wings had been torn off and it was currently drifting toward some of the larger debris from one of the Droxian destroyers. He punched the engines of his remote StarFury and vectored toward her.

"Fillio! Can you hear me? Please respond."

There was no answer.

He expanded his mind and focused his thoughts on her starfighter. Life support was erratic at best. Pushing his mind further allowed him to hear a heartbeat, but it was very faint. He needed to get to her quickly. His StarFury entered tractor beam range in the nick of time, and he successfully locked onto her before her fighter collided with the debris. He brought the ship back onboard the *Hope*.

A few seconds later Chase witnessed the *Destiny* blowing the last Zarlack destroyer to kingdom come with its main guns.

He opened a channel to Yanis.

"Yanis, you should meet me in landing bay three."

"Why? What's going on?"

"It's Fillio."

"Is . . . Is she alright?"

Chase could feel the fear in his friend's voice. "I don't know yet."

"On my way!"

Chase looked at Sarah for a second and then flew out of the bridge.

When he arrived in landing bay three, his StarFury was just arriving with whatever was left of Fillio's fighter in tow.

The damage to her StarFury was extensive. Smoke still escaped from the engines. Most of the armor plating on one side of the craft was gone, revealing circuitry that spewed sparks onto the deck. Her cockpit's windshield was cracked.

He flew above the nose of the craft and saw her. He could no longer sense her life signs. Losing no time, he tore off the canopy and threw it to one side. He carefully took her in his arms and levitated back toward the deck, where he gently laid her on the cold metal floor.

Yanis arrived.

She was badly wounded, with many electrical burns and bleeding wounds. Probably some internal bleeding as well.

Chase put his hands on her and started healing her. The surface wounds were taken care of quickly, but something was wrong. He could usually sense a positive feedback and life being injected back into the people he healed, but for some reason it didn't work this time. Was she too far gone?

"Is she going to be okay?" asked Yanis, barely able to breathe.

"I . . . I don't know."

"Don't you dare let her die! You promised you would protect her."

Chase's eyes burned with the beginning of tears.

Why isn't it working? Why isn't she healing, dammit?

Chase emptied his mind and tried to push his healing abilities to the maximum, but to no avail. He could not sense life flowing into her.

That's when he heard a voice inside his mind. *It's okay, Chase, you can let me go now.*

No! Fillio, please fight this! Let me revive you.

I'm tired, Chase. I've been tired of all of this for a while now. Please, if our friendship ever meant anything to you, then you'll let me go.

I can't. I promised your brother I'd protect you no matter what.

It wasn't your fault. I've always loved you, you know that. Please tell Daniel and Yanis I'm sorry. Goodbye, Chase.

Chase removed his hands and looked down in horror, still in shock.

What was that? Could he speak to souls now?

"I'm so sorry, Yanis. She's gone."

"NO! I beg you, please save her."

"I did all I could, trust me."

"Bullshit! I've seen you heal people before. Why can't you heal my sister?" Yanis' eyes were filled with tears. "I beg you, Chase, please, try again!"

Chase gave her mouth to mouth then opened his palm. Multiple electrical bolts ran between his fingers. He put his hand on her chest and sent an electric shock to her heart. He did it again and again, alternating it with his healing light.

"Don't give up," said Yanis, his hands trembling uncontrollably.

"Yanis," tried Chase.

"No, you keep doing it! No matter how long it takes."

Chase knew she was gone already. There was nothing more he could do. He kept trying to resuscitate her for ten more minutes, even though he knew it was in vain.

Then, when he couldn't take it anymore, he stopped and rose to his feet.

"Don't stop, Chase!" ordered Yanis.

"I'm sorry. She's gone."

Yanis rose and pushed Chase.

"She's not gone until I say so. Get back to her, NOW!"

Chase shook his head.

"You son of a bitch! She's my sister. You killed her with your dumb-ass bravado."

That stung Chase right in the heart. Fillio and he had been very close at one point, and he never imagined he would be responsible for her death. Was he responsible? Could he have anticipated the Zarlack's destructive strategy? He could have at least made sure she had jumped with them, but in the midst of it all, the truth is he only thought of Sarah and Chris. So perhaps it was his fault.

Yanis pounded Chase's chest.

"I'm so sorry, Yanis, and perhaps you're right, it is my fault. Please forgive me."

Yanis took a step back and looked at him with a mixture of anger and despair in his tear-filled eyes.

"Forgive you? No way! I don't forgive you. I fucking hate you!"

Then Yanis fell to his knees and let himself fall on his sister's dead body as he sobbed uncontrollably for what felt like an eternity.

General Arkoolis was not used to seeing his own blood, but he liked the fact that finally this mission was turning into something other than a borefest of meaningless destruction with no real challenge.

"That was an impressive display, and the gravity's shift a neat trick. But I haven't used my full powers yet. You are going to regret spilling my blood."

Seven of the droids answered by launching themselves toward the general.

"I don't think so," he said, sending a powerful shockwave their way.

It stopped them in their tracks and they stayed paralyzed in midair.

"This has gone on long enough."

He slashed both his hands in the air and all seven droids were cut into pieces. He finished them off with a series of powerful fireballs.

The ground shook and the gravity increased even more. The general looked down for a brief moment.

The rest of the droids, all of them except the red-and-silver droid, launched themselves at him and a terrible battle ensued. They were less affected by the gravity shift than he was and they landed more blows over time. The tactic seemed to work as more bruises formed and more blood was spilled.

The droids were everywhere around the general, landing more blows, when he jumped high in the sky. He lost no time preparing a gigantic fireball and sent it back toward the ground, right into the midst of the droids. Thanks to the high gravity the fireball reached the ground in a fraction of a second, preventing Gaia from intervening and siphoning its energy as she had done before.

The resulting explosion unearthed trees all around, and when the dust settled, there was a large crater at the point of impact. Parts of destroyed droids were disseminated over the crater's surface.

"Mechanical fools."

When the general landed back near the crater, the Gaia droid, the only remaining one, approached him.

"Looks like I've missed one."

"I won't be that easy to dispatch."

"So these things talk."

Gaia took an offensive posture.

"You don't really think you have a shadow of a chance of defeating me? No matter how strong the gravity is."

"We're about to find out."

Gaia extended both hands with open palms and fired two extremely powerful shots of plasma.

The general blocked the attack with both his palms but was surprised by the strength of the streams of plasma. He clenched his teeth, showing a little blood on them.

Gaia advanced while she maintained the streams of plasma energy. Once she was only a few yards from her target she stopped firing and landed a hook kick to the Fury's head, making him lose balance. She didn't wait and catapulted him into the air with a powerful uppercut. She followed him upwards into the air and fired another stream of plasma energy. It hit him in the torso and sent him flying backward at great speed toward the ground.

"Now, Ares!"

Ares understood what that meant and teleported away into the Alpha Prime system.

When the general hit the ground he skidded for more than three miles, leaving a trail of flying stones, soil and grass.

At 4 Gs, Gaia clearly had the upper hand, but now that Ares was gone, the gravity returned to its original strength.

Fortunately, it took a while for General Arkoolis to recover from the last blow.

Gaia checked the internal power levels of her avatar droid. Power was at sixty percent. She wouldn't be able to use similar attacks too often or she'd run out of juice pretty quickly. The little reprieve allowed her to reprogram her attack matrix with the logs from the fight the other droids had with the Fury. It should prove helpful in devising the best attack and defensive patterns upon his return.

General Arkoolis stood and dusted himself off. He had a few more burns and bruises, but lost no time before shooting into the air and flying back to the fight. He landed only yards from Gaia.

"That was quite unexpected and impressive. For a tin can, anyway."

The Fury grew his aura and soon all his bruises and burns healed. Except for a few scorch marks on his armor he looked as good as new.

THE *PHOENIX* WAS ABOUT to enter Droxia's atmosphere when Ronan thought of something.

"Arknon, are we gonna survive re-entry in our current state?"

Arknon crunched some numbers on his terminal before answering. "There's a sixty percent chance we will. We're about to find out. It's too late to change course."

"This is going to be a rough ride."

"We only have a handful of seconds before we hit the upper atmosphere. Make sure the coordinates are locked."

Ronan double checked the targeted Fury and saw he was on the move.

"Dammit!"

"What is it, Ronan?"

"He's moving again. He's heading toward the next city."

"The one where your uncle lives?"

"Yes."

"It's safe to assume that's his next target. You should probably lock these coordinates in."

"I'm locking it three miles outside of town on his approach vector."

"Why? I understand your feelings, but will it really make any difference?"

"I'm not thinking of trying to give my uncle a chance. He's either gone from there or he's dead anyway. But this particular Fury never entered any of the cities he has destroyed today. He always stood two to three miles away while he launched his destructive attacks."

"Dishonorable bastard. Then shoot for two and a half miles. Law of average kind of thing?"

"Right. Coordinates locked."

"Entering the atmosphere now. I'm boosting the engines to their maximum. We're gonna lose control of the ship soon."

The ship rocked heavily and Ronan and Arknon had to hold their consoles so as not to be thrown out of their respective seats. The lights on the bridge flickered, and the previously damaged bulkheads and dislocated hardware were thrown around, creating a very unsafe environment.

"Why don't these seats have belts?"

"That's a good question, but perhaps we should think of going to the escape pods soon. Less than a minute until impact."

"Right," said Ronan. "We should go n—"

A power conduit next to Ronan blew and engulfed him with blue flames. He was badly burned and thrown to the side. He skidded until his head hit a nearby console.

"Ronan!" Arknon tried to reach his friend but the vibrations and movement caused by re-entry made it difficult for him to walk straight without stumbling.

"Are you alright?"

Ronan had lost consciousness, and had serious burns to half his face.

Realizing there was no more time, Arknon reached his unconscious friend and that's when he saw them.

"Gravity boots."

He quickly removed his own boots and took Ronan's. He activated the gravity lock and grabbed Ronan by the collar as he started running.

There were explosions the whole way to the nearest escape pods, those meant for the bridge's crew. Several times debris and loose plating hit the duo of Droxians, but Arknon, dragging Ronan in tow, arrived at their destination. They only had a few seconds before impact. He threw

Ronan inside the first pod, closed it and pressed the manual release. There was no time to strap him down, meaning much less chance of survival. Ronan's pod flew away from the ship.

He ran to the next pod and punched it, but was rewarded with shooting sparks that burned his face. All instruments within the pod flashed red.

Time had almost run out, but he quickly jumped into the next pod.

Last chance!

He tried to punch the launch control but the ship rocked so heavily he was catapulted out of the pod and thrown against the nearest bulkhead. He heard and felt most of the ribs on his right side shatter. The pain was unbearable.

Then he felt the heat and looked to his side. Approaching rapidly was a series of fireballs, each bigger than the last.

The ship was a few milliseconds away from being obliterated, and him with it. He pushed with his legs with as much strength as he could muster and launched himself back inside the pod, striking his shoulder on the way. He punched the controls for ejection. The doors closed and he was pushed forward by the acceleration, hitting his skull on the pod's windshield.

The last thing he saw before losing consciousness was flames everywhere.

MISEO HAD ARRIVED at the next big city, and as with every other city before, he was greeted by whatever pathetic ground and flying military forces the Droxians had. They were in much greater numbers this time. This city did look like one of the biggest, perhaps even the capital. Not that it mattered. In minutes it would be leveled.

Three waves of in-atmosphere fighters approached and opened fire upon Miseo.

When will these miserable insects understand that their weapons are useless against us?

But Miseo was in a playful mood. He enjoyed ripping the planes to shreds one by one, using telekinesis or fireballs, or sometimes just passing through them with his own body. Soon the sky was filled with explosions from the carnage he inflicted on the incoming squadrons.

Tanks on the ground started firing their energy blasts toward him. He purposefully vectored toward them, deflecting the few lucky shots that managed to come his way with the palm of his hand. When he landed, the full force of his current velocity created a large crater, and the resulting shockwave pushed half the tanks onto their side.

Miseo's eyes flashed red and he fired thin laser beams, destroying one tank after another.

A giant hand made of metal hit him in the face. One of the mechs had landed a lucky shot while he was distracted by the tanks.

Miseo's response was as lethal as it was fast. He waved his hand forward at such speed that the mech exploded from the impact of his kinetic attack.

Pieces of burning metal, wiring and screws landed all around him.

He smiled, but the ground started shaking and he looked behind him. A full platoon of these mechs was running toward him like a herd of wild animals. They all opened fire simultaneously.

He put both his hands in front of him and created a powerful shield that absorbed every shot.

This is rather fun. Futile, but fun.

When the first salvo had ended and the mechs all switched to either giant, metallic knives or light-blades, he sent a volley of fireballs into their midst and destroyed most of them. The cascading explosions knocked the others off their feet and into the dust.

He felt a strange sensation around his waist. The same sensation repeated around his shoulders, and then his arms. Pretty soon he couldn't move.

He looked at his body and saw blue energy bands restricting his movements. The more he moved the stronger the counteracting force was.

Interesting weapon.

A platoon of foot soldiers had fired at him and temporarily paralyzed him.

With a single thought he blew most of the soldiers up from the inside out. Blood and guts splashed the other Droxians. Their eyes filled with terror.

One of those remaining, clearly their military leader, wore a smirk.

"You don't think this is going to hold me for long now, do you?"

"It only has to hold you for a few more seconds, then you're dead, asshole," said the Droxian, pointing toward the sky.

A giant shadow was cast all around. It felt as if night had instantly fallen upon them all.

Miseo looked upwards and what he saw made no sense.

WHEN CHASE WALKED BACK onto the bridge he was still in

shock from Fillio's death. Why couldn't he save her? Had it mattered that she didn't want to be saved?

Sarah saw the look on his face and ran to embrace him.

"I couldn't save her," he said, with tears forming in his eyes.

"I'm sure you did all you could."

But that was of little comfort to him. Until now he thought he could save anyone. Heck, he had brought Daniel back when his injuries seemed even worse than Fillio's. But no matter how bad the wounds were, he was still breathing. That probably was the difference.

"She . . . she wanted to go."

"What? How do you know?"

"I heard her in my thoughts when I was trying to heal her. And I also felt resistance. It was as if she didn't want me to."

"I find that creepy but, then again, a few minutes ago my unborn son raised a shield and saved both my life and Ryonna's. I'm getting used to the feeling."

"It seems the more I get a hold on my powers, the more things I can do. That's probably why I heard her talk to me."

"I understand. If she told you she wanted to go, then you shouldn't blame yourself."

"Tell that to Yanis."

"Put yourself in his place. He must be devastated. In time he'll forgive you. For now he needs to process his grief."

"That's putting it mildly, I'm afraid. I don't know about him ever forgiving me, but you're right. I should let him grieve for now."

"I'm really sorry, Chase. I know she was your friend, but she was also an officer in the Earth Alliance. Like everyone else, she knew the risks. It was her choice to be here with us."

Sarah was right, of course, except she was more than just a friend at one point in his life. Chase decided that now was not the time to speak about that. Would it ever be the time? And did it really matter, under the circumstances?

"Thank you, Sarah."

"Have you told Daniel yet?"

"He's leading the *Destiny*'s away team in their search of survivors."

"He's your best friend. The longer you wait to tell him the more difficult it will be. He might even resent you for it."

"I know. Perhaps I could send him a message telepathically."

"That's a no-no! That's like breaking up with a girlfriend with a text. This requires your presence, and for you to look him in the eyes."

Chase dreaded that moment. He'd rather fight Argos once more than face his best friend in the whole world and tell him he couldn't save the woman he fell in love with.

Like an answer from the heavens, the bridge was illuminated with a golden tinge as Ares appeared in front of them.

Ryonna ran toward them in anticipation.

"We've got to go to Droxia now!" exclaimed Ares.

"Ares," said Ryonna. "Any news of my son?"

"He's one of the only survivors aboard the *Phoenix*, but the ship has set a collision course toward the planet. They're trying to take one of the Furies out of the equation. I need Chase to take care of the other one, who just decimated an entire battalion of battle droids. I had to leave the Gaia droid alone, so let's go now. Perhaps she will still be operational and you can use her help in your fight with the Fury, but we must hurry!"

"I'm coming with you," said Ryonna in a tone not open for discussion.

"No, it's too dangerous. Only Chase should come with me."

"Chase!" insisted Ryonna.

"Ares, take her with us. She has the right to go, no matter how dangerous it is."

"Very well. We've lost enough time as it is. Now, come close and join hands."

Chase looked back at Sarah as he took Ryonna's left hand. "You have the bridge, Commander, please be careful."

He sent another message but this time telepathically. *Looks like you'll have to tell Daniel about Fillio. I have no idea when I will be back. Please convey how terribly sorry I am and that I did everything I could. I love you.*

She nodded back at him and he read, "I love you, too," on her lips.

Ares put one of his energy-based hands on each of their shoulders and they vanished from the bridge.

It took a fraction of a second for Miseo's brain to interpret the image his eyes sent to it.

A Droxian destroyer, with an insane amount of damage, and flames spewing from every deck, was on a collision course with . . . him.

The scene seemed surreal.

He brought all his energy to bear and freed himself from the energy bonds. The resulting shockwave killed everyone around him as they exploded at the cellular level.

Miseo extended both his arms upward, even though he knew he was too late.

As he fired the most impressive column of energy in an

attempt to vaporize the incoming ship, it impacted with him and the ground.

The resulting explosion, amplified by the explosion of the ship's engine, sent such a powerful blast of energy on all sides that half the nearby city was incinerated almost instantly. Glass windows exploded in the rest of the buildings from the shockwave. Buildings collapsed atop one another, and the once beautiful Droxian city was transformed into a burning graveyard in a matter of seconds.

GAIA ADOPTED a defensive stance the moment Arkoolis launched himself toward her. He unleashed a series of powerful blows but she managed to dodge them in the nick of time. But then the Fury started attacking her at increased speed. He landed a powerful uppercut that sent Gaia flying upwards into the air. Before she had time to recover, Arkoolis was already upon her and he hammered her back toward the ground. Gaia managed to recover a few milliseconds before impact, but she had lost visual contact with the Fury.

"Looking for me?" said the Fury from behind her.

Her shield activated, but almost immediately failed. A powerful burst of red energy shot through the chest of her avatar body. Arkoolis' foot hit her back and her avatar body was sent flying forward, ending its course face first in the dust.

When she got up she saw a fist-sized hole in the left side of the droid's chest. She activated repair nanobots immediately, and the hole started mending itself.

But Arkoolis didn't wait. He launched himself toward her once more. His speed had increased tremendously in the last few minutes and she was no longer able to block all his blows. While the force of most of his punches and kicks was deflected by her shields, he was landing too many and her shields were draining quickly. The repeated attack patterns made their usual, super-quick recharge cycle almost useless now. In the middle of a combo she flew upwards into the air and made a run for it in order to recharge them.

"Not so fast."

The Fury was already on her tail, flying faster than her, gaining on her with every passing second.

She redistributed her internal power to boost the efficiency of her right arm to four hundred percent and she stopped short in midair, pivoted on herself and smashed Arkoolis with a terrible blow to the face. He was taken by surprise and flew backward, splashing into a nearby body of water, sending tons of water upwards upon entry.

Gaia's shields were back up to one hundred percent and her nanobots were finishing repairing the hole and damaged circuitry inside her avatar's chest.

By the time Arkoolis had recovered from the attack, her systems were back to one hundred percent. She redirected most of her power to the engines in order to increase her speed, even if that meant lowering her shields and disabling her offensive plasma energy weapons. She needed to buy as much time as possible until Ares returned with Chase.

13

Daniel's away team had arrived at the source of the distress call they had received but there was nobody in the communications tower. They had encountered only a few Zarlacks until now, but each encounter had involved a long and difficult battle. Their thick skin provided them extra protection from blaster fire. The fact that the *Destiny* had left orbit was a little worrisome, though. No doubt the battle on the other side of the planet was still raging and Chase needed the added firepower of the newly upgraded weapons on board *Destiny*.

Daniel wondered how Fillio was doing and hoped she was fine. They had been really close in the past few weeks and he couldn't help but worry about her well-being. Even though she seemed to feel better since they had started going out together, on many occasions her spirits were down. Sometimes out of the blue, and while he made every effort to comfort her, he felt something darker brewing inside her. That worried him the most.

He brushed the thought away. She was a seasoned pilot,

probably even better than him, so there was no logic in worrying. And now was hardly the time to be distracted.

Daniel and a few ground troops arrived at the top of the communications tower. He rested his blaster rifle against the nearest console and started browsing logs.

Most of the logs had been erased except the one containing the distress call, and the file wasn't properly signed.

That raised a red flag.

Had the distress call been planted? If so, for what purpose? Or perhaps the people who sent it weren't of military background and did their best, not knowing the Star Alliance protocols. But then the question as to why the rest of the logs were absent remained.

"Commander," said one of his away team.

"What is it?"

"I've been getting some strange readings ever since we entered the tower."

"What kind of readings?"

"Some unusual power fluctuations on every level of the facility."

"I'll check it with the internal sensors. Thank you, Lieutenant."

"Very well, sir."

Daniel brought up the schematics of the tower on the holo-display of a nearby console. He looked for power fluctuations and detected some, but the readings seemed erratic. This station had seen better days, and perhaps there was a glitch in power distribution. But his instinct told him to dig further.

He re-calibrated the sensors to look for different types of parameters, like energy waves, modulation and frequency. One of the scans displayed something that froze his blood.

The tower showed five different red dots that blinked on his holo-display.

"These," he said, pointing toward one of them. "They aren't part of the schematics."

"Could they be . . .?" said the lieutenant.

"Bombs. We should get out of here."

"What if we've armed them on our way up? That would explain why I got more and more readings as we progressed."

"Smart observation, Lieutenant. You're probably right. We'd better not try to get out until we either get more info on these devices or find another way out of here."

"We could rappel down the outside of the building."

"Depending on the range of the devices—if they are bombs—that could have the same result as retracing our steps."

"But by that same logic we can't really make a visual check. That could trigger them."

"Let me bring video streams into these areas."

Daniel entered a few commands on his console and was rewarded with "access denied."

"That's odd. I should have access to the videos. My credentials worked for accessing the sensors."

Then every light and terminal shut down and they were plunged into darkness. Daniel heard a nearby door open and then metallic steps.

Two orange lights blinked into existence and their small light revealed the shape of a combat droid's face. Then all hell broke loose.

"Take cover!" shouted Daniel as the droid opened fire.

Daniel jumped and rolled to avoid blaster fire. He then grabbed his own rifle and returned fire, but the droid was shielded.

By the time he had taken cover and grabbed the night-vision goggles from his backpack, the droid had killed every member of his away team except the lieutenant, who had also found cover.

"Lieutenant, tell me you have grenades."

He flashed him a thumbs up.

"On my mark. Three . . . two . . . one . . . NOW, Lieutenant!"

Daniel left cover and showered the droid with blaster fire in order to provide a distraction while the lieutenant sent two grenades toward their foe.

Daniel shot one of the grenades which exploded right before impacting the droid's shield and made them blink just long enough for the second grenade to pass through the shields and detonate. But not before Daniel received a laser blast on his shoulder. He dropped his rifle. He crawled back toward cover just as the second grenade exploded. Some metallic shrapnel lodged in the wall nearby.

After a few seconds he looked out from behind cover and saw the top half of the droid body on the ground. But then its hands started moving and the droid began crawling toward his position.

He ignored the throbbing pain in his shoulder, took his sidearm and fired a few shots at the crawling droid, but they were deflected by its strong armor. Sparks from the severed trunk of the droid played havoc with his night-vision glasses and burned his eyes, so he removed them. That didn't help much. He could barely tell where the droid was based on the few sparks emitted by it.

"More grenades, Lieutenant?"

"I'm out, and I've dropped my rifle."

Swell.

Daniel put his night-vision goggles back on and looked

for the nearest downed member of his away team. He ran to the other side of the room and searched the body of his deceased teammate for another grenade.

"We've got to get out of here, Commander!"

Daniel could still hear the metallic arms of the droid crawling its way toward him.

"Stand fast. If we run down the stairs we might trigger the bombs."

"And if we stay here that droid will kill us."

Daniel was well aware of that fact, but wasn't ready to give up just yet. He didn't find grenades on the body he was searching, but when the droids unnerving, metallic crawling grew closer he had an idea. He set the power source of his blaster to overload and faced his incoming foe.

When the intensifying, high-pitched noise of his blaster's power source indicated it would soon explode, he threw it at the droid. The droid caught the pistol with one of its arms, and its creepy, orange, blinking eyes looked at it just before it exploded. The concussion cracked and disabled his night-vision goggles.

WHEN RONAN REGAINED consciousness he felt waves of tremendous pain radiating all over his body.

What had happened? The last thing he remembered was getting up to run toward the escape pods, but then something had exploded nearby.

He opened his eyes and saw he was inside one of the escape pods. He tried to move but was rewarded with sharp pain that told him he had broken a few bones.

He tried to get his bearings inside the pod. He was upside down, the windshield of the pod was cracked and all he could see was parts of the sky covered by humongous clouds of dark, gray smoke.

It took all his energy to just reach the controls. He activated the comms.

"Arknon, come in? Are you there, buddy? Arknon, please respond!"

But there was only silence. He set the comms to the widest band possible.

"Ronan to any Droxian soldier in the area, please respond."

Again no answer on the comms. Perhaps they were damaged in the rough landing.

Some of the walls inside the pod were deformed and Ronan wondered how he'd even survived the trip.

If Ronan made it alive in an escape pod, no matter how badly he was hurt, that could only mean Arknon had thrown him into one. The fact that he wasn't strapped in told him there had not been enough time to do so. But what did that mean for Arknon? Had he had time to eject in another pod?

Ronan used his right foot to kick open the cupboard with the first aid logo printed on it. After repeatedly kicking the damn thing, it finally opened and the first-aid kit fell on his face.

Ronan located the strongest painkiller and injected himself with it. He needed to move and get out of this pod and start looking for his friend. But until the medicine kicked in, which took a few minutes, Ronan watched the sky fill with more and more dark smoke, no doubt resulting from the impact of the destroyer on the surface. Hopefully killing that Fury in the process.

When he felt numb enough to move without aching everywhere at once, Ronan got up inside the pod and grabbed the survival backpack. He then punched the opening sequence on the pad and the engine of the door moaned, but nothing happened.

Ronan activated the emergency release, which sent the door flying in the air.

He crawled backward out of the pod and let himself fall on the ground. That was when he realized he didn't have any shoes on.

Where are my boots?

It made sense to assume Arknon had taken them in order to walk with more ease while the ship entered the atmosphere, since Ronan had been wearing gravity boots. It must have been one hell of a bumpy ride.

Ronan looked ahead.

The view of the nearby giant furnace, no doubt a result of the ship's impact, and the apparent damage to the city beyond, grabbed at Ronan's heart.

So much destruction. Jonas, I really hope you weren't there when it happened.

He looked inside the backpack and found a portable scanner. He scanned the area for a power signature. He saw a faint one in the area that, from where he sat, looked like a furnace. He climbed back inside the pod and grabbed an extinguisher, forced it into the backpack and started walking toward the blinking dot on his scanner.

Arkoolis rose from the water and flew back toward Gaia.

"You keep surprising me, but I think it's time to end this little dance of ours. This has been a fun distraction but I've lost enough time."

"You keep saying that, and yet I still stand."

"A robot with personality. These thousands of years trapped in another dimension sure have brought up the most peculiar things."

"You should have stayed there. No one wants you back in this reality."

The general laughed hard. "Do you think we care what you and these insects want? This universe is ours now. Now that we're back we'll cleanse it from all impurity."

"You're the impurity," said Gaia defiantly.

"I'm gonna make you swallow those words."

"Let me see you try."

"Do you really think you stand a chance? I have barely deployed twenty percent of my abilities up till now."

The planet rocked for a moment and a distant explosion resounded.

"You hear that? It seems my partner is ripping this world apart."

"What makes you think he's not the one getting ripped apart?"

"Miseo is one of the most powerful Furies there is. None of you stand a chance of defeating him. Not that you ever stood a chance defeating me either."

"Ah, the Fury pride. It will be your downfall."

"Speaking of downfall, time to send your body parts back to your creator."

"I'm my own creator, and this is but one body. You'll never be done with me."

"We'll see about that."

Arkoolis moved so quickly he was on Gaia's back before she could react. He planted his elbow deep into her avatar's back, and began pounding her metallic body with more blows than she could count. Her shields quickly failed and each new blow deformed her armor. The end of that avatar body was near but there was nothing she could do about it.

But then something happened.

Arkoolis received a blue fireball right in the face and was thrown hundreds of yards away, crashing unceremoniously into the dirt, face first.

When Gaia looked toward the source of the attack, she saw Chase with his arm extended.

"You okay?" he asked.

"Don't be ridiculous! This is just a piece of technology. But thanks, nonetheless. I have been badly damaged but I can still help you in your fight."

"That's alright. I'll deal with this Fury on my own."

"Don't let your pride blind you, Chase, he is more powerful than you are."

Gaia saw a Droxian in the distance.

"What is *she* doing here?"

"Ryonna ... She's looking for her son."

"If he was in any of the cities that were destroyed, she is too late."

"According to Ares, Ronan was in the ship that crashed not long ago in the southern hemisphere, taking out the other Fury in the process."

"This Fury said his name was Miseo, and that he is even more powerful than him. If that's true, he might have survived."

Chase reflected upon the words of the Gaia droid. "One problem at a time. For now I need to get rid of this one."

"We. You'll need my help."

"Alright then, let's get to work."

DANIEL COULDN'T SEE a damn thing in the darkness. The night-vision mask was totaled, so he threw it aside.

"Lieutenant? Are you alright?"

But there was no answer.

"Are you hurt, Lieutenant?"

Daniel used his hands to try to find his backpack in the dark. After a while he found a rifle on the ground and turned its light on.

The droid laid on the floor motionless. The fact that no sparks shot from its severed body parts told him it was finally destroyed, or at least disabled.

When the light from his rifle landed on the lieutenant, Daniel had to refrain from vomiting. His head had been severed by a piece of armor from the droid.

"I'm so sorry," said Daniel out loud.

But now was not the time to mourn. Daniel needed to find a way out of the building without setting off the unidentified devices strategically placed in the communications tower.

He went into the room where the droid came from and looked around. He found the power control panel for the tower and cycled the power back on.

The main control room was a bloody mess. His entire away team had been wiped out by the battle droid. He looked for a first-aid kit and found one.

Time to mend his shoulder wound. He injected himself with a painkiller and was soon back in front of a control console.

He tried to access the video feeds inside the complex but was again denied access. He punched the console out of frustration.

He found the controls for the shades and activated them. They rose, and finally the light of day filled the bloody room. Outside he saw lush vegetation and large trees as far as the eyes could see. A bird landed on the nearest one. Some of its branches were only a couple of yards away from the control center's large, angled windows.

He tried opening a channel to the *Destiny* but was unsuccessful; with both his own gear and the tower's comms.

What the hell is going on up there?

He ran a system-wide diagnostic. It would take a few minutes to complete.

But then he felt it. Something exploded on a level below and it shook the entire complex.

Crap! Perhaps running these diagnostics wasn't the best idea.

Shortly after the first detonation, another rocked the facility, and then another. Alarms wailed and Daniel knew he only had seconds to react. The third explosion cracked the large window in the control room. He grabbed what was left of the droid's left arm and threw it against the cracked window, which gave out and shattered into a thousand pieces. He took a few steps back as the latest explosion caused the structural integrity of the tower to fail. The entire tower started leaning forward. He ran and jumped out of the window as far as he could, hoping to catch one of the tree branches nearby.

At the exact moment he jumped, the tower's control room exploded and he felt a wave of heat on his back, as well as the pressure from the shockwave of the explosion.

He was thrown so far forward he missed the branch he had been aiming for and crashed against the tree's trunk, hitting his head badly in the process.

He started his descent toward the ground, grabbing the first branch that passed him by, but it didn't hold his weight and cracked. As he fell, he was stopped every now and then by other branches that slowed his descent, but not without inflicting a tremendous amount of pain. Many of his ribs broke, and by the time his body crashed near the bottom of the tree, he had lost consciousness.

AFTER MANY UNSUCCESSFUL hails to try and contact Ronan, Keera decided to cloak the *Valken* and head toward the planet's surface.

The battle between the Alliance fleet and the Zarlacks was still ongoing, and it took some pretty fancy flying to avoid being hit by stray fire. When she entered orbit of the planet her cloak failed. Fortunately, she didn't need it anymore, at least for the time being. She headed toward the coordinates where the *Phoenix* had crashed. She really hoped Ronan had managed to escape. A new dot appeared on her scopes. It was similar to the signal Ronan had asked her to amplify before.

Could that be the receiving device of that signal?

She locked onto the area and opened a channel.

"Is anyone receiving me?"

"Identify yourself," answered a familiar female voice.

"Ryonna?"

"Who's this?"

"It's Keera. I'm looking for Ronan."

"Where is he?"

"I don't know. How did you get here so fast?"

"That's a long story. Can you please come and pick me up?"

"I'm adjusting course to your position."

"I'm not gonna stay in the area for long. Chase is about to battle a Fury and we all know what that means. I've just secured a military ground craft but this thing is way too slow. Let's meet at the following coordinates."

Keera received the transmission.

"Rendezvous coordinates received. See you soon."

Keera adjusted her vector for the new rendezvous point and flew above the city that was destroyed by the *Phoenix*.

The damage was surreal.

I doubt many people could have survived that blast.

RONAN ARRIVED near the coordinates indicated on his portable scanner and was horrified to see a pod in the distance, in the middle of a large field still on fire.

He ran as fast as he could toward the pod, finding a path amongst a labyrinth of flames. The temperature around him became unbearable but he kept at it nonetheless.

He reached a large and deep crevasse that blocked his way forward.

Dammit!

The crevasse ran as far as the eye could see on both sides and he needed to make a choice. His first instinct was to try to jump over it, but that would have been a risky proposition even if he was in full possession of his abilities. With his multiple wounds and the lack of oxygen around him, it was suicide, plain and simple.

He decided to go left and hoped to find a way across.

He tried hailing his friend again but there was no response.

After ten more minutes of running it became clear that he would need to build some sort of bridge in order to pass to the other side. He looked around him for anything to help him achieve that goal. There was a tree trunk not too far away but it was on fire. He checked his survival pack and drank some water. The smoke around him made it even more difficult to advance and his eyes were burning.

He kept going for another three miles when he finally saw a tree near the edge of the crevasse. It hadn't been unearthed or burned. He took his sidearm blaster and shot multiple times at the base of the tree, and soon it cracked and fell forward. The top of the tree landed on the other side of the crevasse, providing him with a bridge to cross. He climbed on the trunk and jumped a couple of times to test its stability. It didn't budge.

Well, that's good enough I guess.

He was halfway over when the ground shook and he lost balance and nearly fell to his death. He fell flat on the trunk and started slipping. Ronan grabbed on for dear life as the ground shook more, hoping the crevasse wouldn't enlarge as a result of the tremor. After some time the tremors stopped and he got back to his feet, increasing his pace. When he was over the other side he ran in the direction of the pod. He hoped with all his heart that Arknon hadn't been cooked alive in the meantime.

He ran as fast as he could, avoiding patches of fire on the way, and reached the pod in under seven minutes. By then he was panting heavily and his head was spinning.

The pod was not accessible. There was fire all around it so Ronan took the portable extinguisher from his backpack and got rid of just enough flames to allow him access to the pod. Then he was faced with another problem. The door of the pod was facing the ground. He tried rolling it to the side but was rewarded with first-degree burns on both his hands.

Okay, dumb idea.

His feet were also burning but he ignored that and

looked around for a large piece of wood. He found one he could use as a lever.

With much effort and pain, he finally managed to roll the pod onto its side. He looked through the pod's window. It was very dirty. He grabbed some leaves from the ground to provide a little heat protection and wiped dirt from the window.

His friend was unconscious, with a nasty cut on his forehead and a lot of blood on his face.

He knocked at the window three times, hoping it would trigger movement in Arknon, but it didn't.

"Arknon! Can you hear me? Arknon!"

Ronan couldn't see well enough to know if his friend and commanding officer was still breathing.

Hang on, buddy, I'll get you out of here.

Ronan looked for the external door ejection system but it was located on a part of the ship still facing dirt. He had to push the pod a little more on the side before accessing the external panel. Soon the door of the pod ejected and he carefully climbed inside.

14

Gaia approached Chase and put her hand on his shoulder. He felt a sting.

"Ouch! What was that?"

"Sorry for the temporary discomfort. I've just implanted you with transmitter nanobots."

Chase rubbed his itchy shoulder. "You could have asked me first."

"We need to be able to communicate without him hearing us. That will give us a tactical advantage."

"Yeah, I get that, but you could still have asked first."

"I'm sorry. I will next time."

Chase looked dubious. "Next time?"

"Never mind that. Our foe is returning. Please be careful. Don't underestimate him."

"Yeah, yeah, Ares already gave me the pep talk. But I'm pissed and I need to blow off some steam, so he might just get something extra from me today."

"No! Do not think this fight will be easy. He destroyed almost one hundred of my battle droids in the space of a few minutes, and if you hadn't arrived when you did I would also be scrap metal now."

Chase preferred not telling her that at this exact moment, it wouldn't have been the worst of things.

"The nanobots are operational. I can hear your thoughts loud and clear."

Chase scratched his head with a dumb smile on his face. "How much of what I just thought did you hear?"

"All of it."

"Right . . . Oops, then."

"Let's move on. I don't care whether or not you think I will be of some help. Together we stand a better chance of defeating him. All I care about is that he is stopped here so he cannot replicate this level of destruction on Earth."

"Perhaps, but you'll let me fight him first so I can gauge him. Then if needed you'll intervene."

"I feel obliged to point out that this is not an efficient strategy, Chase."

"Still, you'll do as I ask, Gaia. I'm grateful for the training facility you provided me, but I need to gauge my own progress now as well as size up this Fury. You have my authorization to intervene the minute anything goes wrong, but I start this fight on my own."

"I should point out I do not need your authorization, but I will abide by your wishes for as long as it doesn't conflict with my own interests."

"Which are?"

"To not let your bravado kill you today, even though that is only a secondary objective, in all fairness."

Chase smiled. "And the first being?"

"Kill both Furies currently on Droxian soil."

"You'd make great friends with Ryonna."

Chase didn't know why he felt so excited at the prospect

of fighting another Fury, but he preferred this sensation to the fear he felt when realizing the role he had played freeing the Furies from their dimensional prison.

When Arkoolis landed in front of Chase, he looked utterly pissed.

"Sorry about that. Are you going to be okay, pal?" teased Chase with an unusual level of arrogance.

"So you're the one they call Laiyos. Argos's brother."

"My name actually is Chase Athanatos. And let's get one thing clear: Argos is no brother of mine!"

"Mine is General Arkoolis. Argos told us you had rejected your Fury heritage and decided instead to fight us."

"That's right."

"That was a foolish decision, and today you'll pay for that dire mistake with your life. I will make sure of that."

Chase decided to antagonize his enemy and gauge his reactions. Perhaps he could get something out of taunting him.

"Not part of my plan for the day, I'm afraid. Let's recap, shall we? First I'll kick your ass . . . *General*. Then I will go kill your other pal. Miseo is it? That's if he survived the Droxian destroyer that got rammed up his ass a few moments ago."

The general's features and expression darkened.

"Awwww . . . You didn't know that, now did you?"

The general clenched both fists. "Impetuous. I'll grant you that. You do seem overly confident for a low-class Fury."

"Low-class?" said Chase, raising an eyebrow.

Go ahead and tell me some valuable information now.

"There are different classes of fighters on our world. Some have a few meager powers but they aren't really any more powerful than the millions of insects whose pathetic lives we've mercifully ended today on Droxia. We call them drones. They are the worker class of the Furies, if you will. They build, we fight. We occasionally use them as cannon-fodder in larger scale assaults when more than one or two of us are required to destroy a world's population and infrastructure, but very few races ever called for such scenarios."

That's it. Keep spilling some more.

"Then there're three distinct categories of fighters, like you and me. The low class. That would be you, by the way. The high-class. I would say Argos sits between these categories. Probably not a fully fledged high class just yet. With the right guidance and training, maybe one day. Then there's the elite, of which I'm part. We are those sent to a world when it needs purifying."

"Mercifully? Purifying? You know what, pal, mercifully purify the shit out of you is what I'm going to do next."

Gaia talked inside Chase's mind.

Is it really necessary to antagonize your adversary at this point?

I'm just making sure he's taking me seriously. I have no intention of losing this fight and I want him to know that, answered Chase.

"I'm sure you're going to try," said the general, "but I'm not Argos, as you'll soon discover."

"Enough with this meaningless banter," said Chase, cracking his knuckles, shoulders and neck. "Let's dance."

"Let's indeed."

The general took a fighting stance and so did Chase.

Chase was fully aware he needed the mental distraction to avoid thinking too much about Fillio's passing and how strongly it would impact his best friend, not to mention the fact that Yanis already blamed him and hated his guts right now. This upcoming battle was about to achieve just that, make sure his mind was focused on something else. Perhaps even channel that rising feeling of anger he felt boiling at the back of his soul ever since he failed healing her. Chase wasn't used to failing. That simply wasn't in his vocabulary. And every time it happened, it hurt him a little more. But who was he angry at really? He wasn't sure he wanted to face this question right now and the universe agreed.

The general started growing his bright red aura at an exponential rate.

Looks like Gaia was right. Looks like this isn't going to be an easy fight.

Still, Chase felt excitement nonetheless. Now was the time to see if his intense training would pay off.

He grew his own purple aura and it matched the general's in size and power. Chase saw the look of surprise in his adversary. He decided to make the first move.

He launched himself at Arkoolis and delivered a powerful blow to Arkoolis's face. The general's head flew backward and blood was thrown into the air, but his body hadn't moved. Chase went for a second blow but found nothing but air. He sensed an incoming kick coming from behind him and dodged it by doing the splits. With both hands on the ground he inverted himself and scissor kicked his opponent. But he was ready for it and grabbed one of Chase's legs and sent him flying in the air.

Chase quickly recovered in midair and saw no less than five fireballs approaching his position. He deflected four of them and caught the last one in his right hand. He crushed it to nothingness with a smirk on his face. He landed back in front of Arkoolis who was smiling as well.

"Impressive."

"For a low-class Fury, you mean?" said Chase, still playfully taunting him.

"Let's see how long you can keep it up at this level of energy, though."

"I'm only getting started here. Let's kick things into high gear, shall we?"

The general disappeared and reappeared behind Chase. He threw his elbow at Chase, who easily blocked it. He retaliated with a kick to the general's chin, who also blocked the blow without breaking a sweat. He took Chase by surprise by head butting him in the face, which forced him to take three steps back. Chase used an index finger to wipe blood from a cut on his chin. He rubbed it between his fingers.

Chase extended both arms out from his sides and grabbed two massive boulders in the distance with his mind. He clapped his hands together and the boulders crashed against the general, exploding into a million little, stony pieces.

It took a few seconds for the dust cloud to clear and reveal Arkoolis still standing there, not a scratch on him.

"You'll need more than boulders to bring me down."

Chase knew that, but he was still gauging his enemy's reaction. He had expected the general to get out of the way of the boulders, so he could get him off guard with his next attack. That obviously didn't happen.

"Looks like it, but we're running out of destroyers," said Chase, grinning.

The general growled.

"Don't worry, General, if he survived, I promise I'll finish off Miseo once we're done here, so you have someone to talk to in hell."

The general laughed hard. "You're funny. I like that. But you're too sure of yourself."

"Not the first time I've been told that."

"I bet. Let's see how you handle what's coming next."

The general ran toward him and disappeared a millisecond before reaching Chase, who had already adopted a defensive stance. When he turned around no one was there. That's when he felt fire rain from the heavens. Without even looking for the attacks but feeling their incoming power, Chase back flipped just in time as the first attack exploded against the ground. He continued his back-flips to dodge all four attacks, but in the middle of the last one he felt Arkoolis' knee impact with the right side of his ribcage and he was sent flying into the dirt.

Before he was back up three more fireballs were on their way. He deflected them all and again, at the end of his last movement, he was taken by surprise by a very powerful uppercut that sent him traveling vertically in the air. Before Chase could recover, Arkoolis unleashed his next attack, an extremely fast combo of punches and kicks, and finished with a full-body, reverse flying kick that sent Chase crashing back to the ground.

Chase's body ached all over as he got back up and dusted himself off.

Now would be a good time for me to join the fight, heard Chase in his head.

It's not needed, Gaia, I have things well under control.

It doesn't look like it from where I'm standing. He is faster than you.

I want him to think that. I haven't yet deployed my full abilities; I need to learn how he fights first.

By getting your face beaten to a pulp?

If that's what it takes, then yeah. I need to be able to anticipate his movements if I want to defeat him.

I see. Careful, he's coming from behind you.

"I know," said Chase out loud as he pivoted his body and landed a powerful right kick into the general's face.

Arkoolis lost his balance and crashed to the ground. Chase unleashed a flurry of icy-blue fireballs his way. The general dodged the incoming attacks by flying upwards. Chase jumped in pursuit and went for a kick to the general's face but only found air. The general reappeared above of him with both hands joined and smashed them down in order to hammer Chase. But he was prepared for it and dodged the blow at the very last moment, putting himself in a perfect position to counterattack.

He lit both his hands with blue flames and unleashed an incredibly fast combo of punches, including hooks and uppercuts. He ended it by grabbing the general's armor with his left hand and head butting him with such strength the general flew away and impacted with a nearby mountain. It exploded upon impact.

Chase flew back toward the ground. After landing he cracked his neck. He checked his internal pool of energy. He had consumed less than two percent.

This fight was only beginning.

Ryonna saw the *Valken* approach her position, stopped her combat cycle and dismounted.

She experienced a strange feeling when she looked around and saw only destruction: her planet, her home, was literally on fire. She had never imagined she would be a witness to anything like it.

And to think only two people were responsible for this.

She was also worried about her son. She hated not having news from him, and the moment the *Valken* landed she ran into the cockpit and sat next to Keera.

"Nice to see you again, Ryonna."

"Likewise. Let's go. We need to find my son."

"Roger that." Keera brought the *Valken* high up in the sky and punched the engines to their maximum. "He's a very resourceful kid. I'm sure he survived."

Ryonna felt a sting in her heart. He was still an adolescent, and no matter how proud she was of him, she still felt overly protective. But Keera's words filled her with pride. "I take it you two have met?"

"Only via comms, but he gave me the feeling he was a bright and courageous kid."

Ryonna smiled. "Thank you for helping my son, Keera."

"I was just at the right place at the right time, I guess."

"Still, this isn't your fight. I appreciate what you're doing for us."

"If I've learned anything during my time with Chase and his friends—you included—it's that one doesn't back down in the face of overwhelming odds."

"Yes, as difficult as it is for me to say this, Chase does have that effect on everyone who gets into his orbit. We all strive to be better versions of ourselves since we met him."

"Do you think he can defeat the Furies today?"

"I have no idea, but if anyone can, it's him. We're clearly not equipped to deal with the Furies ourselves."

"Yeah, I got that. But he's only one man, Fury— Well, whatever he is."

"He's willing to risk his life to save us all, even when he gets flak for his efforts."

"What are you referring to?"

"Never mind. I shouldn't have said anything."

Keera looked at her instruments. "We should reach the impact location in about ten minutes."

"Very well. I haven't eaten anything for more than a day. Anything I could sink my teeth into?"

"There are plenty of provisions in the mess hall. Help yourself to anything you'd like."

Ryonna got up from the co-pilot's seat and put her hand on Keera's shoulder. "Thank you."

"Anytime."

WHEN DANIEL OPENED his eyes he was no longer in the forest. He found himself resting on a bed with a wet towel on his forehead.

What happened? Where am I?

"Anybody here?" he asked.

There was no immediate response, but then a young woman with long blonde hair came into his room.

"Hello," said Daniel, not sure what else to say.

"Hello, sir, my name is Sendra. You don't have to worry. We don't mean you any harm."

"We?"

"My mom and I. We found you near that building that exploded a while back."

"I see. I take it I have you to thank for all of this," said Daniel, pointing at his bandages.

She nodded and smiled.

"Well, thank you. Any chance you brought some of my gear with me?"

She opened a wooden cupboard, took a few things out and put them on Daniel's bed. He tried to sit up but was rewarded with a strong pain that traveled his spine. "Ouch."

"You shouldn't try to move too much for the time being. You seem quite injured."

"Yeah, a hundred-yard fall will do that to anyone, I guess."

"How did you survive?"

"Let's just say a tree helped."

"I should get my mother. She will want to talk with you."

"Very well. I'll be right here. Looks like I'm not going anywhere for a while."

Sendra smiled and left the room.

When she returned with her mother, Daniel thought he recognized her from a photo on the commodore's desk.

"Are you the Saroudis family?"

The mother sent her daughter out of the room, closed the door and took a blaster out and pointed it at Daniel. "Who are you? How do you know our names?"

"Relax. Your husband is my commanding officer."

Her eyes watered and she dropped the blaster to the ground.

"He will be really happy to hear you survived. Are your other two children around as well? We should try to get the commodore on the line."

She wiped some of her tears, "Commodore?"

"Your husband was promoted."

She smiled for a second, but her expression quickly turned back to sorrow. "I'm afraid neither of our sons made it."

"I'm so sorry to hear this. Please accept my deepest condolences for your loss."

"Thank you, mister . . .?"

"Tharraleos, Commander Daniel Tharraleos. It's an honor to meet the wife of Commodore Saroudis. Without him we would all have been killed."

"Why did it take you guys so long to come back to Alpha Prime?"

"It's a long story. We were stranded on the other side of the galaxy. Outside the known regions, in fact."

"Where is my husband, Daniel?"

"In orbit. I lost contact with the *Destiny* a few hours ago, but I'm sure they're fine. We just need to find a way to communicate with the ship."

"What's the status of the Star Alliance? It's been so long that we have lost all hope."

"It has been mostly annihilated. Only a few ships survived the Zarlack attack. In fact, we thought they had completely destroyed Alpha Prime."

Daniel put himself in her shoes. It must have been hard to not know if anyone had survived in the Alliance, and to wonder if her husband had been one of the victims. He could see in her eyes a mixture of pain, sadness and a smidgen of hope.

"I see. Here it's been hell. When the attack began it rained fire from the heavens. In mere hours the biggest cities had been bombarded from space, and only a few survived. When we first met other survivors we thought at first that we could rebuild. But then they sent these lizard men to the surface. They tracked us and killed us by the thousands. Joshua, our first son, was killed in the bombing of the cities, and Ethan died sacrificing himself so we could escape certain death when a battalion of lizards came hunting us."

Her tears now streamed down her tired face like wild rivers.

"I'm so sorry for what you had to go through. How did you manage to survive for so long?"

"We hid in underground complexes, caves, and moved farther and farther away from the big cities. After a few months the enemy seemed to have left, but they had left booby traps all around. We were attacked by vicious droids.

Those that were once our servants had been reprogrammed to exterminate us."

Daniel remembered his deadly encounter with one such machine.

"Did a resistance build? We came back the minute we received a distress call coming from the tower where you found me."

"I don't know. We're always on the run. We never stay in one place more than a few weeks. It's been more than two months since we saw another soul."

"I see." Daniel tried to sit up in bed.

"I'm not sure it's such a good idea to move just yet. Your injuries are severe. We don't have the necessary equipment to see if you have any internal ones. Perhaps you should rest until the *Destiny* finds us."

"I have to contact your husband. The sooner I'm in med-bay on board *Destiny*, the sooner I can get patched up."

He still throbbed with pain, but he forced himself through it. Once he sat on the bed he looked through the gear Sendra had put by his legs but he didn't see any communications devices.

"You wouldn't happen to have a communicator, Mrs. Saroudis?"

"Call me Alexandra. And I'm afraid not. Anything that emits strong electromagnetic signals could attract the wrong crowd."

Made sense.

"How far are we from the tower?"

"About ten miles."

Daniel realized the effort it must have taken to bring his unconscious body back from so far away and was really grateful. "Thanks for getting me out of harm's way. It must not have been easy."

"Reaper helped."

"Reaper?"

"Our wolfen pet. He's very strong. Once we made a structure to lay you upon, he dragged you back most of the way."

Wolfens were very difficult to tame but it was said that once they had formed a bond with humanoids, they were loyal for life.

"I'll have to thank him personally then."

"If he takes a liking to you. He can be very aggressive with strangers. He saved our hide more times than I care to count."

Daniel nodded. "I need to get back out there. Hopefully our shuttle is still intact and that's the fastest way of rejoining the *Destiny*."

"If you do you'll have to go on your own. It's pure luck we found you. We were gathering mushrooms in a forest nearby when we heard the explosion. I didn't want to come but Sendra can be very persuasive. However, the area where we found you is notorious for droid patrols. Many have lost power by now, but if we have learned anything it is that we can't be too cautious these days."

"Then I should try to get my shuttle, swing back to pick you up here and bring you back on board the *Destiny*."

"Do what you have to do, Daniel, but as far as coming with you, I'll have to discuss that with my daughter."

Daniel frowned. How was it possible that she didn't want to jump at the opportunity to get back on board her husband's ship? "I thought you'd want to see Adonis."

"Daniel, don't get me wrong. I'm grateful he survived, but he abandoned us here. For months we had to fend for ourselves. Both my sons are dead. I don't know what to think anymore."

"It's not his fault, Alexandra. We also have been fighting for our lives on a daily basis ever since the fall of the Alliance."

"And you are still fighting off the Obsidian?"

"It's complicated. The lizard men you talked about are called the Zarlacks. We've been fighting them mostly. A Fury named Argos commanded their forces, and while we took out a lot of it—thanks to an alliance with the world that sheltered us after the fall—he has now freed the rest of the Furies."

"Furies? You must be mistaken. They were defeated thousands of years ago."

"I'm afraid not, and they're back and wreaking all sorts of havoc. In fact, the Obsidian is now part of the newly formed Earth Alliance. They are helping us fight them back."

"I'm not sure I like the world you're describing, Daniel. Perhaps things aren't so bad here after all."

Daniel bit his lip.

Good job selling her on coming with you.

Daniel tried to get up from his bed but a cascade of pain radiated all over his body.

"You should try and rest some more."

Daniel didn't want to rest. He wanted to get to the shuttle and return to the *Destiny*, but his body didn't seem to want to comply at the moment.

"Just an hour or two, then I'm going."

15

Ronan checked the state of his friend Arknon. He was relieved to find a pulse but was worried by the multiple wounds all over his body. He used his portable scanner to try to get a better picture of his state of health and cringed at the result.

Arknon had internal bleeding and it was a miracle he was still breathing, even if ever-so-faintly. The temperature inside the pod was rising fast due to the proximity of the furnace outside, more so since the pod had been opened. Ronan had to act fast. He grabbed Arknon and put him on his shoulder.

"Hang on, my friend, I'm getting you out of here."

Moving him this way was highly risky, but better than letting him cook inside the pod.

Ronan climbed out of the pod as carefully as he could. He put distance between them and the nearby towering inferno until the temperature was more bearable.

He laid Arknon's body in the grass, went for the first-aid kit in his backpack and bandaged Arknon's visible wounds.

When he ran out of bandages, Ronan removed Arknon's

boots, put them back on his own feet and quickly ran back to the pod to get the other first-aid kit. When he was about to climb out again he heard the comms on the pod activate.

"R-nan. Do --- hear? --ease respond."

Ronan thought he recognized his mother's voice but it couldn't be her. She was too far away. Perhaps Keera had managed to patch her through.

He climbed back inside the pod and tried clearing the signal.

"This is Ronan. Is it you, Keera?"

"Thank the prophets you're alive, son. I'm on board the *Valken* with Keera. We're on our way. We should be there shortly."

"It's good to hear your voice, Mom. Weren't you supposed to be on Alpha Prime? How did you get back here so fast?"

"It's a long story, Ronan. I'll tell you later."

"Alright. Please hurry up. Commander Arknon is badly hurt. He needs urgent medical attention."

"See you soon, son. Stay near the pod."

"I'll be a few hundred yards east of it. It's too hot here. Plus I need to watch over Arknon."

"Very well, son, see you shortly. Take a portable comms with you so we can contact you; and please be careful."

"Right. See you soon."

He looked around the pod for an earpiece communicator, put it in and activated it.

"Checking comms. Do you hear me, Mom?"

"Five by five, son. Our ETA is four minutes."

Ronan ran back toward Arknon when a nearby explosion made him lose his balance and fall to the ground. When he got back on his feet he looked in the direction of the blast and what he saw made his blood freeze.

There stood a man in the middle of the fire, with his arms slightly extended to the sides, while pieces of burning ship and tons of soil and stones were sent flying all around him. A piece of the *Phoenix* rebounded only a few yards from him.

This is not possible. He can't be alive!

But there stood the Fury, his skin burned to a crisp. His eyes shone red, giving him a demonic look. He levitated. While in the air he curled into a ball and suddenly extended his limbs, unleashing a powerful shockwave that extinguished most of the fire around him. He unleashed the most ear-piercing, powerful and animalistic roar Ronan had ever heard. A bright red aura engulfed his entire body and his burns quickly healed.

What kind of monster is this?

After a few seconds the Fury's skin was smooth, and he looked in perfect health.

Ronan was terrified. His brain simply could not interpret what he had just witnessed. He had to get back to Arknon but his limbs simply refused to move as fear enveloped him from head to toe. He couldn't help looking at the Fury. Then their gazes met. The look on the Fury's face intensified and he flew toward Ronan.

That sent the biggest jolt of adrenaline throughout his body and his legs started moving. He ran as fast as he could toward Arknon, but before traveling half the distance, the Fury landed in front of him with a look of murder in his glowing eyes.

"You! Are you responsible for this?" asked the Fury as he pointed toward whatever was left of the *Phoenix*.

"What's it to you?"

"I'm gonna kill you anyway, but if you're the one responsible, I might actually take my time and enjoy myself."

Ronan swallowed hard. He had never felt so afraid in his entire life, but his Droxian pride wouldn't let him show it.

"I really thought that would kill you, asshole."

Miseo's teeth clenched.

"Someone had to do something. You were destroying my world one city at a time."

"As it should be, and I'm glad you told me the truth."

Ronan didn't wait. He sent a powerful right hook toward Miseo. When his fist impacted with the Fury's face, not only did it not budge, but Ronan felt a horrible pain as the bones in his hand cracked upon impact. It felt as if he had just punched a twenty-inch-thick wall made of quadrinium-reinforced alloy.

"A destroyer didn't take me out and you think you can hit me with your fist? Your kind is so pathetically stupid; we're actually doing the universe a favor by wiping you out."

Ronan held his broken hand in the other, his face deformed from the pain. He was not sure what had been wounded more, though, his hand or his pride.

Miseo smirked and shook his head from side to side.

"Proving my point. Now for some real pain."

He extended his index finger toward Ronan and started levitating him upwards.

Ronan's ear-comm activated. "Hang on, Ronan, we're near."

"You'd better hurry up," said Ronan out loud.

Miseo, who thought Ronan was talking to him, smiled. "You're courageous for a boy your age, I'll grant you that, but I'm going to enjoy taking my time with you."

A thin, red laser beam shot from Miseo's finger and pierced Ronan's shoulder. The burning sensation radiated around the point of entry.

For a moment Ronan thought he would pass out.

SARAH WENT to see Yanis in engineering but he wasn't there. She tried his quarters, but there was no answer. She tried getting him on the comms.

"Sarah Kepler to Yanis, please come in."

Still no answer. She had no doubt he was in no mood to answer right now, but the *Hope*'s internal power distribution was a mess. The engineering crew were doing their best to repair the broken conduits but they could use Yanis' expertise. He had designed the ship, after all. Sarah knew how cruel it was for her to ask him to get back to work in a moment like this, but she also wanted to see how he was doing.

She resorted to asking the computer for his current position. He was inside a bulkhead tube near one of the damaged power conduits. After climbing three flights of ladder and crawling through the access tunnel, she was exhausted. Not really easy in her condition. Little Chris was really starting to show on her. In fact, she had no doubt that both Chase and the doc would reprimand her if they knew she was putting herself in such uncomfortable positions.

She felt a little worried about her pregnancy. Not only had she never really envisioned having kids, but Chris was going to be something else altogether. Reviving dead people, protecting her with in-womb shields and god knows what else. What human mother wouldn't be terrified of what was growing inside her under these circumstances?

She saw Yanis with his head between his knees, sobbing, and it stung her heart just looking at him.

"Yanis, mind if I talk with you a little?"

Her voice startled him and he quickly wiped his tears. His voice trembled a little. "Sure thing, Cap."

She sat next to him and put her hand around his shoulder. "I'm so sorry for your loss, Yanis."

"Thank you. I still can't believe she's gone."

"I know. You want to talk about it?"

"I appreciate what you're trying to do here, Sarah, but I'd rather be alone right now."

"I understand, but perhaps it's better if you have someone to talk to."

"Don't take this the wrong way, Sarah. You know I like you, but right now you just remind me of Chase, and that's not a good thing."

"You do realize he did everything he could to save her?"

"So he says. But if he wasn't coming up with one ludicrous tactic after another, she'd still be alive."

"I think you've got it backward, Yanis. If Chase wasn't doing what he does, I think we'd all be dead ten times over by now. But I can understand how you feel at the moment. I'm sorry to have bothered you. I'll let you be alone now."

He embraced her and started crying on her shoulder.

She felt so sad for him. Fillio was all that was left of his family. He must have felt terribly alone right now.

"We'll always be here for you," she said as she patted his back softly. "I know you hate Chase's guts right now, but trust me, he feels like crap as well."

"I keep thinking this is a nightmare and I'm gonna wake up soon. I really thought he would get her back."

"I know."

Yanis released his hug and looked down. His eyes were red. "I said horrible things to him. Not only that, but I might have been partly responsible for her death as well."

"What are you talking about? You did nothing wrong."

"When Chase put her on the ground in front of me, I saw the multiple electrical burns all over her body. I think I caused this trying to improve the StarFury. I'm sure Chase told you that the new revisions could overload?"

"He did."

"Well, it's a design flaw I thought wouldn't happen often. But when three Zarlack destroyers sacrifice themselves to take an entire fleet, that incommensurable burst of energy certainly overloaded her fighter's power conduits, and the electrical burns on her body before he healed them were proof of that. So you see, in fact I might have killed my own sister."

"No, this war killed her. Neither you nor Chase are responsible. You both did what you thought was best. When you feel better you can tell him you didn't really mean it."

"I guess so. I was never too keen on him at first. I really hated that he dated her back at the academy."

"He did what now?"

"I'm sorry, I thought you knew. They were pretty close once."

Sarah felt a little jealous for just a moment, and then realized she had nothing to be jealous about. So what if they had dated before he met her? She had dated other men as well. Chase went through hell and back to rescue her, and even though she was still a little mad at the consequences, she couldn't blame him for it. In fact, she was fully aware there was no bigger proof of love, and yet she had given him so much grief for it. Nah, it really didn't matter that he dated Fillio in the past.

"She never really recovered when he ended it."

"Why did he?"

"Mostly because I asked him to. In fact, they had both been assigned to the *Cronos*, but after our talk he agreed to take his commission on the smaller *Destiny* with me, to make it simpler and use that as a reason to distance himself from her."

"That's quite a bro move, right there."

"Yeah, I know. And I wasn't even being such a good friend to him until then. But he saw how important it was for me, and he backed off. That's why I feel so bad telling him I hated him earlier on. But I still can't fathom she's gone and I'm still angry. I'm not so sure that I'm angry at him. He just was an easy target, being there when it happened."

"I understand, Yanis, and so will Chase. Don't worry about that right now and take all the time you need to grieve. I came here to tell you that whenever you need to talk to anyone, you can come see me."

"Thank you, Sarah. You and Chase are the best friends a man could ever ask for."

She patted his shoulder affectionately and started walking back toward the access shaft.

"Sarah?"

"Yes, Yanis?"

"Was that all you wanted to say?"

"No, but it doesn't matter. You need your alone time and I respect that."

"You know what, Sarah, I could use a distraction, so if there's something I can help you with? Perhaps it will help me think about something else."

"In that case, we really need to repair power distribution. In fact, I thought that's what you came here to do."

"I did initially . . . until I broke down."

"Well, take all the time you need, okay?"

He nodded. "Thanks."

"Sure thing, buddy. I need to go back to the bridge now. I'll see you later, okay?"

SAROUDIS WAS SITTING on his captain's chair on board the *Destiny*. The moment the last Zarlack destroyer had been dispatched, he had coordinated multiple search and rescue teams in their attempt to find survivors in the debris field that was once their battleground. A couple of ships had been disabled, so these received shuttles with engineers on board to help with repairs of their main systems. These could still be salvaged. But locating survivor pilots in their disabled starfighters, or other crewmen within severed parts of the capital ships, took a long time.

"Any news from the away team?" he asked his communications officer.

"I'm afraid no answer from Alpha Team. I dispatched Beta to look for them an hour ago," answered Lieutenant Brents.

"I don't like it. It's not like Commander Tharraleos to miss a scheduled report."

"There might simply be too much interference from the debris field."

Saroudis didn't buy it. Something was definitely amiss.

It had been a very hard day, and Saroudis hated the fact that they couldn't travel back to Droxia right away. He really hoped Chase could defeat the opposition there, but he hated not being there as backup. Commodore Saroudis rose from his chair as the rest of the bridge crew looked at him.

"Major Bradis, you have the bridge. Commander Philis, you're with me. We're going to the planet's surface to help Beta Team locate Daniel and his team."

Twenty minutes later Saroudis, Philis and three more armed soldiers were doing flybys on the surface of their now derelict home world.

"Would you look at the damage?" said the commodore.

"Yes, Commodore, it's hard to believe anyone might have survived down there."

"I sure hope you're wrong. I haven't lost hope my family could have survived."

"I'm sorry, Commodore, I didn't mean anything by it. The way you talked about them in the past, I didn't know they were on Alpha Prime. I thought they had been killed earlier in the war."

"That's alright, Commander, I should never have talked about them in the past tense. It sent the wrong message. At least not before I was sure. But the fall of the Star Alliance had been so fast and brutal I didn't really think there was a shadow of hope in that regard. Think nothing of it, Commander."

The commander looked at his controls. He clearly didn't know what else to say. "I'm picking up some readings one hundred miles southwest of our current position."

"We should have a look at it. Adjust our course, Commander, and punch it."

"Course adjusted, Commodore."

They soon saw the column of smoke rising from their target destination.

"Seems something went wrong over there," said the commander.

"Let's check it out."

WHEN SARAH ARRIVED at her quarters she felt dizzy. Something was happening inside her belly. She felt a warmth build up within her.

I can't be due already. It's too early! What the hell is this?

She managed to crawl onto her bed and rested on her back, trying to calm herself down with deeper breaths. She was petrified by what was happening. Chris was very agitated. She could feel him moving inside her as if he wanted to get out.

When she lifted her shirt she saw her belly glowing: it did nothing to reassure her. When she was about to call a medical emergency, something happened.

She was no longer in her quarters but, instead, she stood on an alien world. From the description Ryonna had given of her home world, she sensed it was Droxia. The planet was in ruins. Cities had been leveled and fires burned as far as her eyes could see.

"Hello, Mom," said a voice behind her.

Startled, she turned around and saw a fully grown young man, looking at her with a big smile on his face. He was an awesome young man. His face reminded her of Chase somehow, but also bore some of her own traits as well as her father's. He had flaming-red, long hair like hers, and had one green eye and one purple one.

"What . . . what did you call me?"

"It's me, Mom, Chris."

"This cannot be. I must be delirious from the pain and you're just a figment of my imagination."

"I've brought you here to calm you down. I sensed your fears and wanted to let you know everything will be alright."

She shook her head. "This is not happening. It can't. You haven't been born yet. How can I stand here speaking with you?"

"Listen carefully, Mom, Dad is in serious trouble, and I will need to send some of my own life-force to help him fight our enemies."

"Is that what's happening with my glowing belly?"

"Yes, but fear not. You won't be harmed, but I'm afraid some discomfort cannot be prevented."

"How can you help your father? We're gazillions of miles apart!"

"You shouldn't worry about that, Mom. I just want you to breathe deeply and trust that I won't hurt you. Only then can I send some of my energy to Droxia. As long as you're agitated and afraid I can't do it without hurting you in the process."

She was so shocked that she had practically forgotten where she stood. "Is this how things are at the moment on the planet?"

"Yes, but Dad is fighting with all his might to make it stop. There are still hundreds of millions of souls that can be saved on Droxia today. He knows that and right now he needs a little help."

"Let's say for one second that I am indeed talking to you and this isn't just in my head."

"Well, technically it is, but it's real nonetheless."

"Right. Chase is fighting Furies on Droxia right this moment?"

"He's fighting one of them at the moment, yes."

"And you're going to send some of your life energy to him?"

"That's correct. But we must hurry. Soon you'll wake up. Please remember what I said and just breathe deeply and trust me. Nothing bad will happen to you."

"What about you?"

"I'll be fine. Don't worry, just breathe."

The scene in front of her eyes changed and morphed back into the familiar bulkheads and viewport from her quarters. Except everything was tainted with a golden light now.

She closed her eyes.

Relax, everything will be okay . . .

She took deep, long breaths and forced herself to calm down.

That's when it happened. She felt the skin on her belly burn for just a second and all the previous discomfort faded away.

When she opened her eyes a golden sphere of energy pulsated a few inches above her. The radiant glow enveloped her with warmth from head to toe and she felt as light as a feather.

Thanks, Mom, she heard in her thoughts.

The sphere of energy started shaking uncontrollably and soon it collapsed into nothingness before her eyes.

WHEN ARKOOLIS UNLEASHED three series of side kicks, exchanging feet as he pivoted on himself in between each attack, Chase blocked the incoming blows with his forearms, but soon the speed of the general's attack increased tremendously and three successive kicks hit Chase respectively on the right leg, torso and finally on his head, sending him down.

Arkoolis created a big red fireball and threw it at Chase before he could recover. The explosion launched him into the air. Arkoolis went for the kill with a flaming uppercut, but Chase spun in midair and countered the attack by erecting a shield, successfully blocking the incoming punch.

Chase spun multiple times in the air before landing on the ground, skidding a few yards backward as he did.

He unleashed a series of blue fireballs toward the general, who deflected them with his hands. The deflected fireballs exploded all around them, sending soil, stones and grass into the air.

The fight was well balanced up till now, but then the ground shook briefly. Chase felt a tremendous amount of power at that exact moment.

Crap, that has to be Miseo.

Chase realized what it meant. Soon there would be two Furies to fight and that would make things much more difficult. While he had no doubt the other Fury had survived the impact with the *Phoenix*, he had hoped he would have more time to finish this fight.

He knew all along that the general was a formidable warrior, but expected his training to have been enough to enable him to defeat him any time he felt like it. Up till now neither had any serious advantage over the other, and it was not for a lack of trying on Chase's part.

Perhaps it's time I gave you a hand, said Gaia in his mind.

Chase remembered she could actually hear his thoughts now.

Yeah, okay. We need to dispatch him before Miseo arrives.

Agreed.

Feel free to intervene whenever you feel like it.

Keep attacking him. I will surprise him, and then you can finish him off.

Chase was not keen on that tactic as he felt it wasn't an honorable way to fight, but he went with it anyway.

The general made the first move and attacked Chase with all his might. He was fast, even for Chase. Even after his 10 G training he had to use all his energy to keep up. But he dodged the first three combos Arkoolis threw at him.

Then Gaia made her move. Her avatar droid sent its knee toward the general's chin. He didn't expect it and he was sent flying upwards. A little blood was expelled from his mouth.

Chase took advantage of Gaia's attack and sent two dozen small fireballs toward the general. They all found their target and he was thrown left and right, each new explosion inflicting more and more damage.

But then Chase stopped.

What are you doing, Chase? Finish him off while you can!

I can't. This is not how I want to win this fight.

Chase, only the result matters! He killed millions of Droxians today.

Why am I not surprised an AI would say that? An incomplete one at that. I'm sorry, Gaia, I will avenge the Droxian people by defeating these two Furies, but I need to win this fight on my own terms.

Very well. I can sense you won't budge on this, so I'll finish him off myself.

I don't think you stand a chance; you should really stand down, Gaia.

But Gaia didn't answer. She was already flying upwards, both fists extended, and hit the general in the back as he crashed back down toward the ground, still not having recovered from the brunt of Chase's repeated attacks.

Chase felt a little annoyed. But then it all went south really fast.

Gaia landed a series of powerful combos and bruised the general's face, but then she missed with three of her punches and Arkoolis grabbed her droid arm.

"You shouldn't have intervened in this fight, tin can," said Arkoolis, just before ripping Gaia's arm off the rest of her body.

He threw the robotic limb to the ground. Sparks flew and oil squirted from the droid's now armless shoulder.

"You're done," said Arkoolis, extending his open right palm in front of him.

From it shot a powerful column of red energy that impaled the Gaia droid and left a basketball-sized hole in the droid's chest. Arkoolis then flew toward it and decapitated it with a powerful, flying kick.

Gaia's droid head rolled and landed not far from Chase. Its eyes blinked madly for a second and then faded to nothingness.

Chase felt sorry for the Gaia droid, but he had been adamant about not winning the fight this way.

Sorry, Gaia.

Arkoolis concentrated his aura and healed his wounds.

"Now, where were we?"

Chase grew his aura and took an offensive posture.

The general rocketed into the air. Chase went in pursuit but couldn't fly as fast as his Fury opponent. When he had gained enough of a head start, Arkoolis stopped and grew a gigantic fireball above him. It was almost a mile in diameter. When Chase caught up with him, Arkoolis launched it toward the south. It slowly advanced toward the nearest city.

Bastard!

"That's for letting that piece of metal intervene in our fight. To each action there are consequences."

Chase's reaction was instantaneous. He flew as fast as he could toward the slowly advancing fireball. He was by its side pretty quickly and fired two powerful columns of blue energy into it, trying to detonate it in the air. But it had no effect. He flew in front of it, positioning himself between it and the city, hovering about two miles above the surface. He launched a huge column of blue energy toward the fiery inferno that approached relentlessly.

When Chase's attack impacted with the general's fireball

it slowed its descent a little, but it kept coming toward him and the city. The resulting shockwave traveled all around him and shattered most of the nearby skyscraper windows into millions of pieces. Chase increased the power of his energy stream, which further slowed down the incoming attack, but soon it was upon Chase. He stopped firing and tried blocking the fireball with both his hands extended before him.

The amount of energy was such that Chase couldn't slow its descent fast enough, and soon he was descending as well, being pushed little by little toward the city with the giant ball of fiery energy.

"You fool! You can't stop this attack with your bare hands," shouted Arkoolis from afar.

I have to! I can't let more millions of lives perish here today. Whatever it takes I will stop this monstrosity from hitting the city.

Soon he was approaching the top of the highest skyscrapers and everything shook for miles around. More windows exploded and the temperature rose to dangerous levels. Chase could sense the panic from the Droxians below. He could hear the screams of people witnessing the scene unfold.

When his back touched the nearest building he went through the concrete and metal and the fireball started consuming the skyscraper little by little.

Chase intensified his aura to the maximum and all his muscles doubled in size. He pushed with all his might.

I can do it! I have to! he kept repeating to himself.

Then he felt an energy added to his own. The energy was loaded with love and warmth. It gave him a much-needed boost in power.

Chase pushed the gigantic ball of fire back as blue waves

of energy emanated from his hands. The enormous sphere of energy soon turned blue. Chase repelled the attack, and he soon cleared the city's skyscraper area.

"Careful, Dad, he's coming at you. Push hard, NOW!"

Chase pushed as hard as he could and the sphere of energy shot into the heavens at tremendous speed. A fraction of a second later, he sensed Arkoolis approaching him from the left and dodged his flying kick at the last possible instant. Losing no time he grabbed the leg of the general and whirled around. Soon he whirled so fast he looked like a miniature cyclone. He released the general's leg and sent him crashing miles away into the dirt. When the general impacted with the ground at such high velocity he skidded for miles, destroying everything in his path and leaving a deep trail.

16

On board the last remaining Zarlack destroyer still in the fight, Argos now had to contend with the four remaining Alliance destroyers still battle worthy. Their combined firepower in their current state wasn't enough to drain his shields completely, but he often needed to use evasive action and retreat away from the theater of battle in order to let them recharge.

Suddenly a massive attack sphere of blue energy grazed his ship and illuminated his entire ready room with a blue tinge, for just half a second. The ship rocked and he was thrown away from his throne and unceremoniously dumped on the ground. Sparks flew from power conduits nearby and a large crack appeared in his viewport window.

What the hell was that?

He rushed back to his throne to check his instruments.

His destroyer's shields were now offline. The ship rocked several more times as the enemy fleet started pounding its armor with battery fire and whatever torpedoes they still possessed.

A violent explosion on the bridge sent flames through to

his ready room, obliterating the door that separated the rooms in the process.

Looks like it's time to go.

Argos erected a force field around himself and levitated a few feet from the deck. He then flew downwards at incredible speed, punching through the different decks on his way to the landing bay, where his ship awaited him. He left a trail of red-hot burned metal as he traveled through his ship. Everything around him exploded and the Zarlack destroyer was only seconds from blowing up entirely.

He reached the *Dark Star*, sat in his pilot's chair and boosted the engines to the maximum. He saw a Droxian destroyer on a collision course with his destroyer and lost no time activating his jump engines the second he was off the landing-bay deck. He micro-jumped away only a few thousand miles and activated the *Dark Star*'s cloak.

"This day isn't going as well as I had hoped, but the general and Miseo have destroyed most of the planet already. It's time to scoop them up."

Or is it?

Argos pondered if perhaps he should leave them down there in the hope that Chase would dispatch them both, but there was so little chance of that happening that he quickly resigned himself to entering the atmosphere and vectoring the *Dark Star* toward Arkoolis' and Miseo's last known coordinates. If any of them survived and he ran, he would be executed by the supreme commander. Of that he had no doubts whatsoever.

~

Miseo still held Ronan in the air and was about to send another of his piercing laser attacks, when he was suddenly hit by an invisible object traveling at an extremely high velocity.

The *Valken* had just rammed Miseo. The collision lit up its shields and sent the Fury tumbling to the ground hundreds of yards away. At the moment Miseo's grasp on Ronan loosened he fell to the ground.

"Are you alright, son?" asked Ryonna over the comms.

"Thanks. I'm okay, I guess."

The *Valken* phased back into view as the cloaking field was turned off.

The back ramp of the ship was already lowering as it approached Ronan's position. He got back up and jumped inside the ship.

"We should go," said Ryonna.

"We need to get Arknon first. He's over there." Ronan pointed toward his unconscious friend.

The ship hovered over Arknon's unconscious body and Ronan brought him on board. A fireball came from Miseo, but Keera saw it coming and dodged it at the last second.

The rocking of the ship sent both Ryonna and Ronan crashing against the wall.

"Hang on, everyone, we need to get out of here fast."

The *Valken*'s ramp closed and Keera started her ascent. She still needed a minute to activate the cloaking device that needed to recharge. But then three fireballs impacted with the ship's shields. The first two drained the shields and the third one damaged the ship's engine.

Keera lost control of the craft and it plummeted back toward the surface of the planet.

~

DANIEL HAD LEFT THE SAROUDIS' cabin and been in the

woods for half an hour when he thought he heard footsteps trailing him. He turned around to check it out but couldn't see anything.

"Anyone there?"

When no one answered he put the steps down to his imagination. He had been through quite a trauma, and it was entirely possible he had imagined it.

It took him almost two hours to reach the destroyed tower in his condition. He looked around the wreckage for any tech he could use to contact the *Destiny* but found nothing useful. He found his pocket communicator near the tree he'd fallen from but it had been damaged beyond repair.

"Just great."

He retraced the steps his now defunct team had taken to arrive at the tower and soon reached the shuttle. He heard the recognizable sound of a tree branch cracking behind him. He took the blaster that Alexandra had kindly given him for the journey and pointed it at the trees.

"Alright, you'd better show yourself before I start shooting."

"Don't shoot, Daniel!"

It was Sendra's voice.

"What the hell are you doing here? Does your mom know you followed me?"

"She thinks I went to get mushrooms for tonight's meal."

"You shouldn't have come along. What if a Zarlack patrol or a battle droid had found us?"

"Then Reaper would have protected us."

The pet wolfen walked from behind the tree where Sendra had been hiding. The wolfen barked.

"That seems like a very courageous animal, but Zarlacks are incredibly tough to kill."

"And yet he has killed his fair share. They have a weak spot in the back of their necks where their scales aren't as tough as the rest of their bodies. Reaper has killed many that way."

"Impressive. I didn't know about that weak spot."

"Neither did we until Reaper killed his first prey. Later, when we had to fend off a couple of their attacks, it became clear that sniping them in the back of their neck would kill them with a single shot."

"Good to know, but we shouldn't stay here in the open. Let's climb into the shuttle and try to contact your father."

"My father? He is alive?" Tears filled Sendra's eyes.

Daniel realized that Alexandra must not have shared the talk he had with her. It also explained why she had sent her away prior to it.

"I thought your mom told you."

"She is bitter lately; she blames him for everything that happened to us."

"But you don't?"

"Why would I? He would never abandon us on purpose. But my mom never liked that he went for a career in the military. Ever since the war with the Obsidian escalated on all fronts, my mother had a real tough time dealing with the long tours he had to do."

"That's war for you."

"And is it still ongoing? My mom often tells me that the war must be over by now."

"Let's just say things have changed. But I think it's best you talk with her about it or with your dad. Now come, let's try to call him from the shuttle."

She joined him and Reaper shadowed her.

Daniel opened a channel.

"Commodore Saroudis? Do you hear me?"

There was a little silence and Daniel grew worried for a moment.

"Commander, it's good to hear your voice. We're on our way to your position. When you missed your scheduled contact time we worried something happened to you."

"It did. I lost my whole team, Commodore."

"I see. Did you manage to find out who sent the communication?"

"I'm afraid not. The communications tower was booby-trapped and I was lucky to escape it with my life."

"Are you injured?"

"I'll live, thanks to someone who would like to talk with you."

"What? Who?"

Daniel waved for Sendra to join him on the co-pilot's chair. She had stayed quiet until now, probably still in shock at hearing her father's voice.

"Talk with him."

"Dad?"

"Sendra?" The commodore's voice was trembling. "Is it really you?"

"It's me, Daddy." Tears flowed like rivers on her cheeks.

"Thank the gods. Are your mother and brothers with you?"

"Mom is well, but . . ."

There was an awkward silence.

"I'm so happy to hear your voice, munchkin. You'll tell me more about it soon when we get off this planet."

"I don't think Mom wants us to leave."

"Let's not worry about that right now, baby. For now I'm just so happy to hear your voice."

"Me too, Daddy. I've missed you so much."

"So have I, Sendra, so have I."

CHASE HOVERED a few miles away from the city and then let himself fall toward the ground. The moment he felt the ground under his feet, he closed his eyes and concentrated a lot more energy within himself. He checked his power levels and they were, surprisingly, at more than sixty percent. His son's help deflecting the general's giant fireball into space had probably also acted as a top up of his own internal pool of energy. Chase focused to bring more of it to the surface, to continue his fight.

That's it, Chase, said Ares in his mind.

Hey, I wondered where you had been.

I'm not really here; only a part of my consciousness is.

You'll have to explain how all this works one day.

I'm honestly not sure I could explain it. The usual laws simply don't apply in this non-corporeal form, I guess.

If you're not really here, then where are you?

We have very little time to talk. I'm visiting my Olympian brothers and sisters.

What about Zeus?

Well, I tried earlier but he didn't seem keen to listen to me. I'm trying to gauge how other Olympians are reacting to the resurgence of Furies.

I'm about to attack Arkoolis, so I'd love to stay and chat but . . .

I've slowed down time at the exact moment you started powering up, so don't worry about it.

Practical. So what did they say?

It's a little early, but I feel we could enlist a few of them. Perhaps in time they can help us make our case with Zeus. If he would agree to help us, every Olympian would fall in line.

I thought not many of you were left.

We're only a few compared to how many we once were, but the most powerful of us . . . Let me rephrase that, most of the powerful ones are still alive.

Is that what you came to tell me?

No, not really.

What is it then, Ares?

You're just inches away from accessing the power you managed to attain when you fought Argos before. With that intensive training of yours you've really got a better grasp on your powers and it's within your reach.

Why do I sense a but coming?

However, that last inch requires an emotion to trigger it.

And that emotion would be?

I wish I could say love, and one day it might very well be, but at your current level of power and state of mind, I think you need to feed yourself some anger, or even rage, to reach your higher level of power.

How am I supposed to do that? The other times it was Argos who brought these emotions to the surface, like when he nearly killed Daniel. I'm far less angry and prone to rage now than I was back then. You've always told me I let my emotion get the better of me, and now that it's taken me months to get them in check you actually want me to let them guide my actions again?

I know, and that's actually a good thing. You might have felt that boost of confidence in you.

Yeah, I even surprise myself.

It's all a matter of balance, Chase. You should not overdo it either. If your ego is too strong, you may become overconfident, and in a fight against the Furies, you really don't want that.

I see. So how do I reach my maximum potential?

You need to use anger as the trigger. Perhaps try remembering how you felt when you had to shoot Sarah's ship?

I don't want to go back there, Ares. Once was hard enough.

I'm not telling you to relive the scene, just let the anger that memory brings infuse and overload your current powering up.

Look, Ares, I had a really hard time putting all this behind me. Thanks to the training I managed to control these emotions and I'd rather not go there.

It's your choice, Chase, but these are powerful memories. They deal with life, death, love. No matter how much pain they bring they might be needed one day.

Let's say today isn't that day, then what?

Can't you bring another moment of grief to the surface? Perhaps something more fresh, that you haven't really dealt with yet, like the fact you couldn't save Fillio? I can sense the bottled frustration within you, even though it was not your fault and you know it. She didn't want to go on. There was nothing you could have done.

That does make me angry and I haven't really expressed it.

This could work, then. Just focus on that anger and let it blow. I'll resume normal time now. Hang on to this feeling. Make it grow a little if you have to. Good luck, Chase.

Chase felt Ares' consciousness leave him, and as he powered his aura he brought back the memory of losing Fillio, the anger he felt not being able to save her from the claws of death. Chase felt a surge within him but didn't feel that spark he was looking for.

Got to dig deeper, I guess. Here goes nothing.

He then brought the memory of Yanis telling how he hated him. He felt his anger, frustration and self-hatred grow and something in him snapped.

When he opened his eyes his aura was no longer glowing purple but orange. He could feel his hair flowing on top of his head. His muscles tightened and he felt a jolt of pure energy flow through his veins, amplifying every one of his senses and bringing a tremendous amount of power for his disposal.

Arkoolis was already flying back toward Chase, an expression of utter madness on his face. But it all seemed to happen in slow motion. Chase saw his attack coming a mile away and then some. As the general threw a powerful, fire-ball-enhanced right hook, Chase moved his head out of the way and grabbed the general's wrist. He snapped it with little effort and heard bones break.

The general screamed from the pain and took three steps back.

Before he could react, Chase was all around him, phasing in and out of thin air at such speeds the general had trouble following him with his eyes. Every time he thought he saw him, Chase was well into his next move.

The general flailed his good arm, trying to hit Chase but hitting nothing but air.

"Who's the low-class Fury now?" said Chase, before appearing yards in front of the general.

He disappeared again, and when he reappeared right in front of him, he hammered Arkoolis with a single punch. He heard facial bones crack under the pressure of his punch. Blood flew from both his nose and mouth, and a few teeth flew out.

Chase didn't let the general hit the ground. Before that happened he had already created an extremely powerful fireball with crackling, purple lightning bolts dancing around it. He threw the attack at the general's torso. The impact was devastating. The general's armor blew up as if it was made of glass and he crashed onto his back. Smoke rose from Arkoolis' burned and bloody ribcage.

Chase walked toward the general and caught a glimpse of fear in his eyes.

Arkoolis got back up and unleashed a flurry of powerful fireballs at Chase. The multiple explosions lit up the valley one after the other. The sheer power in these attacks would have taken out a city. But when Chase walked through the flames unscathed, the general could not believe it.

"This is not possible," said Arkoolis.

Chase launched himself at Arkoolis and planted his knee deeply into his enemy's stomach. Blood shot from his mouth as he staggered a few steps back, blood still dripping from his mouth.

"What are you?" he spat.

"You tell me. I thought I was just a low-class Fury. Then again, I didn't buy into that bullshit of yours about classes."

The general cast two basketball-sized black fireballs in each of his hands. Red, crackling lightning shot between them. He merged them together and shot a column of dark energy toward Chase, but it hit nothing but air. Chase was already behind Arkoolis.

"Game over, *General*," said Chase, before thrusting his right fist through the general's back. It burst through the Fury's ribcage as if it was made of silk paper. Bones and blood were thrown outwards from the power and speed at which Chase's hand had traveled through the Fury's ribcage. The last thing the general saw was his own heart stop beating in Chase's bloody hand. Chase squeezed it into nothingness and forcefully removed his arm from the general's back. Arkoolis was dead long before his corpse hit the ground.

Then Chase heard Ryonna's voice in his head.

He reacted instantly and vanished into thin air.

～

INSIDE THE *VALKEN* the gravitational forces prevented Ryonna and Ronan from moving. She had grabbed him by the collar the moment the ship lost control. He in turn had grabbed his friend, not ready to let him be crushed against the nearby bulkheads.

Ryonna felt a sensation that she hardly knew. She was terrified by the sound of the engines and the disorienting G-forces that pulled on them from every direction. She had just laid eyes on her son after all these hours of worrying whether or not he was alive, and their ship was about to crash onto the planet's surface.

She closed her eyes and only one thought came to mind. *Chase, please help us.*

The *Valken* crashed into the middle of a forest and uprooted many trees as it skidded along and emerged into a clearing. Smoke rose from the damaged ship's engines.

When Ryonna opened her eyes, she felt a tremendous pain in her right arm. The one that had held onto Ronan's collar with every last bit of energy and strength. It had dislocated upon impact, but she never let go, even when she eventually lost consciousness.

Ronan was still unconscious, and she feared that Arknon couldn't possibly have survived the rough landing.

She was still holding Ronan's collar, even though they were both on the floor. She checked her son's pulse and found one. His shoulder wound bled alarmingly. She tried waking him up but was unsuccessful. Smoke from a nearby conduit filled the cargo hold at an alarming rate.

"Keera! Can you please open the *Valken*'s cargo-hold ramp? Keera! Please respond?"

But there was no answer. She was probably also unconscious or worse. But Ryonna couldn't be everywhere at once, so she needed to focus on the most pressing issue and that was to get some much needed air inside the cargo hold, before the ever-thickening layer of smoke choked them all to death.

She crawled toward the nearest console, ignoring the throbbing pain, and tried opening the cargo-hold ramp, but she was unsuccessful and sparks from the damaged console shot into her eyes. When that failed she crawled toward the manual release.

She popped the lid, grabbed the mag-lock release handle and pulled on it. She then rotated it counterclockwise for forty-five degrees and pushed it back in. More smoke was released from the grinding emergency hydraulics systems, but soon the ramp jerkily lowered toward the ground, revealing the large and long trail of dirt the ship had created upon landing, as well as a gap in the tree line.

The smoke vented from the opening and fresh Droxian air filled the cargo hold. Ryonna decided to check on Keera. She would need her help to revive Ronan and tend to Arknon. That is, if he was still alive. But the moment she was back on her feet and walking toward the cockpit, she heard a loud noise behind her.

She turned around and her blood froze.

There stood Miseo. He had a huge gash on the left side of his face, no doubt from the *Valken* ramming into him.

His eyes were bloodshot and he looked utterly mad. His teeth were clenched. Thin lines of blood showed between them.

"You're gonna pay for this, you scumbags."

He raised his left hand and opened his palm toward the interior of the shuttle. A red fireball was created out of thin air.

Ryonna grabbed her blaster with her good hand and shot toward Miseo, but the blasts never reached him.

He had stopped them with his mind. In the meantime, Miseo's fireball grew to soccer-ball size.

Then Ryonna's motherly instinct kicked in and she lurched forward to cover Ronan. She didn't care if that made a difference or not. In the middle of her jump she saw someone's knee impact with Miseo's face. The impact was so violent that the Fury flew out of view at an impossible speed, just as he fired his fireball toward the inside of the ship. It went higher than intended and burned through the ceiling of the cargo hold as if it was made of plastic, letting more daylight into the ship.

Ryonna adjusted her landing at the last moment and instead of landing on top of her son she rolled forward. That's when she saw him.

"Chase!"

"Sorry I couldn't get here any faster. Are you alright, Ryonna? Anyone need healing? This guy," said Chase, pointing his thumb in the direction of the Fury, "will be back very soon. And probably even more pissed than he was before."

Her entire face lit up and she pointed at Arknon. "I think Ronan is just unconscious but his friend over there . . ."

Chase moved so fast that Ryonna felt a strong current pass her. By the time she had finished pointing at Arknon, Chase was already healing the Droxian commander.

"His wounds are critical. Another few seconds and he would have been beyond my help," said Chase. It painfully reminded him of his failure to save Fillio earlier.

Keera stumbled into the cargo hold, her entire face covered with blood. She tripped on some equipment that had fallen during descent. Before she hit the deck she was in Chase's hand. He healed her in less than a second.

"He's coming back," said Chase, sensing the approach of Miseo.

"What about Ronan?"

Chase shot a bolt of white light at Ronan's body. It startled Ryonna, and she was about to complain when she saw all his wounds recede and his eyes started blinking. Before she could say thank you, Chase was already flying out of the shuttle, but he rotated in midair and shot yet another white bolt of light at Ryonna, who felt the weirdest sensation. Her arm relocated itself into her shoulder socket and all pain vanished.

"That's new. Thanks Chase—" but Chase was already outside and fighting with the Fury.

17

W hen Saroudis landed his shuttle at the rendezvous coordinates Daniel had given him, a few hundred yards beyond the cabin where his family had found refuge, he ran toward his daughter the moment the back ramp had been lowered. A terrifying growl stopped him dead in his tracks.

"Reaper! Watch your manners. That's my father you're growling at. Stop it at once!"

The wolfen understood from the tone that he had been unwise in his overzealous attempt at protecting Sendra and took a few steps back, lowering his muzzle and gaze to the ground.

Sendra ran the rest of the way and jumped into her father's arms.

Daniel looked at the scene with a smile on his face. The commodore was crying tears of joy as he kissed his daughter on her face and hair. Daniel could read in his eyes that he still couldn't believe what was happening.

"I'm still unsure if this is real or if I'm dreaming," he said as he hugged her tightly, his hand caressing her golden hair.

"I know what you mean, Dad."

But then Saroudis saw his wife approach.

"Give me a second will you, Sendra."

She wiped her tears of joy and nodded at him with a beaming smile.

"It's about time!" Alexandra said in an icy-cold tone.

"Alexandra," said Saroudis, with more than enough caution in his voice as he approached her.

Daniel didn't know what would happen next. She looked utterly pissed.

But then she took him in her arms and started crying as well. "The boys . . . I'm so sorry, Adonis, I couldn't save them."

Saroudis affectionately patted his wife on her back. "There, there. None of this is your fault. I just wish I was there with you when all hell broke loose."

Daniel decided it was way past time to go back into his shuttle and let the reunited family have their deserved moment of privacy.

Now was as good a time as any to try to get some news from Fillio. He looked forward to holding her in his arms the same way the commodore had held his wife and daughter.

When he established a channel with the *Hope* and Sarah's face appeared on his holo-display, he immediately understood that something was wrong.

"Daniel," she said with watery eyes.

"What is it, Sarah? Is Chase alright?"

"Chase is fine. At least I hope so. He left for Droxia a while ago now and I haven't had much news since then. But I'm afraid I'm the bearer of very sad news . . ."

Daniel's heart skipped a beat and before Sarah told him more he knew something had happened to Fillio.

WHEN MISEO RETURNED he was infuriated.

"You'll regret taking me by surprise!"

"Hello to you as well. Miseo, is it?"

That only further inflamed Miseo and he threw himself at Chase.

Chase dodged Miseo's first set of attacks with ease. He was still partially in angry mode. He had little difficulty anticipating his enemy's attacks, and when Miseo least expected it, he planted a powerful, fireball-charged right punch to his stomach. Miseo staggered backward and his expression changed. He looked really surprised to have been bested so quickly in the fight.

"What the fuck are you? You shouldn't be able to move that fast."

"Says who? If you're thinking of your friend the general, he wished he could come. But at the last minute he had a *change* of heart."

Miseo took a deep breath and calmed himself.

"Impressive. Argos might have undersold your actual level of power. Fortunately, you're still no match for me."

Chase tapped a finger on the right side of his mouth. "You still have a little blood running from your mouth. I hear Fury acid reflux is a bitch."

Miseo chuckled. "You seem pretty confident. I can already feel that it will be your undoing."

"Beside my asshole brother, I've only met two other Furies, but you guys are walking clichés."

A vein in Miseo's right temple started throbbing.

Am I annoying you? Good!

Chase smirked.

Miseo crossed his arms across his chest. "It's too bad you aren't fighting on our side, though; you'd be a great ally."

"I bet you'd think so. Your former friend Arkoolis also voiced his disappointment about which side I chose."

"Where is General Arkoolis? Your brother told me you are *not* a killer."

"Afraid I'm gonna have to disappoint you on that one. You and I are the only two remaining Furies on the surface of this planet. The only ones with a beating heart, anyway."

"General Arkoolis is dead?"

"Afraid so, unless he can regrow the heart I ripped out of his chest."

Miseo frowned.

"My father will be displeased. He was very fond of him."

"Don't worry. I'll make sure to attach an apology card when I send him both your heads."

"Enough! You may have bested the general, but this planet will be your tomb. I will make sure of that."

"Like I said, walking cliché. But you know what? I'm sure you'll give it your best. Doesn't seem to me you're nearly fast as I am at the moment."

"My best? Very few adversaries ever lived to see my best. It does look like I might have to push myself more than usual, though. But between you and me, it's been so long that I find that thought particularly enthralling. General Arkoolis was a great warrior, but there are many more strong Furies still alive today. They are all aching to see this universe burn for what it did to us."

Miseo grew his aura as he powered up and the entire planet shook. Every stone within a ten-mile radius started levitating upwards.

Looks like he wasn't kidding when he said he hadn't shown all he is capable of. I'll have to tread carefully. I've spent a lot of energy in my first fight. I'll have to be smart in how I manage the rest of it.

Chase extended his consciousness and checked Miseo's power level. He was still at more than ninety percent.

Yep, definitely not a good sign when one factors in that he received a Droxian destroyer full-on not long ago. I had hoped the experience would have drained him much more than that.

Chase also brought more power to the surface. Blue lightning bolts danced and crackled all around him.

He was surprised how naturally he did that nowadays. It briefly reminded him of his first training session with Ares and how difficult and frustrating it had been to access even a slight portion of his power. He had certainly come a long way since then.

Miseo made the first move and sent a powerful black fireball at Chase, who blocked it with his right hand. But something went wrong. Dark-red lightning shot from it and hit Chase on the torso, head and left knee. He lost balance and had to put a knee on the ground. By then Miseo was already upon him and landed his own knee on Chase's left cheek, which sent him crashing hundreds of yards away, leaving a trail of dust behind him.

Chase got up and wiped some blood from the corner of his mouth.

I guess this is gonna be a tougher fight.

Miseo walked toward Chase with a smirk on his face.

"Still thinking you're gonna save the day, hero?"

Chase wanted to answer something sarcastic but he knew he was mistaken in thinking that because he dispatched the general, he could take care of Miseo with ease. Clearly these two were in a different category, and this would be the most difficult fight of his life. But he had no choice now. The only way out was to defeat his new adversary, no matter the cost.

Billions had died today on Droxia and Chase knew that it was all his doing. He hadn't meant to, of course. He hadn't seen Argos' bigger picture at the time, but the fact remained: every new life lost on Droxia would be on his hands. He couldn't reconcile himself with the thought of letting one more person die today because of his actions. While his heart still beat, he would fight to avoid any more casualties.

"You're fast and powerful, but this fight has only begun."

"That's where you're wrong. You've spent almost half your energy killing the general. So you're already dead. It's just a matter of time. How long do you want your suffering to go on? I can make it quick for you, if you like, if only for the respect I have for the abilities you've displayed today. You're a true warrior, which I frankly did not expect. At least you should be proud of how far you've gone before you die."

"I'm not dead just yet."

"Very well, shall we continue then?"

Chase answered by adopting an offensive combat stance.

WHEN SAROUDIS CAME BACK on board the *Destiny* with his family, he felt something that he thought he had forgotten in the last few months: hope. They would have to send another fleet here soon and try to locate more survivors, but right now it was time to go to Droxia. Last news they had they were still under attack. The commodore had no doubt that by the time they reached there the main battle would be well over. It was a very long jump, after all.

But that family reunion also meant a real feeling of grief in his heart. His two boys were gone, forever. He would never see Joshua and Ethan again. At first he had been so happy seeing Alexandra and Sendra, but upon returning to the ship he realized the full implications that both his sons were gone, forever. It hit him hard and he had to force himself not to show his emotions.

He didn't want his crew to see him weak. It wasn't a matter of pride. Saroudis knew they had all lost everything and everyone they held dear with the fall of the Star Alliance. And he came back on board with part of his family, so he wasn't sure how showing sadness in that moment would be interpreted. There would be time for grieving later.

He made a conscious choice to bottle up his emotions for the time being and contact the *Hope.*

Sarah's worried image filled the holo-screen.

"Commander? I was expecting Chase."

"Chase is on Droxia."

Saroudis looked dubious. "How can he be on Droxia already?"

"Ares beamed him there, or something."

"Looks like Ares is way more powerful dead than when he was alive."

"Yeah, it's disconcerting, I agree, but at least he's on our side."

"Do you have a status report on what's happening there?"

"Sort of. Oh boy, how do I explain this without sounding like a total nut job . . ."

"Sarah, with everything we've been witnesses to since we met, I don't think there's anything you can say that will surprise me at this point."

"Alright then. My unborn son appeared to me in a vision. In that vision I was standing on Droxia. The place looked utterly destroyed, leveled really. I got the feeling that billions died today. He told me he needed to send some of his life force to Chase to help him fight the Furies on the surface responsible for all the destruction. Which I guess he did. And to say the whole experience was weird is to put it mildly."

Saroudis chuckled. "I stand corrected."

"Tell me about it, sir. I heard you brought your family on board? I'm so happy for you."

"Thank you, Sarah. I . . . It still feels surreal, but I'm over-joyed. I never thought I would see any of them alive. Of course, I'm also grieving for my two boys that weren't so lucky. It's one thing thinking your family is dead. It's another when you know."

Saroudis wiped a tear from one of his eyes.

So much for bottling up my feelings.

"I'm so sorry to hear that. My condolences, Commodore. At least your wife and daughter made it."

"Thank you. Yes, it's already more than I could ever have hoped for."

"We've also lost Fillio today, amongst the hundreds that died onboard the fleet at the same time."

Saroudis' expression darkened. So many deaths. And this was just the beginning.

"I'm so sorry to hear that. She was such a kind person."

"And a great wing commander."

"We must ready ourselves to lose many more people in the future. This war has only just begun."

Saroudis saw Sarah's hand move to her belly. He regretted voicing his last remark. She was probably worried enough as it is, with her unborn son already in contact with them. That had to be scary in and of itself. Then there was the world they would bring the child into. The same world in which he had to try and protect whatever was left of his family. For a brief moment, he wondered if perhaps they wouldn't be safer on the surface of Alpha Prime. He brushed the thought away.

"So, Commodore? Can we jump to Droxia?"

"Absolutely. What's the status of the *Hope*?"

"The damage is extensive, but she'll fly. We've got power back to seventy-five percent and we should be back to full power by the time we end our jump."

"Very well, Commander, slave your jump engines to ours. We'll jump within the next five minutes."

"Roger that."

Saroudis ended the communication and rose from his chair. He approached the viewport and, for just a moment, he let his thoughts get lost among the stars.

RONAN GOT up and saw Arknon doing the same.

"Arknon!"

"Hey, Ronan, I take it I have you to thank for still being alive? Thank you, my friend."

"I don't really remember much."

"Glad to see you both up," said Ryonna.

"How did we get healed?" asked Ronan.

"Chase. He arrived in the nick of time."

"Where is he? I want to thank him for saving us."

"He's outside, fighting with that Fury that almost killed you."

"I really thought crashing the *Phoenix* on him would take him out."

"I second that," added Arknon.

"Let's hope it injured him enough so Chase can finish him off."

"I'm worried about that, Mom. When he rose from the furnace he was burned to a crisp and he healed himself like it was nothing. How are we supposed to defeat an enemy like that?"

"By never giving up. But I won't lie to you, son, this is going to be the most devastating war ..."

Ryonna hadn't had time to really think about anything but Ronan these past few hours, and she was happy he was alive, but she felt a sense of urgency in her soul. This was not over, and they would still have to find some sort of shelter or get evacuated if any of the ships in orbit had survived. Right now, staying so near a battle involving two Furies was not safe. She knew it with every fiber of her being.

"We need to get out of here. If one of Chase's or his enemy's attacks comes our way we'll be obliterated."

"Right. Can the ship still fly?"

"I was about to go check that with Keera. I'll be back shortly. Please don't go outside just yet."

As if to enhance her warning the planet started to tremble.

Ronan nodded. "Right."

When Ryonna entered the cockpit, Keera was hitting her controls with both her fists.

"That bad, huh?"

"Yeah, the *Valken* isn't going anywhere I'm afraid."

"We couldn't have flown into space anyway, not with half of the cargo bay's ceiling missing."

"That's for sure. I'll miss this ship. It got me out of many jams."

"If Chase manages to defeat Miseo my people will help you repair it."

Keera raised an eyebrow and gave her a look.

"That's sweet, Ryonna, but I don't think so. Your people have almost been wiped out today. It will take years to rebuild your planet and that will only happen if Chase defeats his opponent. Too many things can go wrong."

"Then the Alliance will."

"Ryonna, what's wrong with you? It's just a ship. You do realize that your world is in ruins, right?"

"I don't think it's fully sunk in just yet."

That's when it actually hit her and she changed color.

"What is it, Ryonna?"

"Jonas . . . My late husband's brother, he . . . he lived in one of the destroyed cities."

"Perhaps he left before it was attacked. As soon as this is over I'll help you look for him. But we need to get out of here."

"Yes, that we must."

A minute later the four of them exited the *Valken* to board the all-terrain buggy Keera owned for planetary exploration. The moment it was down the ramp Keera caught a glimpse of something moving a hundred yards in front of her. She veered to the left abruptly, skidding and drifting heavily. Two of the vehicle's wheels left the ground for a second. They reconnected at the end of her turn.

The passengers looked at the fight between Chase and Miseo. Their eyes only saw blurry shapes traveling way too fast to follow.

ARGOS MADE A FLYBY NEAR GENERAL ARKOOLIS' last position.

Upon descending near the planet's surface he had seen the extent of the damage inflicted in the area. It wasn't pretty. Almost every city had been leveled and fires still burned as far as the eye could see.

Droxia had been obliterated in only a few hours. It had been thanks to his ingenious plan of distracting their large protection fleet, most of which had been destroyed by only a handful of Zarlack destroyers. Argos caught himself feeling bad for the Droxians.

What the hell is happening to me? Why would I even care ...?

He landed the *Dark Star*. A battle had clearly occurred in the area. When Argos stepped out of his ship he saw obvious traces of fighting, not only with Droxian military but also between two Furies. The landscape had been devastated, with crevasses and craters in the ground, as well as large trails that went for miles. These were clear signs of two powerful beings fighting. Argos wondered who had won, but was again surprised when he hoped Laiyos had been the victor.

Could it be that I'm losing respect for my own race? I wonder ...

After all, they had treated him like nothing while he was clearly the only reason for their resurgence. No matter how badly he tried to put his public humiliation behind him, he hated the supreme commander with a vengeance. Miseo was a more tolerable Fury to work with, but he had sensed something a little off about him as well. Perhaps the son aspired to replace his father. He wouldn't put it past him.

Argos took some altitude and scanned the area. Then something caught his attention. It was pretty far away, but it definitely looked like a humanoid body. He flew there and landed near Arkoolis' corpse.

Argos smiled.

Impressive. Looks like Chase is getting better by the day.

Good for you, brother. I take it you've now moved on to fight Miseo. But if that's the case, if you're not dead already, it won't be long now.

He felt a sting in his heart and clenched his fists. Rage filled his entire being.

I hope that nosy brat remembers that he promised me the final blow.

Argos flew back into his ship and vectored toward Miseo's last known location.

18

A res stepped inside Athena's temple on Olympus. The place was huge, with large white columns all around, but also inside the temple.

"You're not exactly welcome around these parts. But you know that, right?" said a beautiful yet intimidating woman with long, golden hair.

Athena was a tall and lean Olympian. She was dressed in white, with flower motifs embroidered into her beautiful gown. Above her throne, mounted on the wall, stood her golden shield. It caught the sunlight from the outside and diffused it nicely into a soft, warm light all around it. It gave the entire area around the throne an ethereal quality.

"But I would be remiss if I didn't say it's good to see you. Well, whatever is left of you."

"Hello, sister, you always had a way with words."

"Some things never change."

"They ought to if we want to survive."

"Don't waste your time. Artemis and Apollo both told me you visited them not long ago."

"I see. Can we still discuss the issue, though? Father was not very receptive, to say the least."

"What did you expect, Ares? You broke the old man's heart."

"I was unaware he possessed one."

Athena laughed for quite a while. "Now who has a way with words? But thank you, it has been a long time since I laughed that much."

"I wish I could tell you I came so we can reminisce about the past and have a few good laughs, but the hour is grave."

"So I hear. Your protégé singlehandedly managed to free the Furies from their timeless prison," said Athena, shaking her head from side to side.

"Well, in his defense, he didn't know he was helping his evil twin brother achieve that objective."

"We sure don't have the monopoly on family feuds, even though ours are legendary."

Ares smiled. Of course, in his current energy form, she couldn't see it, but evidently she sensed it.

"I'm glad to see your sense of humor has improved. You were a much less fun Olympian in the old days, you know? Pre-banishment times."

"I try to not think of those days too much."

"I bet. You wreaked havoc. But let bygones be bygones, I say."

"I'm glad to hear it."

Athena rose from her throne and went to a beautiful marble table nearby to serve herself some wine.

"I would ask you if you want a glass . . ."

"Funny."

"I'm teasing."

"I know, sister. Believe me, there are things we said to each other in the past that I wish I could take back."

"You were blinded by your thirst for power. I don't think you need to worry about that now."

She walked back to her throne, sat back down and took a sip of the delicious beverage.

"How is it, being in a non-corporeal state?"

"It has its advantages. And I'm still learning everything I can do as days go by."

"Except you're not supposed to stay here, at least not forever."

"I know. I just can't stand idly by while the universe around me is destroyed, at least not if I can do something about it."

"Did you ever ask yourself if perhaps that it's destiny?"

"Was that Athena talking or my father?"

"Touché. But now that most inhabitants of this universe don't really pray nor fear our wrath, it's a little more difficult to care about what happens to them."

"We both know you don't mean that. I never took you for one that craved such things."

"And you'd be right. But lately I have been wondering what it meant to be alive. Immortality has the disadvantage of making things really boring after a while."

"Well then, perhaps you should hear me out."

She took another sip. "Why the hell not."

"The Furies have risen from the dead."

"They were never dead, and there lies the problem."

"Indeed. Still, they haven't yet had time to manufacture their armada of old. Their ships fell during the last war. Before coming here, I took a tour of their world, and they're almost done building their first exterminator-class destroyer. But now that Argos has managed to feed them a continuous stream of resources, they've started building others, many others."

"And you want us to stop them?"

"My thinking is that we have to try. It took our participation in the universe-wide coalition of worlds to defeat them back then. It stands to reason we'll have to play a part in that once more."

"Unless we let the younger races take care of it, like we all promised we would."

"The others races might want to rethink that old pact as well. If it was a new race trying to rise to power I would be inclined to agree with you. But the Furies are almost as old as us. The new races don't stand a chance. In fact, for a long time it also looked as if we wouldn't stand a chance."

"You're forgetting something. It took the legendary spirit ships to make that happen. Without them the Furies had reached a level of technology even higher than our own."

"Then why don't we just get them back? If Zeus didn't destroy the key to the dimension prison, I bet these ships are also still lying somewhere, taking dust until they are again needed."

"I wish I could tell you more but I simply don't have this information. Perhaps they are ..."

Athena lowered her eyes and she looked at her empty glass. She lifted her other hand with grace and the jar containing the wine flew to her, poured her another drink and went back to the table.

"Couldn't you have done that before?"

"Like I said, Ares, I'm bored. Sometimes I need to stretch my legs."

"About the ships. Any information you can give me, even sketchy, would be welcome."

Ares saw something in her eyes. There was something she wasn't telling him.

"Please?" he pleaded.

"Look, Ares, I'm really happy to see you and I am glad for this talk, but I'm unsure you want to know the information I have, which—and I must stress this point—might or might not be true."

"Why don't you tell me anyway?"

"Very well. But you're not going to like it."

"Will you tell me already?"

She sighed.

"According to some information I came by three thousand years ago, the legendary spirit ships were destroyed."

"Are you certain of this?"

"What part of 'might not be true' didn't you understand?"

"Right. Anyone who could let us know? Do you remember who told you this?"

"Father, but he did it in passing really, so unless we ask him directly, which I doubt he would like coming from you . . ."

"And what about if you asked him?"

"Sure, I will go to him and say, 'Father, didn't you tell me the spirit ships had been destroyed? I vaguely remember a conversation we had eons ago, please tell me more.'"

Ares didn't appreciate the sarcasm but she had a point. Zeus would immediately know he had put her up to it. At the moment he'd rather have Athena as a potential ally rather than alienate her from their father. Athena was a very powerful Olympian, and an incredible tactician. The Earth Alliance sure could use her help.

"You're right, he would see right through that."

"Of course he would."

"One thing, though, why are these ships so special? Do you know?"

"Again, I'm not the right person to ask."

"Anything you can remember, even a small detail?"

"I don't know about detail, but I remember that they were a piece of extremely advanced technology that came from the previous age, possibly pre-dating our own creation."

"Creation?"

"Well, Zeus likes to tell tales about how we came to be, but there are those amongst us who think we had creators. The very first race to travel the stars."

"They have a name?"

"They probably have one, but I'm sure father burned every reference to it from history. Anyway, it is said that these ships have the ability to channel and focus one's internal power and deliver that energy into space safely."

Ares' blood froze. The implications were huge. If such a ship existed, someone like Chase could use his power in space without creating black holes and other tears in the space-time continuum. He could probably wipe out an entire fleet with just one of these ships. Ares knew then and there that these spirit ships would be the key to the whole Fury war.

"I wish I could tell you more, really. And I will think about carefully slipping a kind word in your favor with father if the occasion arises."

"Thank you, sister. You've actually been more helpful than you know today. I'll probably swing by to see you again in the future."

"It's been nice talking with you, Ares. Don't let it be centuries this time, and please make sure to visit me at least once more before you decide to sail on the Styx."

"It sure won't be centuries, and the Styx will have to wait until after the Furies have been dealt with. Thanks again for your help."

"Anytime."

Ares vanished into nothingness as Athena took another sip of her drink.

～

CHASE PARRIED Miseo's next incoming wave of front and back kicks, but Miseo was now on a par with him with respect to speed. He had to stay incredibly focused to not get hit by the incoming blows. It didn't let him breathe, though, and he couldn't find an opening.

For the time being he had to contend with just blocking, dodging and parrying. But then Miseo threw him a curveball and hit him square in the face with a heel kick. Chase temporarily lost balance but managed to recover quickly.

Miseo switched to a series of punches next, alternating between jabs, hooks and uppercuts. Then Chase got an idea. It was risky, but he had to try something. He couldn't stay on the defensive forever.

Chase let Miseo execute his next punch combo and feinted being sucker-punched by one of the uppercuts, but then he grabbed Miseo's forearm and swiped his left leg with enough force to make him lose balance. He then pulled Miseo forward and hit him with a scorpion kick, a move his Fury enemy was clearly not prepared for.

Miseo stumbled back, disoriented. Chase lost no time lighting up two fireballs, sending one of them low intentionally. It exploded in front of Miseo, who probably didn't understand why Chase hadn't fired at him directly, but it provided him with a dust screen. The second one shot through the cloud and was aimed at his head, but Miseo dodged it by tilting his head to the left. Before he realized it was a ruse, Chase was already in the air, landing an extremely powerful flying kick, hitting Miseo's cheek with the full force with his shin. Miseo fell to the ground a few yards away.

Chase flew in pursuit, but Miseo pushed hard on his hands and back-flipped into a standing position. He threw both his clawed hands forward. Chase felt an invisible force field slow him down in midair. The more he tried to push through the more he slowed down.

An idea took form in his mind. He consciously pushed even more and saw veins on Miseo's arms grow bigger in order to increase his hold on Chase. It now looked as if he was stuck in midair.

Chase then suddenly stopped pushing and flew backward, helped by the opposing kinetic energy blast from Miseo's counter. The moment Miseo let go Chase was already twirling madly in the air, curled into a ball, and out of the blue shot two columns of energy. But he didn't shoot them at Miseo. He used them to increase his thrust as he flew toward Miseo like a shooting star, head first. When his head impacted with Miseo's torso, Miseo was clearly unprepared for that ingenious move. His armor cracked upon impact and Miseo was thrown backward for miles.

Before Miseo could hit the ground Chase was already under him, hands firmly planted in the ground as he catapulted Miseo into the heavens by extending both his feet upwards. Miseo whirled uncontrollably during his ascent and was only stopped when Chase smashed his face with a fireball-infused right hook. Miseo saw stars before his eyes and Chase lost no time grabbing him from behind and locking his arms at shoulder level.

Chase twirled with Miseo locked in. The resulting whirlwind soon created a powerful cyclone as Chase then forced them both to shoot back toward the ground from miles high. They looked like a comet about to impact with the planet.

At the last second, Chase released his grasp and somersaulted in midair, using kinetic energy to pull himself backward. Miseo crashed into the ground with the force of a thousand bombs. The resulting explosion could be seen from space, with a giant shockwave traveling for hundreds of miles around the point of impact.

Chase's hair flew madly in the air as he witnessed the spectacle from above. He checked his power levels and worried when he realized he was at less than twenty percent. He would need to finish Miseo with his next set of attacks or he would run out of juice.

When the dust had settled, there was a fifteen-mile-wide crater on the surface of Droxia.

Chase wondered if perhaps he had defeated his enemy, but his instincts told him otherwise.

That was confirmed when a huge mound of soil started moving in the middle of the crater.

19

Miseo rose back up as the ground that covered him trickled down around him. His face had seen better days. Deep cuts under the left eye, on his right temple and right cheek, still gushed blood. He looked enraged, with most blood vessels in his eyes having popped, aggravating the already mad look he shot toward Chase.

Chase checked his enemy's power levels and was pleased to see they had been cut in two, but he was still around forty percent, more than double what Chase still had left.

Miseo levitated into the sky and reached Chase's altitude, although he was still a couple of miles away. He passed his hand over his face and looked at it. It was covered with his own blood. He healed himself and Chase felt a little dip in Miseo's power level as he did so.

Perhaps it was something to be exploited.

A nearby engine hummed, but no ship was visible. But Chase felt his brother's presence inside the craft and shot a warning fireball toward it. It briefly lit the shield and revealed its position a couple hundred yards east of him.

What do you want, Argos? asked Chase telepathically.

I just want to be here for your demise, that's all.

I am not going to fall today. Are you waiting your turn so once your competition in the Fury ranks is diminished you can cowardly finish me off and take all the credit?

Come on now, brother, I'm just curious, that's all.

Stop calling me that. And stay out of this fight.

We shall see. Miseo promised me I could be the one to kill you.

Not if I have anything to say about that.

Chase flew down and landed inside the crater. Miseo did the same, landing only a few yards away. He crossed his arms over his chest.

His armor had been thoroughly damaged and half of his clothing had been torn to shreds.

"I must congratulate you on your last attack. I did not expect such a powerful display, but it did cost you a lot of energy. I can feel you're running on fumes now."

"It cost you a lot as well and you know it."

"Perhaps, but not enough for me to lose this fight. You should have made sure to finish me off after sending me to the ground. Waiting for me to get back up was a terrible mistake."

Had he made a strategic error? he wondered.

"I enjoyed fighting you today, Miseo, more than I thought I would."

"You're finally discovering what your Fury heritage is all about. We love to fight. It's in our blood. We also love to kill. I'm sure you felt a surge of pleasure when you ripped out Arkoolis' heart."

Had he enjoyed killing Arkoolis? Chase didn't really know at the moment. He felt it was necessary to avenge the billions that had died at his hands today, but did he feel personal pleasure in doing so? Chase decided that now was not the time to think about that.

"Perhaps. But I think using our powers on lesser beings is the trademark of cowards. Why don't you fight between yourselves and leave the universe alone?"

Miseo laughed. "We have a score to settle as a race. You wouldn't understand."

"I understand better than you think."

"Shall we continue?"

"Unless you'd like to leave this world now. Your fleet in orbit has been reduced to ashes. You and Argos are all that's left, and perhaps it's time to pack it up and call it a day?"

"Do you really believe I would let you live after killing Arkoolis? No, you must pay for this crime with your life, today."

The next few minutes would see the end of this confrontation, one way or the other.

"Alright then, let's finish this once and for all, Miseo."

Chase smirked.

Argos landed the still-cloaked *Dark Star* atop the crater and exited the craft.

Miseo looked at him. "Do not intervene. That's the one order you do *not* wish to disobey."

His icy tone sent shivers down Argos' spine.

"I won't," replied Argos. "But remember what we agreed upon."

"We shall see," said Miseo as he launched himself toward Chase with all his might.

ARGOS LOOKED at the fight unfolding before his eyes. Both

Laiyos and Miseo were incredible fighters. As much as it pained him to admit it, they were both vastly superior warriors to him now. That hurt his pride more than he was ready to accept.

He probed both fighters' energy levels and saw the difference between them.

You've overextended yourself, Laiyos. You will run out of juice soon.

But then Argos' response to that thought was a mixed bag of positive and negative emotions.

He waited patiently for his chance to finally take his life, and take revenge for all the pain Laiyos had been responsible for. Both after and before Argos had removed all his memories, in fact. Some of these painful memories ran deep inside Argos' psyche.

Laiyos had parried Miseo's first combo and counterattacked with a combo of his own. They had very different fighting techniques. Miseo had a more raw and powerful approach to his blows, while Laiyos had more grace in his movements, even though some of them weren't executed most efficiently.

Argos wondered if Laiyos was aware of that, or if he fought this way naturally. Perhaps it all came down to his training. Which brought back the memories of his own fight with Ares. Ares also used fully formed attacks and had that quality of delivering moves that were beautiful to look at, but not always efficient or fast enough.

Ares had trained Chase well. In fact, he had done with him in just a few days, more than Chase had learned in his entire life before Argos had been forced to wipe his memory.

Did I just call him Chase?

Argos was surprised by that, but he felt that it mattered

not what he called his twin brother. As long as the fight was headed this way, he would lose for sure.

But then Chase broke one of Miseo's combos and his counterattack was brutal. He pounded Miseo with more and more powerful blows and sent him to the ground.

Reminds you of some bad memories? he heard Chase say in his mind. *I can sense your thoughts, Argos. Is that worry that I might lose this fight I sense at the moment?*

Argos was stunned he could do that and fight at the same time.

I'm just enjoying the show, and you should concentrate on your fight instead of diverting your focus.

I'll take that as a yes.

Chase kept grinding at Miseo and he sent him flying upwards in the sky, right before unleashing a series of icy-blue fireballs. Miseo was hit by a couple of them, but quickly recovered and deflected the next ones away.

Miseo then unleashed his own set of fireballs, but Chase deflected a few and blocked the last two and assimilated them. He received a small boost in energy doing so.

One of the deflected fireballs ran straight toward Argos and he blocked it with ease. He closed his fist around it and it was reduced to nothingness.

Argos saw what his brother was trying to do, but Miseo made sure to only send small-powered attacks toward him.

The end is near . . .

BEFORE RETURNING TO DROXIA, Ares decided to make a little detour via Erevos.

The first thing he saw sent a shiver through his non-corporeal being. There orbited a ship that was as black as the night. It was spiky, and massive. Bigger even than the Zarlack behemoth destroyers, it looked like a shadow from hell, with long spikes arching forward, and soon the Alliance would have to face this new, formidable technological foe in their upcoming battles.

He was surprised not to find Aphroditis and the soul-sucking machine she was now a prisoner of. The destroyer that once was her newly forced home was still there, but she wasn't onboard anymore. Ares expanded his consciousness to the entire planet and it didn't take him long to detect the now faint remains of Aphroditis' trapped consciousness and ever-drained life force.

Ares understood the strategic value of moving her to the surface of their world. It made sense. If someone was to find a way to remove her from the machine, it stood to reason that the Furies would be sent back to their dimensional prison, but then whoever had done so would be as well, and this time forever. Still, Ares wouldn't put it past Chase to accept such a mission, even if it meant sacrificing his own life. But not enough was known about the device itself to make that assumption. Only the device's inventor could say with exact precision what would happen in such a case. Ares made a mental note to try to learn more about the device.

The device was better guarded on a planet filled with extremely powerful Fury warriors, and Argos had surely told Supreme Commander Arakan what Chase had promised Aphroditis just before she willingly accepted her fate and fused with the machine. Perhaps Arakan even intended to use her to attract Chase to him if needed.

Ares teleported inside a very dark room with no windows. It was a cold and humid place, a hostile dungeon in which to spend every living moment of one's life. But could Aphroditis still be considered alive at this point? Certainly her heart still beat, but was she anything but a shadow of her former self?

Ares could not sense that.

He appeared inside the windowless cell and illuminated it with his golden presence and warmth. He could have stayed invisible, of course. The room was probably being recorded and monitored, but no Fury could hurt him in his current form. Not that he knew of, anyway. And on some level he wanted them to know that he could not only visit her anytime he saw fit, but he also would know every time they moved her around.

He scanned the room for a recording device and saw one on top of the closed and reinforced door. He waved at it, but then felt compelled to extend his golden middle finger at it. Such an impulse achieved nothing, and was very childish for a being that had lived for thousands upon thousands of years. But the damp and cold hole in which they had put his sister had that effect on him. It gave him the impulse to tell them to go fuck themselves.

Ares wished he could retake corporeal form and give Arakan a piece of his mind right this instant. But that would not be wise. If Argos had easily dispatched him, he could never dream of bringing the supreme commander down, at least not if he was the one on the other side of this fight.

Hopefully Chase one day . . .

Ares realized he had got carried away, and that was not why he had come here. He approached his sister. The warm glow he was emanating cast a light golden hue on his half-sister's face, but even so she looked more livid than the last time he had visited. He caressed her cheek affectionately and talked to her telepathically.

I don't know if you can hear me. I haven't been around much lately and I'm really sorry about that. Things have been kinda crazy. Chase has trained and he is now a formidable warrior. He killed General Arkoolis today, one of the Furies' top generals. He is now fighting Miseo, and I guess I should go to see how he fares as soon as I leave here. He has come a long way. He is more focused, more aware of his own weaknesses, and I sense more hope and determination in his heart than ever before. Perhaps you were right. Perhaps all of this needed to happen. Still, I wish I could take your place. I wish I was in there while you were out here, still advising him.

Ares thought he saw one of her eyelids move just a tiny bit.

Aphroditis? Can you hear me?

But there was no answer.

Anyway, where was I? Oh yes. Unfortunately, today Droxia fell. Whether Chase manages to save the few million souls on it or not remains to be seen, but the main attack fleet has been destroyed and there is a good chance that his fight with Miseo will give him pause. I have no doubt Argos is behind it all once again. He knows how powerful a message it sent the rest of the universe when Droxia joined the Alliance, so I'm sure he decided that it should be the first to fall. Things are going awry all over the place. The Furies have colonized, destroyed or enslaved worlds rich in resources. All of that in order to destabilize the trust in the still growing Alliance, but mostly for Argos to secure the Furies the right amount of resources to build their new fleet of shadow vessels, like the one in orbit right now.

This time Ares was certain he saw a twitch on Aphroditis' face.

Can you hear me? Try and twitch again if you can.

But nothing happened, and he sighed.

Ares shouldn't raise his hopes about communicating with Aphroditis while she was inside the machine. In fact, she might never get out of it, which frustrated him more than he would care to admit to anyone.

But he understood why she did it. And why she put all her trust in Chase. One could debate all day long that if he hadn't done this, the Alliance would have won the war against the Zarlacks, but who was to say if someone else, later on, wouldn't have released them anyway?

No, deep inside his soul Ares knew that the one truly responsible for their current predicament was his father Zeus. He should have dealt with the Furies once and for all when he had the chance. Trapping them was always going to be a ticking bomb, and that bomb was already in the process of exploding and taking the universe with it.

Chase's unborn child, Chris, also has demonstrated impressive abilities already. Perhaps he will play a role in all of this yet. Though I wonder what will be left of this universe by then. Will anything be left? I don't even dare let my thoughts go in that direction.

Aphroditis blinked. It was the first time Ares had witnessed it and he wondered if perhaps some of her natural bodily functions simply acted automatically. Her eyes were still all white, and she looked more like a scary, gray-skinned flesh-statue than the smiling and full-of-life Olympian he remembered.

I really hope you don't mind me telling you all this. If there's even the slightest chance you can hear any of this, then I hope it helps you a little. I'm sure if you feel anything at all, these days spent here must feel like centuries and a little change of pace could probably help you.

Something started shining on her forehead. At first Ares thought his own golden light was shining on some dust or a particle of some kind. But, much to his surprise, a hair-thin golden energy wire grew and connected with Ares. He heard her in his thoughts, but her voice felt weak and far away, as if she spoke from the top of a canyon that was hundreds of miles away and Ares only heard a very weak echo.

Ares, I am still here. Thank you for coming. But listen to me carefully. Chase is in trouble. His fight with Miseo . . . I . . . Her mental voice was trembling, as if she was in such pain that the act of speaking was excruciating. *I've lost most of my powers. My mind and body are constantly bombarded with darkness and it takes all my energy just not to succumb to utter madness in here.*

Ares was deeply hurt, just listening to her feeble and tortured voice, and anger rose within him.

I will get you out of here, soon. Chase and I will find a way.

Ares, no . . . listen . . . I saw Chase . . . vision . . . he . . . will . . .

"He will what?" exclaimed Ares out loud.

Go . . . Droxia . . . before . . . late.

The energy wire connecting them solidified and turned black for just a second, before it turned to dust.

Ares felt her fear resonate deeply within his entire being in the last moment of their brief communication, and knew what it meant.

He instantly teleported out of the cell and back to Droxia.

20

Chase was starting to feel tired, having fought for hours now, first with the general and now with Miseo, who was a much stronger opponent.

He needed to find a way to end this fight, and soon. Perhaps he needed to provoke Miseo and hope his anger would force a dip in concentration, because it had been near perfect up until now.

When Chase back flipped three times in a row to escape Miseo's current combo, he landed on his feet and adopted a defensive stance.

"Where's your maximum, Miseo? If that is it then we both know that if I had all my energy, I would easily win this fight."

"Think what you will. Argos told me how you let your emotions guide the way you fight. Everyone with power can use hatred and rage to unleash more potential for brief moments. Doing it while not letting emotions get in the way is the true way of the Fury warrior."

Chase wondered if that was true. He was proud to be a little more in control now than before, but he didn't feel as much power flow through him as when he went after Argos in Tokyo, for example. His rage really made him that much more powerful. Was that the key to defeating Miseo as well? he wondered.

"To be honest, I'm a little disappointed by your technique, or should I say, lack of? You're a skilled warrior, but you lack the mental discipline to best me, whether your energy levels are low or high. You have witnessed how I can also raise my power levels at any time, and I don't need hatred to boost them."

Miseo's aura doubled in size, and before Chase could react he had planted a powerful blow into Chase's stomach. He then took Chase by the hair and unleashed three terrible blows to his face with his knees. He then struck Chase with a powerful kick to the torso and sent him flying and crashing backward. Blood flowed from Chase's mouth.

"See what I mean? I did not need hatred to put you down just now, just perfect control of my powers and emotions."

Chase's ribcage hurt really badly, and he had to heal at least half a dozen broken ribs as he stood back up, using energy he was running out of.

"Perhaps, but at least I'm not a heartless robot intent on destruction of all life in the universe."

"Not all life, just the weak and useless. And as distracting as it has been fighting you today, I'm starting to believe you belong in the ground with them."

Chase spat blood on the ground. He looked for any doubts to exploit in Miseo, but he only sensed utter confidence. Whereas Chase's doubts, which started as a small nagging thought at the beginning of the fight, were slowly but surely taking over his entire psyche.

What if I fail? What then? Will the universe fall? Will Sarah and Chris be killed?

"I believe these people will rally even if I lose today," said Chase, though he had no idea what would happen if that came true.

"*When* you fall, not if! You have lost, and deep inside you already know it. I can smell it on you now. It would take a miracle for you to win now."

Chase regretted appearing overly confident before. "This fight isn't over. I may have been arrogant but not more so than you and your pathetic friend the general."

"Do not speak ill of the dead!"

"Or what? I'm not afraid of you. I think I've proved that much."

"All you proved today is that you've been training to become a formidable warrior, but one that has no sense of true technique. You should have left this world after defeating Arkoolis. But you let your pride convince you that you could take two of the most powerful beings in existence in a single day. You bit off more than you could chew and I will look forward to bringing your head to my father."

"Fuck you, daddy's little boy. My father this, my father that . . . Why don't you call him to your aid right now?"

A vein bulged on Miseo's forehead.

Chase decided to antagonize him even more, see if he could break his icy-cold demeanor now that he sensed anger in his enemy.

"So much for controlling your emotions, asshole! This one right here is anger. The truth is you are just as unsure as I am about how this fight will end up. Sure, you're better at hiding your emotions. But that doesn't mean they aren't buried behind that ugly mug of yours."

"THAT'S ENOUGH!" shouted Miseo as he shot a fireball at Chase in an attempt to shut him up.

Chase blocked and absorbed the attack with his hand. That gave him a small but needed boost in energy.

"That one's called rage."

"I'm going to make you regret this. So let's finish it once and for all. I'll tell you what, once I'm done with you here, I'll make it my personal mission to find your wife and show her what a true warrior is, just before I rip your unborn child from her still-living body."

Something in Chase snapped and the sky darkened almost instantly. A thick layer of cloud covered the sun and soon it felt like nighttime on Droxia.

Chase unleashed the most inhuman of all animalistic growls as his pupils shone a bright orange before disappearing altogether. His aura was also tainted orange, and golden lightning sparked madly all around him. A powerful lightning bolt crashed down on Chase and boosted his energy. His hair flew upwards.

"You will not touch a hair on their heads. I won't let you!"

Chase flew so fast toward Miseo he left a trail of light behind him. He started by unleashing a powerful butterfly kick upon Miseo, who didn't have time to react as his head was thrown downward. But it was thrown back up quickly when Chase kicked it again and again with his right leg. He then alternated between shin kicks and powerful elbow blows to the face, and finally sent Miseo flying with a spinning crescent kick.

One of Miseo's teeth flew from his mouth, as well as a huge amount of blood. Before Miseo hit the ground again, Chase extended his arms and mind as he grabbed two of the biggest boulders around and crashed them into Miseo.

Chase then grabbed Miseo with his mind and held him there. Miseo's limbs dangled. He hadn't recovered yet from this powerful cascade of attacks.

Chase approached a floating Miseo with fire burning in his pupil-less eyes.

He prepared a powerful fireball and let it grow until it almost engulfed his entire arm.

He thought he heard Ares in his mind—*No, Chase, don't do it!*—but he ignored it.

"Time to join Arkoolis in hell!"

He sent the fireball toward Miseo with all his might, but then everything went wrong. It all happened very quickly. Miseo's crimson aura exploded out of nowhere, firing impressive, red bolts of lightning all around him. The entire planet shook. The debris from the boulders Chase had crashed into him a few seconds before all rose from the ground, and sizzling, dark-red lightning bolts shot between them, obliterating every one of them.

He released himself from Chase's mental hold with ease, extended both his arms in front of him and sucked in every last bit of Chase's extremely powerful attack. He siphoned it all.

Chase did not believe his eyes. He was certain that he had just landed the finishing blow of this fight, putting most of his remaining energy into it.

Miseo smiled from ear to ear.

"That's the difference between a true Fury warrior and a pathetic traitor like you. Would you like to know what just happened? I used your emotions against you. I willingly provoked that transformation in you and you fell for it. Partly because I wanted to see how powerful you might become when you unleashed all that raging power of yours, but also to make sure you hit me with everything you had next, like Argos told me you did when you entered that furious mode of yours. I knew I could use the power of your own attack to replenish mine, and I did. Thanks for the power up."

Chase's hair fell down his back and his aura returned to its usual purple.

He played me all along.

"I told you from the start that very few warriors ever live to see me deploy my abilities to the fullest. Well, now you have. And like the very few others before you, it is time to die. You're on empty now. I can feel it. Let me give you some of that energy back."

He extended his arm toward Chase and unleashed a super-fast series of small fireballs. In less than a second, Miseo had fired one hundred of them, all flying toward Chase.

Time seemed to slow and Chase realized how foolish he had been.

He heard his son's voice in his mind. *Dad, you can't die here today. You must survive!*

Chase used the last of his energy to fly upward into the air in an attempt to dodge the attacks. He traveled miles in an instant, but Miseo closed his fist and all one hundred of his attacks arched upwards at various angles and they all hit Chase simultaneously. The resulting cascade-explosion and shockwave pushed back every one of the dark clouds in the sky and soon the light of the sun burned Chase's broken body while he plummeted back toward the planet's surface.

WHEN ARES ARRIVED on Droxia he realized he was too late. He saw Chase falling from the sky and felt that he had no energy left. Miseo had also expended most of his own. He had a lot of battle damage on both his armor and face, but he was smirking while Chase plummeted from the heavens toward certain death.

Dammit! I should have come back earlier.

But what could he have done? Perhaps affect gravity around Miseo at a strategic moment, or try to add his own energy to Chase, to give him just a nudge when he most needed it. Instead, he saw his friend, his protégé, hit the ground at tremendous velocity head first. Chase lay there, defeated and unable to move a single muscle.

I'm sorry, Ares heard.

Chase, no, you can't die now. You promised you'd stop the Furies and save Aphroditis. You have to!

I failed you just like I failed everyone else. Please promise me you'll tell Sarah and Chris how much I love them both.

Chase, I can't let you die!

I don't think there's anything that can prevent that now.

Ares' mind raced to find a solution.

Miseo took a few steps toward Chase and stood above him. He extended an open palm toward Chase's face. A dark-red fireball crackled into existence.

This can't be happening!

To Ares' surprise, Argos shouted toward Miseo, asking him to stop.

"Not now, Argos!" answered Miseo.

Ares flew toward Chase. He needed to teleport him away from Droxia before it was too late. He had no idea if Chase would survive the trip in his current weakened state but there was no choice. He couldn't let Miseo finish him off. In order to do so he had to materialize into his energy-based form, and so he did a few yards before reaching Chase. But Ares hit an invisible wall.

Miseo looked at him and Ares saw that he had extended his other arm toward him.

How is this possible? How can his telekinetic energy affect me in this form?

"I expected you damned Olympians to try to intervene. I can't kill you in your current form, but I can make sure you don't move another inch."

Ares pushed with all his might but he was stuck, paralyzed even. He couldn't do anything. He couldn't travel the last three yards separating him from Chase.

"I take it you're the one who trained him? I'm glad you came by to see him die."

The fireball in Miseo's hand grew a little more.

I'm so sorry, Chase, said Ares

But Chase couldn't hear him anymore.

WHEN ARGOS REALIZED Miseo had no intention of honoring his promise he flew toward Miseo and hit him square in the face with a flying kick. Miseo skidded on the ground, leaving a trail of dust behind him. The fireball in his hand receded.

When Miseo got back up and saw who had attacked him he was furious. "You're going to die for this, Argos!"

"I can't let you kill him! I'm the one who has to do it."

"Then you'll die here as well."

"That won't be necessary and you know it! You said you'd let me finish him if it was at all possible. You have won. He cannot move anymore so you have nothing to prove. Don't forget it is thanks to me and me alone that you're standing on the surface of this planet today! It is also thanks to me that you had plenty of time to wage your destruction today. I have fully earned my right to kill my brother as promised!"

Miseo took a few deep breaths and calmed himself down while he reflected upon Argos' words.

"This," said Miseo, pointing at his bruised cheek where Argos had kicked him a moment before, "is the last time you touch me."

Argos nodded.

"Very well then, finish him."

Argos levitated Chase's body toward him and grabbed him by the throat.

CHASE WAS ONLY semi-conscious when he felt his body levitate toward Argos. Soon the entire weight of his body dangled from his neck where his brother grasped his throat. Chase could barely keep his eyes open.

"Look at me, brother. I want to see the look in your eyes when I rip you from existence once and for all."

Chase felt some energy enter his body from his throat, just enough to open his eyes.

Argos stood there with a grin on his face. He prepared his final blow by raising his other hand a little over his shoulder. He lit up his palm with a bright, crimson layer of energy. His entire forearm looked like a glistening sword.

"You have been a thorn in my side for far too long, brother. It ends now," said Argos coldly.

Chase thought he saw a brief, golden reflection in Argos' eyes. He thought he heard Argos in his thoughts, but his voice sounded slightly off. *Chase, stand very still and let it happen.*

Argos thrust his hand inside Chase's stomach and

impaled him. When Argos' palm shot through Chase's back and appeared within his long, dusty, black hair, it was covered with Chase's blood.

Chase didn't feel pain anymore, but he felt darkness invade his soul and cover him like a cold blanket. His consciousness started to wither away and was slowly replaced by a terrible void made of loneliness.

Argos removed his hand from his brother's stomach and let him fall to the ground. Blood gushed from his large, open wound, and soon Chase's skin had lost all color.

A gag reflex made him spit a large quantity of blood all over his own face as the veil of darkness extended inside his very being.

Chase's eyes closed.

I love you, Sarah.

Argos walked toward Miseo when the *Dark Star*'s cloaking dropped. "We should go now."

"What are you talking about? We should finish this planet off once and for all."

"Miseo, my ship," said Argos, pointing at the *Dark Star*, "is the only thing we have left from the fleet we came here with. Its cloaking field just ran out of juice and now it will show on sensors. We either leave now or risk being obliterated from orbit."

"I thought you said you'd guarantee us a victory against that fleet of ships."

"Well, they were more resilient than expected. We can stay here and be shot like sitting ducks while we debate that fact, or we can get the hell out of here. In any case, now is not the time for reprimands. I have no doubt I'll be punished for failing my part of the mission."

Miseo looked at Argos' eyes and then his gaze shifted to Chase's inert body.

"First, I want to bring your brother's head as a trophy to my father," said Miseo.

"Wait! I think it will have a much more demoralizing effect on whomever finds his dead body if they can see it's him."

Miseo shot a look at Argos while he thought it over.

A powerful shot of plasma fell from the sky and hit the *Dark Star*'s shields.

"Miseo, my ship won't be able to take many more of these. We should go, *now*!"

Miseo nodded and they both flew inside the *Dark Star*. It flew away and disappeared into the sky.

Chase was barely breathing anymore; his heartbeat had fallen to less than ten beats per minute.

ONBOARD THE *HOPE* Sarah was resting in her quarters. They were still heading toward Droxia and she was looking forward to being reunited with Chase. She had spent most of her time in her quarters since they had made the jump, thinking of her vision with Chris. She also thought about Chase a lot. She missed him and was looking forward to holding him in her arms again. With a baby on the way now was not the time to hold a grudge.

For the first time since he had rescued her, she only felt love for him in her heart and didn't care why he had chosen to potentially sacrifice everything to save her. What mattered was that he loved her more than life itself, and at that moment she felt the same.

Her belly grew icy cold and it startled her. She sat up and put her hands on it.

She felt a tremendous sadness permeate her entire body and it flash froze her blood.

Then she heard his voice in her thoughts. *I love you, Sarah.*

She didn't know how it was possible, but she instantly knew that Chase was at death's door.

She fell to her knees. Tears flowed like rivers, and she cried uncontrollably. "Chase! No! I beg you, no! Please god, no . . ."

End of Book IV . . .

Get Book V here: Rise of the Ultra Fury (Universe in Flames Book 5)

AFTERWORD

Publishing books is an extraordinary but difficult challenge. If you reached this point, I guess you liked my work. Please help me support the book by leaving a review and/or a rating on Amazon. You'll also be helping new readers find books they want to read. For further information about the *Universe in Flames* saga, please refer to my website: www.christiankallias.com. I would also encourage you to subscribe to my newsletter to get notified about new publications, be informed about sales and additional content available only through my website as well as some premium free content (like early access to the online Heroic Fantasy series I've started writing: **The Kyrian Chronicles**).

*Please note that I will gladly offer my books for free to anyone in exchange for an honest review. If you are interested, please contact me at **christian@kallias.com** .*

Thank you for reading and supporting me.

ABOUT THE AUTHOR

Christian Kallias is an Award Winning & Best Selling Science Fiction author. He writes Science Fiction Space Opera with a Mythology twist and Fantasy influences.

Keep in touch
www.christiankallias.com
christian@kallias.com

Made in the USA
Lexington, KY
02 December 2019

58022466R00207